THE FRONTLINE FUGITIVES

BOOK IV

SS WEREWOLVES & WAR CRIMINALS

NICK JACOBELLIS

THE FRONTLINE FUGITIVES

BOOK IV

SS WEREWOLVES & WAR CRIMINALS

CONTENTS

INTRODUCTION

T he Frontline Fugitives Book IV is a plot driven, police procedural historical fiction war story, that takes place in the European Theater of Operations (ETO) in 1945. In addition to the introduction of a few new characters, Book IV includes a cast of primary and supporting characters who are carried over from Books I, II and III.

The Frontline Fugitives Book Series comes to an action packed conclusion, when Lt. Colonel James Beauregard and Captain Al Parker lead a contingent of U.S. Army Criminal Investigation Division Agents, U.S. Army Counter Intelligence Corps Agents, U.S. Army Military Policemen and two civilian German policemen during the Invasion of Southern Germany. In addition to engaging in combat operations against regular German troops, Nazi Werwolf resistance fighters and members of the Volkstrum militia, Jim and Al lead their men in hot pursuit of Nazi SS personnel, who are wanted war criminals, in the closing days of the war in Europe.

While Jim and the other members of the American Liaison Unit serve with the French Army during the Invasion of Southern Germany, a team of CID Agents under the command of Captain Don Lorenz investigate black market activities at the supply dump known as Q179. Shortly after Captain Lorenz and his partner begin observing the main subject of their investigation, CID Agents Cal Parker and Benny Greene volunteer to work undercover and infiltrate the black market activities at this supply depot. Scenes such as these were included in Book III and in the beginning of Book IV, because CID Agents did serve in an undercover capacity during World War II. In addition to operating in uniform, armed CID Agents also wore civilian clothes when they visited cafes and walked the streets of Paris, while looking for deserters and black market operators. As a result, U.S. Army CID Agents operated like civilian police detectives and federal agents from other government agencies. However, what really makes U.S. Army CID Agents unique, is that they are also soldiers.

Just as the black market investigation at Q179 was being successfully concluded, Jim Beauregard and his men arrive in Liege, Belgium. Because their services as undercover agents are no longer required, CID Agents Cal Parker and Benny Greene are allowed to join the American Liaison Unit. After picking up additional supplies, Lt. Colonel James Beauregard and his men rendezvous with the French Army along the Rhine River.

The moment this composite unit of American personnel and the French Army cross the Rhine River and enter Southern Germany, every member of the Allied invasion force becomes a combat soldier. This becomes evident, when the French troops and their American Allies end up engaging regular German soldiers, SS troops and SS Werewolf fighters as they make their way through the remains of The Third Reich.

The enemy commander behind these attacks is SS Major Gunther Kessler, a ruthless Nazi stormtrooper who is determined to prolong the war for as long as possible. While aided by SS Werwolf resistance fighters, members of the Hitler Youth and regular German military personnel, who are staunch supporters of National Socialism, SS Major Kessler and his band of SS troops continue to fight the Allied invaders.

After the French and American column is ambushed in the Black Forest, Jim Beauregard, Al Parker and a recently recruited German policeman develop the leads that identify SS Major Kessler as the principle enemy officer, who is organizing the Nazi resistance movement in Southern Germany.

This is accomplished by examining captured maps and the personal effects that are taken from the enemy combatants who were killed during the ambush in the Black Forest. Al Parker and this German policeman also obtain additional intelligence information about SS Major Kessler, when they interview the father of a young SS Werwolf fighter, who was killed while trying to oppose the Allied occupation of Frueudenstadt.

When Allied Intelligence confirms that SS Major Gunther Kessler and the other members of his SS unit are wanted for committing war crimes, General Tremble directs Jim Beauregard, Al Parker and some of their men to leave the French column, for the purposes of capturing this Nazi Officer and his SS troops. In addition to keeping with the original theme of The Frontline Fugitives Book Series, participating in a manhunt behind enemy lines, proves to be an excellent way to use fictional characters to describe certain historically accurate events, that actually occurred in the closing days of the war.

While doing the research for this four part book series, I became fascinated by the fact that during World War II, there were people who lived in various Axis nations who opposed the Nazis and the aims of National Socialism in various ways. Some of this opposition involved armed civilians making a stand, against the attempts by hardcore Nazi fanatics and Fascists to prolong the war. This happened in a number of countries that were under the control of the Axis Powers.

While some people took this stand because the so called "handwriting was on the wall," others challenged the Nazis and other Axis forces before and after the Allies invaded Axis nations, or the territory they controlled. Once the Allies drove deeper into German held territory, some of the more aggressive resistance units assisted Allied Forces in various ways, including by offering armed opposition to The Thousand Year Reich.

One of the most interesting acts of anti Nazi armed resistance took place in Oberstdorf, the southernmost town in Germany. As documented in the footnotes in this book series, Oberstdorf was the home of a community of Bavarian Catholics who reportedly had no love for the Nazis. In the final days of the war in Europe, a home defense force known in German as a Heimatshutz, rose up against the Nazi personnel who administered this town, or were stationed in Oberstdorf.

As a further act of defiance, the members of the Oberstdorf Heimatshutz wore armbands that displayed the blue and white colors of the "Bavarian Flag." Clearly, the act of taking up arms against the Nazis, while displaying the flag of Bavaria, before the surrender of the German Armed Forces on May 8, 1945, was tantamount to committing treason.

Even though the actions of the Oberstdorf defense force is not widely known, what occurred in this Alpine region of Southern Germany in the closing days of the war, was significant for three reasons. First and foremost is the fact, that when this group of armed German citizens took over control of their town, the invading French Army was heading their way, but wasn't exactly "down the road." The available research also reports, that several kilometers north of Oberstdorf, was an SS Werwolf training camp in Langerwang, Germany and a Nazi training school in nearby Sonthofen.

Members of the Oberstdorf defense force also reportedly observed SS troops and other German military personnel moving into the nearby

Alpine trails and passes. This was a critical piece of intelligence information, because German propaganda radio reports had been broadcasting for some time, that a well supplied pro Nazi resistance movement would be operating in Southern Germany. In fact, the headquarters for this Nazi SS Werwolf resistance movement was called The Alpine Redoubt. This means, that the residents of Oberstdorf who opposed the Nazi occupation of their town, were surrounded by an ample number of potential threats to their very existence until Allied help arrived.

This particular armed militia of Bavarian Catholics did such an impressive job of securing their town, that when the French Army occupied Oberstdorf on May 1, 1945, they allowed the members of this Heimatshutz to retain their weapons. In addition, the French Army reportedly allowed the armed members of the Oberstdorf defense force to help hunt down and capture the German SS troops and regular soldiers, who were operating in the surrounding Alpine trails and passes. Doing so, prevented these Nazi holdouts from continuing to wage war against the Allies and any German citizens who opposed the aims of National Socialism. It is also important to note, that the pro Nazi resistance movement did cause casualties and some level of concern, even though SS Werwolf operations did not prolong, or change the outcome of the war. (In order to keep things simple, I elected to use the name Werwolf and Werewolves when referring to this Nazi resistance movement. As you will see in the footnotes, different reference sources spell this word differently.)

Combining the actions of fictional characters with historically accurate events, provided the perfect way to tell a riveting story, that fit the theme of The Frontline Fugitives Book Series. Just like Book II ends with the pursuit of two fugitives during the Battle of the Bulge, Book IV ends when Jim Beauregard, Al Parker and a select group of Allied military personnel, along with two civilian German policemen and German Heimatshutz fighters, pursue die hard Nazi SS troops into their Alpine Redoubt on May 1, 1945.

Combining fact with fiction was also an appropriate way to pay tribute to the brave German citizens from Oberstdorf, who sided with the Allies and risked their lives, to rid their town and the surrounding area of Nazi holdouts. Another group of anti Nazi partisan fighters known as the Austrian 05 Organization, also offered their assistance to the invading

Allied Forces. In an effort to acknowledge the contribution that was made by these anti Nazi Austrian fighters, the actions of 05 personnel were also woven into the fictional plot of Book IV. This was accomplished, by having a unit of 05 personnel escort Jim Beauregard and his men through Austria to the German border.

Book IV continues to explore the different personal and professional relationships that developed between the various characters. This includes the relationship between friends and colleagues, superior officers and subordinates, fathers and sons, men and women, cops and criminals, as well as between the Allied troops who served together. Even the relationships between different enemy combatants and civilians is explored in different ways, to help describe the war from every possible perspective.

In Book IV Jim Beauregard is once again leading troops in battle, while he and his composite unit of U.S. Army CID Agents, MPs and Counter Intelligence Corps Agents, pursue Nazi resistance fighters and war criminals in the closing days of the war. Like all good commanders, Jim feels the pressures of being in command, when he is compelled to lead men in battle, in order to complete a very dangerous mission. Fortunately, Jim has Al Parker by his side, to help him get through the more demanding days, when they serve as "cops in a combat zone."

Rather than conclude this story with the events that occurred during the war, or at the end of the war, I included an additional chapter that describes what happened to Jim Beauregard, Al Parker and some of the more significant supporting characters in the post war years. I included this chapter, because doing so, allowed me to tie up a few "loose" ends and give Jim, Al and a few of the best supporting characters the send off that they deserved.

*The names that were used in this book to identify different primary and secondary fictional characters were selected because I liked the sound of these names. With one exception, the names that were given to fictional characters have no connection to any "real life" individuals from the past or present times. As a tribute to my father's best friend, from his days growing up in the Flatbush section of Brooklyn, I named one of the CID Agents Sam Carubba. In real life, Sam Carubba is a decorated U.S Army soldier, who served in the 7nd Armored Division during the war in Europe.

I also included a "surprise" of sorts in Book IV. This particular "surprise" seemed like the right thing to do, for reasons that I decided to explain at the end of this book.

While every effort was made to make The Frontline Fugitives Book Series as realistic and historically accurate as possible, it is important to remember that this is a fiction story set in the European Theater of Operations (ETO) in 1945. As a result, certain liberties had to be taken, in order to combine fictional characters and a fictional plot, with historically accurate events that occurred during World War II.

On a personal note, I cannot express how happy I am that the men and women who have read The Frontline Fugitives Book Series, have enjoyed this historical fiction story as much as they have. As a writer, I hope that Book III and IV will be just as well received. Enjoy!

DEDICATION

This book series is dedicated to those who served in military and civilian positions and protected the United States and our allies during World War II. Clearly, the victory that was achieved in 1945 was made possible, because decent law abiding human beings from different backgrounds banded together to defeat the Axis forces.

Special thanks also go to my wife, my sons, all of my loved ones and close personal friends. Their support and encouragement means more to me than they will ever know.

CHAPTER 1

TRYING TO FIND A NEEDLE IN A HAYSTACK

When Jim Beauregard, Al Parker and their convoy of vehicles arrived at The Rhine Meadow POW Camp, also known as the Rheinweisenlager, they could not believe their eyes. For as far as their eyes could see, the entire barbed wire enclosure was jammed packed with tens of thousands of German Prisoners of War. This included the young, the old and even men who were wounded.[1]

It was also blatantly obvious to Jim and his men, that there were no buildings, no tents, no cots and no camp fires to protect the German POWs from the elements. The fact that these prisoners were being held under guard in an open muddy field, was a clear indication that the conditions in this so called prison camp, were at best considered appalling.[2]

While Jim turned to his left, he made a face then said, "This place looks twice as bad as it smells."

After agreeing with Jim, Al Parker added, "Maybe this is one of those temporary camps, where they hold prisoners until they move 'em to a regular POW Camp?"

"Let's find out," responded Jim as he faced forward and motioned Al to proceed to the makeshift MP guard post that marked the entrance to the camp.

As soon as the Jeep driven by Al Parker came to a stop, the MP on guard duty presented the two officers with a salute, before he addressed the highest ranking officer in the vehicle, "Good morning, Colonel. Welcome to The Rhine Meadow Camp."

After seeing the conditions in this sorry excuse for a prison camp, Jim Beauregard was not in a very good mood and proved it when he produced his CID credentials and responded in a businesslike tone of voice. "Colonel Beauregard and Captain Parker from CID to see your commanding officer. The men behind us are with us."

Even though the MP on guard duty was curious why a contingent of Army Agents and MPs were asking to see his CO, he performed his duties as required, as he leaned closer to the Jeep and said, "Major Hampton can be found down the road on left in the command tent, Sir."

"Thank you, Corporal," responded Jim as he returned the salute, while Al put the Jeep in gear and proceeded through the check point.

As the convoy of CID Agents, CIC Agents and MPs drove along the perimeter of the open air prison camp, Jim sat in silence while he made eye contact with a long line of German soldiers, who stood shoulder to shoulder on the other side of a makeshift fence, that was made out of a few strands of barbed wire.

"This must be the command tent," said Al as he pulled over and parked.

While the other vehicles parked behind the lead Jeep, Jim and Al were getting out of their vehicle, when a succession of shots were heard being fired from the direction of the Rhine River. The sound of shots being fired, caused every MP on duty, to level their carbines and submachine guns on the German POWs.

"Standby the vehicles, men. Lieutenant Kelly you're in charge. Captain Barnes you're with me and Captain Parker," said Jim, before he turned to Al and said, "Let's go," just as Major Daniel Hampton left the command tent in an obvious hurry.

While Jim, Al and Captain Barnes walked over to where Major Hampton was standing, a Jeep containing a young MP Lieutenant drove up and came to a stop.

"How many this time?" asked MP Major Hampton.

Two killed, four wounded, Sir," responded MP Lieutenant Steven Tyler, who quickly added, "We ordered them to stop, Sir, but they kept going. The ones we recaptured said all they wanted was a drink of water and that they weren't trying to escape across the Rhine River."

"I want a pipe from the Rhine River run into this camp, so the Krauts won't be tempted to escape just to get drink of water. See to it, Lieutenant," remarked the MP Major.[3]

"Yes, Sir," responded the MP Officer.

"Carry on, Lieutenant," said Major Hampton. Once again, the MP Officer acknowledged the order, before he motioned his driver to turn their Jeep around.

Just about the time that Jim, Al and Captain Barnes approached the American MP Commander of the Rhine Meadow Camp, Major Hampton saw that he had three visitors coming his way. Once the four officers exchanged casual salutes, Jim Beauregard, Al Parker and Captain Billy Barnes produced their credentials, while the Colonel from CID introduced himself and his two fellow Army Officers to Major Hampton.

Despite the rather unpleasant nature of his duties, Major Hampton seemed to be in good spirits when he said, "What can I do for CID and CIC today, Colonel?"

As Jim produced his orders and he handed the envelope to Major Hampton, he responded as if he was performing a routine mission. "My men and I have orders from SHAFE to interview German POWs and recruit captured enemy personnel, who are familiar with Southern Germany and are willing to serve as scouts and civilian German policemen with a combined CID, CIC and Military Police liaison unit. We're particularly interested in locating a German Military Police Master Sergeant from the 26th Volksgrenadier Division by the name of Hans Sigmann."

While Major Hampton reviewed Jim's orders one last time, the officer in charge of The Rhine Meadow Camp remarked, "It sounds like you and your men have a very interesting and potentially dangerous mission to perform, especially since we haven't captured the southern part of Germany yet."

"That's why we're taking the time to recruit some special help and gather whatever intelligence we can, before we head deeper into Germany," responded Jim.

As Major Hampton handed the orders back to the Colonel from CID, he went on to say, "I'm curious, Colonel, but what makes this Kraut MP Sergeant so important?"

Even though Jim really didn't want to explain himself, he decided to do so to move the process along. "Master Sergeant Sigmann and his squad of military policemen had my men and I dead to rights and could have taken us prisoner, after we successfully engaged an SS unit near the village of

Longchamps last December. As soon as Sergeant Sigmann heard that the American glider pilot we pursued behind the German lines was wanted for killing a New York City Policeman, he turned the fugitive over to us and let us return to Bastogne." After pausing for a split second Jim added, "You see, Major, Sergeant Sigmann was a cop in Munich before the war. I guess you can say that Sergeant Sigmann extended us a professional courtesy, because besides being soldiers, Captain Parker and I, along with Hans Sigmann are policemen in civilian life."

As Jim continued, he removed a pack of cigarettes from his field jacket pocket and offered one to Major Hampton. "If Sergeant Sigmann was willing to help us then, he might be willing to help us now that the war is all but over for Germany."

While Jim produced his Zippo and offered Major Hampton a light, he went on to say, "We hope he's willing to do so, because Germans like Hans Sigmann can help us keep the peace and combat the Nazi fanatics, who are reportedly hell bent on causing trouble after the German Army surrenders."

After taking a cigarette from the pack for himself, Jim paused to light his own cigarette as he continued. "The reason we're here is because according to Army Intelligence, the survivors of the 26th Volksgrenadier Division who were recently captured are being held in this encampment. If Hans Sigmann is in this camp, our orders are to find him and take him with us. If we find one or two other Germans who can help us successfully complete our mission, we'll be taking them with us as well."

After hearing what Jim had to say, Major Hampton responded after having his memory refreshed. "I remember reading about the arrest that you and Captain Parker made behind enemy lines, with a mixed bag of GIs during the German offensive in the Ardennes. If I remember correctly, the article in The Stars and Stripes never said anything about you and your men being helped by a friendly German MP Sergeant. Including that piece of information in that story, would have made it a lot more interesting."

"We purposely left that part out, to protect Sergeant Sigmann and his men from being put in front of a firing squad for aiding the enemy in time of war," responded Jim.

"I assume this Kraut MP speaks English," asked the MP Major.

"Yes he does," responded Jim, who quickly added, "Captain Parker also speaks fluent German and can help your MPs locate Sergeant Sigmann, if he's being held in this camp. Captain Parker will also be assisting Captain Barnes and his men from CIC when they conduct their interrogations."

After taking a quick drag on his cigarette, Major Hampton extended his hand toward the command tent and said, "Why don't we discuss how we can help you find your German inside the command tent, Sir?"

After following Major Hampton into his tent, the POW Camp Commander invited his guests to have a seat at the makeshift desk, that was made out of wooden ammo crates and ration boxes.

While everyone removed their helmets and got comfortable, Major Hampton remarked, "Your Sergeant Sigmann sounds like one Kraut who deserves a break after helping you out the way he did."

"He sure does," responded Jim, before he took one last drag on his Lucky Strike and continued, while he crushed the cigarette butt out in an empty ration can that served as an ashtray. "Tell me, Major. How long before these prisoners are transferred to a regular POW Camp?"

After extinguishing his cigarette as well, Major Hampton responded to Jim Beauregard's question in a very matter of fact tone of voice. "As far as I know, Sir, this is the last stop for a lot of these prisoners. I also heard that we'll be sending train loads of POWs to help rebuild France and other Allied countries that were badly damaged and destroyed by the Krauts and anyone who sided with them during the war. There's also a rumor going around that enemy personnel who are taken prisoner after the official surrender takes place, will not be considered POWs and will receive a new designation, that will not afford them the protection of the Geneva Convention."[4]

Being briefed by General Tremble about how different classifications of German prisoners were going to be treated was one thing, but seeing the deplorable conditions in the open air Rhine River Camp was an eye opening experience for Jim Beauregard and the men who were serving with him. While it was true that certain units, including those from the SS and the Gestapo, committed horrific war crimes, the German Army and Air Force ran a large number of POW Camps that provided the basic amenities to Allied POWs, especially to American, British, Commonwealth and French troops.

Even though some Allied POWs were treated better than others, the German run POW Camps included a building to live in, running (cold) water and a very basic food ration.

The fact that the U.S. Army accurately estimated the number of German troops who would need to be cared for at the end of the war, meant that there was no reason to be unprepared to cope with the mission to confine and care for millions of captured enemy personnel. After all, in addition to the massive stockpiles of Allied military rations, blankets and medical supplies, there were also large quantities of captured German supplies that could be used to care for enemy POWs, as well as the civilian population.[5]

About the only thing that Jim Beauregard could think of saying at that moment was, "All I can say, Major, is that this is a real mess and you for one have a job that I wouldn't want."

"You know the drill, Sir. We go where the Army tells us to go and we do what the Army tell us to do," responded the Major.

After nodding his head in agreement, Jim remarked, "You're right about that." When Major Hampton asked the Colonel from CID if he could explain some of the difficulties that he and his men will encounter, when they try and locate Sergeant Sigmann in an open air encampment," Jim responded and said, "By all means, Major."

Major Hampton proved to be a competent officer with a difficult mission, who was trying to help, when he went on to say, "If this was a regular POW Camp I could have the prisoners assemble in front of their barracks, which would make it very easy to find your German MP Sergeant.

Unfortunately, Sir, this open air camp is jammed packed with tens of thousands of German Prisoners of War. As a result, Sir, I have no idea how you and your men are gonna find your Kraut MP, in the sea of bodies that have filled this open field beyond its intended capacity. I certainly can't let you, or any of your men go beyond the barbed wire and enter the actual compound. In addition to being potentially dangerous, there's not much room in there for the prisoners to move around, let alone a search team."

As soon as Al Parker saw a look of despair cross Jim's face, he spoke up and said, "Excuse me, Colonel, but why not use food as the carrot on the stick to get the Germans to cooperate? Maybe Doc Keller could help out as well, Sir," suggested Al, who quickly added, "It might keep the crowd under control, if we tell 'em that our doctor will do his best to treat their more seriously sick and wounded, while using all of our available medical supplies."

Jim Beauregard and Al Parker had been working together long enough to think alike. Jim proved it when he remarked, "Excellent idea, Al," before he contributed an idea of his own that added more weight to Al's brilliant suggestion. "Since we're looking for a German MP Sergeant from the 26th Volksgrenadier Division, why not make our job a little easier and ask all German MPs to come forward to assist in the distribution of the food that we have on hand. Instead of trying to find one needle in a huge hay stack, we'll bring the needle we're looking for to the entrance to this camp."

"Providing, Sir, that your Kraut MP got captured and he was taken to this camp," remarked Major Hampton.

"Think positive, Major," remarked Jim, who sounded as confident as ever when he continued and said, "That's the plan we'll go with."

After pausing to remove a pack of smokes and his lighter from his field jacket pocket, Jim faced Captain Barnes and said, "Have the men save enough food and water for us to operate in the field for three days. Once that's done, have all of our vehicles parked in front of the entrance to the camp, but keep both machine guns manned at all times. Lieutenant Miller and his MPs can provide additional security while the supplies are unpacked and laid out for distribution. In addition, tell Doc Keller to get ready to treat some of the more seriously wounded and sick prisoners. Also, tell the men that we need to put on a show for the Germans so they remain cooperative."

As soon as the Captain from CIC acknowledged his orders and left the command tent, Jim turned to Al and said, "Have Sam drive you around the perimeter of this camp in our Jeep, while you direct all German MPs to assemble by the main entrance to help distribute the limited amount of food that we have on hand at this time. We'll also need all German medical personnel to bring the more seriously wounded and sick forward, so they can be treated to the best of our ability. We'll start the ball rolling once you get back to the main gate."

"I'll get right on it, Sir" said Al as he put his helmet on and left to complete his assignment.

Jim then turned to Major Hampton and said, "Tell me, Major, when do you normally feed these prisoners?"

After lighting one of his own cigarettes, Major Hampton responded and said, "We have no set time, Sir. Whenever we receive a food delivery we issue what we have."

Jim didn't like what he just heard, but rather than jump to conclusions, he quickly asked the Major when the German POWs were fed last.

"Two days ago, Sir," responded the Major.

"Two days!" remarked a shocked Jim Beauregard, who stepped closer to the camp commander as he continued reading him the riot act. "What kind of an outfit are you running here? Haven't you ever heard of the Geneva Convention?"

"I do what I'm told, Sir and I work with what I've been given," responded Major Hampton who quickly added, "If the Army wanted me to feed these prisoners more often, they'd give me more food. If the Army wanted me to house these Germans in a suitable shelter, they'd give me tents, or the materials to construct buildings. If the Army wanted me to issue clean clothing, blankets, mess kits, hot water and soap to these POWs, they'd give me the means to do so. I know this sounds harsh, Colonel, but this is the way it is, Sir."

While Jim Beauregard did his best to calm down, he stood up and took a few steps off to the side of the command tent, as the Major stood up as well and did his best to explain the situation in more detail. "You have to understand, Sir, that thousands of Germans are either surrendering or being captured on a daily basis. The simple truth, Colonel, is that the only place we can keep the number of prisoners that are pouring into our custody, is in these open air encampments."

"I'm sorry, Major, but I never thought I'd ever see anything like this," remarked Jim, who quickly added, "Personally, I wouldn't lose any sleep if this open muddy field was filled with SS troops and members of the Gestapo who committed war crimes, but captured regular German soldiers, sailors and airmen deserve to be treated properly, unless we can prove they deserve to be treated otherwise."

Major Hampton knew that it was an overwhelming experience to observe the conditions in these open air POW encampments. In an effort to explain the situation further, the Major continued and said, "When my men and I were given this assignment, we didn't have enough barbed wire let alone the material to construct a typical POW camp. About the only thing we can do for these prisoners is give them whatever food the Army provides for their use. I know it's not much, Sir, but we've been handing out the cardboard from the ration boxes to the POWs who don't have a coat or a blanket. They use the cardboard as ground cover to try and stay dry and warm. I also don't have any way of providing these prisoners with anything close to a steady supply of water. In fact, even if I had access to a thousand buckets, I couldn't provide enough water to these prisoners on a daily basis.

That's why I ordered my MPs to rig a pipe that can carry water from the Rhine River into this camp. Fortunately, this is the rainy season, so the POWs in this camp have been able to drink some rain water whenever it rains." Then, after pausing for a split second, Major Hampton ended his remarks by saying, "I'm sorry, Sir, but my men and I are doing the best we can, with what the Army gives us."[6]

After hearing what the Rhine River POW Camp commander had to say, Jim Beauregard asked Major Hampton when he and his men planned to give the prisoners their next meal.

"We received a food delivery just before you and your men arrived, Sir," responded the camp commander, who went on to say, "We planned on passing out cold rations tomorrow morning when our medical officer returns."

While doing his best to remain composed, Jim remarked, "Due to the urgency of our mission, it would help a great deal if we could pass out whatever you have on hand, with whatever we can spare as soon as Captain Parker gets back."

"If some of your men can give us a hand, Sir, I'll have all the food that was delivered earlier today distributed to the prisoners," responded the Major.

"You got a deal, Major," said Jim, who quickly added, "Let's get it done," as he put his helmet on as he left the command tent.

Once outside, Major Hampton ordered an MP Sergeant to have the five trucks that arrived earlier with the prisoner's food, brought up to the entrance to the camp and parked next to Colonel Beauregard's vehicles. While Jim stood next to Major Hampton, cases of rations, five gallon Jerry cans full of clean water and medical supplies were removed from his unit's vehicles, including from the two trailers that were towed behind the M3s.

As MP Major Hampton admired the rather large stockpile of Army rations, that were being removed from Colonel's convoy of vehicles, he turned to Jim Beauregard and said, "You and your men brought an impressive amount of food along for a detail of seventeen men, Sir."

"What can I say, Major. We planned ahead," responded Jim as he checked his watch, while five of Major Hampton's MPs drove five trucks that were loaded with additional rations over to the area near the entrance where Jim Beauregard's convoy of vehicles were parked.

Inside the overcrowded camp the word started to spread, that the Americans were asking all available German military policemen to assemble by the main entrance, to help distribute food rations to the prisoners. The fact that the message was being delivered by a Negro Captain didn't seem to matter to the German POWs, who were in desperate need of something to eat.

As Al Parker continued, he also asked for German medical personnel to come forward with the prisoners who were in desperate need of medical attention. In order not to exaggerate their capabilities, Al explained that his unit wanted to share whatever they had in the way of supplies, with as many prisoners as possible.

Inside the POW camp, Hans Sigmann was doing his best to care for his youngest son Peter, who was wounded, while flying a combat mission to destroy the Remagen Bridge. After placing his wool coat over his son, Hans looked up, when he heard a German speaking American broadcasting a message about the need for German MPs to report to the main entrance, to help distribute food to the prisoners. When Hans heard the American, who was circling the camp, say that his unit's medic would also be treating the sick and wounded, he decided to take his son with him when he reported as directed.

"You better go, Father," said Peter, who coughed several times before he continued and said, "By helping to distribute food, we should be able to get something to eat."

Even though Hans was unable to see the American who was making the broadcast due to the overcrowded nature of the camp, he could hear the American repeating the same message, while he circled the camp in a slow moving Jeep. While Hans knelt on one knee next to his son, he spoke as he reached out and helped Peter get up on his uninjured leg. "You're coming with me, son. Easy now. Take your time."

Once Hans got his son up on his feet, he helped him make his way to the entrance of the camp. Even though it was slow going, Hans and his son eventually saw the entrance in sight, as they followed a number of German military policemen, medics and wounded prisoners to the location where they were told to report.

While a bone tired Hans Sigmann held onto his youngest son, he continued looking straight ahead as he remarked, "We're almost there, Peter. Just a little further and we can get you some medical attention and something to eat."

As soon as Sam Carubba delivered Captain Parker to the main entrance, Al jumped out of the Jeep and said, "Mission accomplished, Sir," just as a group of captured German Military Policemen, followed by German medics and those who needed medical care started to assemble as directed by the entrance to the camp.

While Jim addressed the POWs, Al Parker translated everything that his Commanding Officer said in German. As surprised as the Germans were that an American Negro Army Officer spoke their language, they were twice as amazed to hear that the American soldiers who recently arrived at their camp, were distributing the food and medical supplies that they possessed, to augment the rations that were being provided to POWs by their Army.

As Jim continued, he asked all German Military Police personnel to exit the camp and form up on the left side of the supplies that needed to be distributed. While the food was being distributed, their medic would do his best to care for the sick and injured, until the Army doctor who was assigned to the Rhine River Camp returned in the morning.

While the prisoners who served a military policemen began to line up, Jim turned to Al and asked if he spotted anyone who looked like Hans? As Al did his best not to act like he was looking for an old friend, he continued scanning the faces of the German MPs who were exiting the camp as he responded and said, "Not yet, but they're still coming."

When a captured German MP Lieutenant stepped forward and saluted Jim Beauregard and the other American Army Officers, the ragged looking German officer identified himself and asked if he could be of some assistance. "Lieutenant Wilhelm Klemper, Sir. If herr Oberst would like, I can assist in organizing these men?"

As soon as the Jim and the other officers returned the salute, Jim remarked, "Your English is excellent," Lieutenant.

"Thank you, Sir," responded the German MP Lieutenant as he held his stomach and looked as if he was about to be sick.

"You don't look too good, Lieutenant. Are you sure you're up to this?" asked Jim. "I'll be fine, Sir," responded the German MP Officer. "OK, Lieutenant," get your men formed up as soon as possible and see to it that the every available MP is put to work distributing this food. I also want some men detailed to assist your medics with the sick and injured."

As Jim continued, he changed the tone of his voice and sounded dead serious when he said, "However, before we start handing out food, I want you to tell your fellow POWs that we will stop distributing food and will not provide medical care if this process doesn't run smoothly. That means no pushing, no shoving, or misbehaving in any way. I also want you to instruct your fellow prisoners to share what they're issued with others, because we don't have enough on hand to feed everyone."

Then, after pausing for a split second, Jim added, "If my men and I are willing to share what we have with you and the other prisoners, we expect everyone in this camp to do the same, or all bets are off.

Do you understand, Lieutenant?"

"I understand, herr Oberst," said Lieutenant Klemper, who quickly added, "I will relay everything that you said to the prisoners. I will also tell the men in the front to relay your instructions to the men who are in other parts of the camp."

After hearing the German MP Lieutenant acknowledge his instructions, Jim directed the young Wehrmacht officer to get all of the military policemen who were still exiting the camp, to get in formation as quickly as possible, so they could move things along. Once that was done, Lieutenant Klemper faced the compound and relayed everything that he was told to say to his fellow prisoners.

As soon as the German MP Officer finished and he returned to organizing his men, Al Parker turned to Jim and said, "He repeated everything that you said word for word."

"Good," said Jim, who quickly added, "As long as everyone behaves, this should run fairly smoothly."

"So far, so good," responded Al.

"The question is, are we gonna find our friend?" remarked Al.

"We'll know soon enough," responded Al.

CHAPTER 2

RETURNING A FAVOR

As much as Jim wanted to continue to comment about the horrible conditions in this sorry excuse for a prison camp, he refrained from doing so. Instead, Jim remained silent, while he and Al Parker looked for Hans, as a number of German MPs, medics and men who needed care came forward. When a frustrated Jim Beauregard remarked, "I don't know, Al. Maybe he's not here," Al Parker did his best to reassure his commanding officer that they were doing their best to find Hans, under what had to be extremely difficult circumstances.

After a few more POWs filtered out of the camp and joined the other German MPs, Al turned to Jim and whispered, "I hate to say it, Jim, but maybe Hans didn't hear me. He could also be sick or wounded and unable to make his way to the assembly area as directed."

As soon as Jim responded and said, "Let's find out," the two men who had good reason to locate Hans Sigmann removed their pistol belts and turned their weapons over to Captain Barnes and Lieutenant Kelly from CIC. The second Jim and Al handed the backup guns that they carried to Sergeant Blair and said, "Hang onto these for us, Hank," Major Hampton stepped in front of the two CID Agents and remarked, "I'm sorry, Sir, but I can't let you and the Captain go in there."

While Jim faced Major Hampton, he sounded like a man who was not about to change his mind when he said, "If Captain Parker and I have to walk every inch of this camp, we're not leaving until we're satisfied that we did everything possible to find the man we're looking for. Sergeant Sigmann kept us out of a prison camp. Now it's our turn to do the same for him."

After hearing Major Hampton once again object to their decision to enter the camp, Jim remarked, "What would any these POWs gain by killing or harming the two of us? Even if they took us hostage, where the hell are they gonna go? Heck, from what we've seen, these prisoners can't make it to the Rhine River to get a drink of water without being gunned down. That means that as much as they might not like to admit it, they're stuck here and will have to hope that things will change for the better, once the Allies can properly cope with the massive numbers of prisoners who are being taken into custody."

After pausing long enough to see Al nod his head to signal that he was ready to go, Jim added, "For the record and in front of witness from CID, CIC and the Military Police, Captain Parker and I will take full responsibility for our actions, Major."

As soon as Major Hampton stepped aside and remarked, "Have it your way, Sir," Jim turned to Captain Barnes and said, "You're in charge, Billy. We'll be back as soon as we have a look around."

While Captain Barnes acknowledged the order, Jim and Al started walking into the POW Camp.

As the massive crowd of German POWs stepped aside and allowed the two American Army Officers to travel deeper into the compound, Jim and Al spotted Hans coming their way, while helping to carry a wounded Luftwaffe Officer. Despite the fact that they recognized him right away, Hans looked like the other prisoners; filthy, cold, tired and wet. Even his soiled uniform looked a lot less flashy, after he was stripped of all his medals when he was captured by a squad of American soldiers.

As soon as Jim and Al approached the German Military Policeman, who made it possible for them to take the fugitive Ivan Larson into custody, a disheveled looking Hans Sigmann was surprised to see the two Americans that he assisted during the failed Ardennes Offensive.

Immediately after Al Parker spoke up and said, "It's us, Hans," Sergeant Sigman slowly raised his right hand and saluted the two American Officers before he remarked, "Somehow I always knew that we would meet again. I just never thought it would be in a place like this."

Once the two American CID Agents returned the salute, Jim stepped closer to Hans while he spoke in a low tone of voice and said, "We have written orders signed by a two star general authorizing us to get you out'a here."

"As much as I would love to be someplace else, herr Oberst, I'm sorry, but I can't leave without my son," responded Hans.

After hearing what Hans just said, a shocked Jim Beauregard remarked, "Your son!"

"Yes, herr Oberst," responded Hans, who quickly added, "Permit me to introduce you to my youngest son Peter. He was shot down over Remagen a few days after I arrived in this camp." Hans then turned to his son Peter and whispered, "These are the Americans I told you about."

Besides being in obvious pain, Peter Sigmann was just as exhausted as his father and barely able to nod his head in a respectful fashion, before he offered Jim Beauergard and Al Parker the best salute that he could muster, while he spoke in a low tone of voice and said, "Herr Obserst, Captain."

As soon as Jim Beauregard remarked, "Then, we'll take him too," he turned to Al and said, "Grab the Lieutenant, Al, while I give Hans a hand."

While the two CID Agents helped Hans and his son back to the line of parked U.S. Army vehicles, Doc Keller was already on his way to render assistance. As soon as he arrived by their side, Doc Keller remarked, "Let me give you a hand, Sir," as he helped Captain Parker take the wounded Luftwaffe Officer over to their convoy of vehicles.

While Major Hampton and Captain Barnes supervised the distribution of food to the German MPs who were POWs, Jim, Al and Doc Keller helped Hans and his son over to the back of one of the half tracks. When Jim asked how the Lieutenant was doing, Doc Keller responded while he began to sprinkle sulfur power on Peter Sigmann's wounded leg. "The Lieutenant is gonna be OK, Sir. He'll feel even better once we get him cleaned up and fed. Right now he needs to be kept warm and dry, while the morphine and penicillin that I'm about to give him takes effect."

After calling Hank Blair over, Jim turned to Hans and said, "While we pass out food, I want you and your son to get in the back of this half track and stay warm and out of sight. Sergeant Blair will get you something to eat and drink and will stay with you until we're ready to leave. Later on when we make camp for the night, you and your son can wash up and get into come clean clothes."

When a grateful Hans Sigmann said, "Thank you, herr Oberst," and he started to salute, Jim extended his hand and said, "The name is Jim. Your war is over, Hans. You and your son are among friends. It's our turn to take care of you."

Once Hans and Jim shook hands, Al Parker smiled wide as he extended his hand as well and said, "My friends call me, Al."

After all that he had been through, Hans became overcome with emotion after being rescued by the Americans that he assisted back in December. This moment was even more intense, because the Americans he helped during the Ardennes Offensive were just as eager and willing to help his son.

While an emotional Hans Sigmann looked at the two Americans, tears streamed down his soot covered face when he responded and said, "Thank you....thank you."

As soon as Al handed Hans a clean handkerchief, the German MP wiped the tears from his face, while Jim Beauregard remarked, "You kept me and Al and all of our men out of a POW Camp. We just want'a return the favor."

While Al Parker handed Hans his canteen, he sounded like an old friend when he added, "You know what they say, Hans. Us cops have to stick together. If we don't take care of each other, who will?"

As soon as he arrived in his assigned area of operation, SS Major Gunther Kessler had his men begin to recruit local citizens, who wished to serve as members of the Werwolf resistance movement. When his second in command returned with two members of the Hitler Youth and eight enlisted men from Luftwaffe and Wehrmacht units, Major Kessler instructed SS Captain Gerhardt Schneider to get their new recruits fed and settled in for the night.

Immediately after Captain Schneider acknowledged his orders, Major Kessler added, "One more thing, Gerhardt. I want you and Lieutenant Weber to issue the regular military personnel weapons and ammunition, but hold off on arming our younger recruits until we can give them some training. We can't afford to lose anyone to an accident."

SS Captain Gerhardt Schneider managed to survive this long for two reasons. First, he was a good soldier. Second, he was lucky to serve under a man like Gunther Kessler. Even though Kessler was ruthless in battle and a strict disciplinarian, his men had the highest regard for their commanding officer. They felt this way, because their unit always achieved their objective, while sustaining the fewest number of casualties. As soon as Captain Schneider acknowledged the order and started to leave the game warden's office, that was serving as their command post, SS Major Kessler remarked, "Once you're finished getting the men settled and fully equipped, I want you and Lieutenant Weber to join me for a drink. We have a lot to discuss before the Allies cross the Rhine and invade Southern Germany."

While SS Captain Schneider stood by the open door to the room, he responded with a simple, "Yes, Sir."

Once they arrived in a tree lined open field along the Rhine River, that was several miles away from the POW Camp, Jim instructed MP Lieutenant Carl Miller to post a security detail, while the rest of the men set up their makeshift campsite. While their tents were being set up to provide protection from the rain, a fire was started to boil water for bathing in the field, as well as for cooking.

With help from Doc Keller, the young Luftwaffe Lieutenant who sustained wounds to his right leg and thigh was cleaned up and issued a U.S. Army uniform that displayed no rank or insignia. As soon as his father finished washing up along the edge of the Rhine River, Al Parker handed the repatriated German MP Sergeant a clean set of U.S. Army uniforms and said, "Once you shave and have something to eat you'll be as good as new."

While Hans dressed as fast as he could to avoid getting cold, he looked at Al and said, "I can't thank you and Jim enough for getting me and my son out of that terrible place."

"We're just returning a favor to an old friend," said Al who went on to say, "As far as we're concerned, you risked an awful lot to do what you did for us last December. If the Gestapo found out that you turned a captured American pilot over to us and you let us go, especially after we wiped out an SS unit, they would'a executed you on the spot."

"And they would have enjoyed doing so," remarked Hans, who quickly added, "Fortunately, my men were very loyal to me and never spoke of the matter again."

"Come on, Hans. Let's check on your son and grab some chow," remarked Al as he started to walk back to camp with Hans by his side. Fortunately, when Hans began to falter and lose his balance, Al was close enough to grab Hans and keep him from falling. While Al helped Hans back to camp, he reassured the German MP who was in his personal care that he was among friends. "Take it slow, Hans," said Al who quickly added, "Once you have some hot chow and get some sleep, you'll start to feel better."

"Do you think we will ever forget the things that we saw during this awful war?" asked Hans.

"I'm still trying to get over the last war," responded Al.

While Hans was helped back to camp, by the American Negro policeman that he called his friend, he nodded his head in agreement then said, "I know what you mean."

Up until the day that he was shot down over Remagen, Lieutenant Peter Sigmann had never met an American up close. Even though he was compelled to join the Hitler Youth at a young age, Peter's strong Catholic faith and the guidance that he received from his family, made him more interested in serving his country than being a Nazi. Peter was further protected by his father's older brother, a World War 1 fighter pilot, who returned to the German Air Force when Hitler began rebuilding the military. Even his older brother was given similar protection, when he was inducted into the Luftwaffe and served as an 8.8 cm Flak 36 gunner attached to a German Army unit on the Eastern Front. In addition to using the famous German "Eighty Eight" to engage enemy aircraft, Luftwaffe Flak Gun crews were also used with great effectiveness to engage tanks, vehicles and other ground level targets.

Unfortunately, Peter's older brother was killed, two days after he was decorated for destroying more Russian tanks than anyone else in his unit.

As a decorated combat veteran and former airline pilot, Peter's Uncle

Carl prepared him for service in the Luftwaffe, by making it possible for him
to get it into flight school. In order to do everything he could to protect his
youngest nephew, Major Carl Sigmann, who was serving on Reichsmarshal
Herman Goering's staff, arranged for Peter to be assigned to fly a single
engine Fieseler FI 156 Storch liaison aircraft after he completed pilot training. Doing so, enabled Peter to fly a military aircraft that had the greatest
chance of keeping him out of harms way. As the war progressed, Peter
applied to be trained to fly a fighter aircraft. By the time his uncle learned
that his nephew was being trained to fly an ME109, he took no action to
prevent Peter from serving in this capacity, because he knew the war was
nearly over for Germany.

As a young Luftwaffe fighter pilot, Peter was lucky to be alive after he
flew a handful of harrowing missions against a sky full of American B17
bombers and P51 fighter planes. His days as a fighter pilot were brought
to an end, when Peter was forced to bail out over Remagen, after being
wounded by anti-aircraft fire from the American units that well entrenched
in the area.

After being captured and receiving some basic medical care, Peter
was transported to the open air POW compound along the Rhine River.
Whether it was by fate or luck, Peter's father was being held prisoner in
the same camp. They met each other in the overcrowded compound, only
because Peter learned that members of the 26th Volksgrenadier Division
were being held in the same camp. After speaking to a number of fellow
prisoners, Peter found his father kneeling by the side of one of his young
MPs who was gravely ill and died during the night.

While Peter Sigmann sat in front of a warm fire, he couldn't believe
that in addition to having his wounds properly cared for, he was clean,
well clothed, well fed, warm and sipping a cup of real American coffee. As
Peter watched his father talking to the Americans, that he assisted during
the Ardennes Offensive, his strong Catholic upbringing made him believe
that miracles do happen. Peter felt this way, because if his father had taken
the Americans prisoner, they would have been left to rot in the hell hole
that they were rescued from. Instead, their lives were spared, because one
German policeman did a favor for some American policemen.

When Jim Beauregard asked Peter if he was feeling better, the Luftwaffe

Officer sounded like a very respectful young man when he responded and said, "Yes, herr Oberst. I am doing much better thanks to you and your men."

"You're here with us because of your father. We owe him a great deal," said Jim as he offered the young pilot a cigarette and a light, before he continued and said, "The main thing is that you and your father are safe now. We'll be taking you both back to Southern Germany. Hopefully, this insanity will be over in short order so we can all go home."

Before they entered The Café Liege Sergeant Davies stopped on the corner to speak to his two new drivers. "There's something I gotta tell you boys before we go inside."

"What's up, Sarge," asked Cal Parker aka Private Andy Carter.

"What'a ever you boys do, don't get involved with any of the women in this joint, 'cause they're nothing but trouble," responded Sergeant Davies.

This time it was Benny Greene, who was working undercover as Private Benjamin Redman, who asked, "Why, Sarge?"

It was obvious that Sergeant Davies was very uncomfortable, to the point of appearing to be a nervous wreck, when he answered Private Redman and said, "Just do as I tell you, or you boys will end up in the same boat as me."

Once again Cal Parker played dumb and said, "Are you worried we're gonna get the clap...cause if you are, we're not?"

"This has nothing to do with catching something from these girls," responded a very frustrated Sergeant Davies, who went on to say, "This is real trouble I'm talking about. The kind that can't be fixed up with a shot of penicillin."

Cal Parker proved that undercover work was in his blood, when he asked the right question at the right time in their conversation with the obviously very worried Sergeant Davies. "If you're that worried about us going into this place, why are you taking us there?"

After pausing to nervously light a cigarette, Sergeant Davies exhaled a lungful of smoke before he faced the two undercover agents from CID and said, "You boys have already been in trouble with the MPs in Paris. The last thing you need is to ruin the fresh start that you got, by volunteering to drive supply trucks to frontline units."

Once again Benny Greene played his role perfectly when he asked, "You're not making any sense, Sarge. How are we gonna get in trouble by having a few drinks with the First Sergeant?"

After pausing to take another drag from his cigarette, Sergeant Davies almost came unglued when he responded to Bennie's last remark. "Because the Top Sergeant in charge of Q179 owns my ass and he doesn't need to own yours. Hell, I'm trying to do you boys a favor, so just do as I say. We go in and have a few drinks then leave. No matter what happens, don't go off with any of the local women and don't agree to nothing you're gonna regret later on. In fact, I want you to get real sleepy after one drink and call it a night."

Cal Parker knew exactly what he needed to do to push Sergeant Davies over the edge and apply the right amount of pressure on him to open up all the way. While transforming himself into one tough son of a bitch, Cal stepped closer to Sergeant Davies and said, "Me and Benny are big boys, Sarge. We don't need you to hold our hands and tell us what to do when we have a few drinks with the First Sergeant. We also don't need you telling us what we can put our dicks in and when we need to go to bed."

While Cal played the rest of his hand, he grabbed Benny by the arm and said, "Come on, Bennie. The drinks are on the First Sergeant," before he glanced back at a stunned Sergeant Davies and remarked, "Why don't you go back to camp, Sarge, and get some sack time. You look like hell."

Cal and Benny didn't take more than three steps before Sergeant Davies called out, "You want'a know why I'm worried about you boys? I'll tell you."

As Cal and Benny turned around and walked back to where the NCO from the transportation company was standing, Sergeant Davies field stripped his cigarette while he continued and said, "Some white whore was going to the MPs to say I forced myself on her when no such thing happened. When she told the owner of The Café Liege what she was gonna do, Sergeant Ross paid her the two grand she wanted to keep her mouth shut. From what the First Sergeant said, she wanted three grand, but he managed to talk her down to two. That bitch knew she had me over the barrel, 'cause the Army would'a hung my colored ass for sure for raping a white woman, even if she is a whore."

While doing his best to sound surprised, Benny Greene remarked, "Two thousand dollars?"

"A pile of money that I didn't have and probably never will," responded Sergeant Davies.

"And now you owe First Sergeant Ross for keeping you from being arrested by the MPs and sent to the damn gallows," said Cal.

"That's right and I've been paying him back for some time now and he ain't never let me forget what he did for me," responded Sergeant Davies.

While sounding like a concerned friend, Cal remarked, "And you're worried that he's gonna get us to help pay back the money you owe him?"

"Worse than that," responded Sergeant Davies, who quickly added, "He'll turn you boys into thieves as a way for him to make all of his money back, plus the interest that he says I owe him."

"Excuse me for asking, Sarge, but how much interest on the two grand do you owe that man and where the hell did First Sergeant Ross get his hands on two thousand dollars?" asked Cal.

After pausing to nervously light another cigarette, Sergeant Davies looked around before he answered Cal. "I don't know for sure, but according to the Top Sergeant, he put up five hundred and he borrowed the rest from his girlfriend. Her name is Emma. She's the widow lady who owns The Café Liege."

"What a fucking mess," remarked Cal as he removed a cigar from his coat pocket.

"Now you know why I don't want you boys to get involved," said Sergeant Davies before he took a quick drag on his cigarette and added, "As soon as I told the First Sergeant that you and Benny got in trouble in Paris and have no love for the MPs, I knew that he was up to no good when he told me to bring you here for a drink after we got off duty. I know how that man works. He's got six other colored boys working for him, that are making all kinds of money helping him steal everything from Army gasoline, to smokes, food, medical supplies, blankets, clothing and shoes."

"It sounds like the Top Sergeant has himself some racket?" said Bennie.

"And he ain't greedy either," responded Sergeant Davies, who seemed almost relieved to tell someone what was really going on at Q179 when he continued and said. "You want'a hear how smart Ross is? I'll tell ya. This man has the GIs running the POL dump short filling truck loads of five gallon Jerry cans on every other run that we make. He's got them trained to never take more than a half a gallon from every can that we take to frontline units so no one gets suspicious. If anyone asks why the cans aren't filled to the brim, Ross told everyone to say that the POL stopped filling Jerry cans to the top to limit the amount of fuel that's being spilled and wasted. He's even got that young second lieutenant so convinced that he's saving tons of fuel from being spilled, Ross got put in for a commendation. Meanwhile, every drop of gas that isn't being put into the cans, is being put into the First Sergeant's private stash of Jerry cans. Heck, he even has his own deuce and a half that's kept loaded with his supply of fuel cans that no one pays any attention to. When the time is right, Ross makes a run into Liege and sells the stolen Army gasoline for twenty bucks a damn gallon."

After taking another quick drag on his cigarette, Sergeant Davies went on to say, "And that ain't all he's stealing. When a truck is being loaded and a crate of cigarettes accidentally hits the ground, Ross writes off eight to ten cartons as being damaged and sells them to the locals for two bucks a pack.

To keep the men who work for him happy, he gives them a piece of the action, or a few cartons that they can sell on the black market. Hell, that SOB had me run my truck off the road outside of camp, just so he could steal a case of C rations and ten cartons of cigarettes that were written off as badly damaged and destroyed in the accident. He even covered my ass by saying that the accident was caused when the left front tire blew, when I was going around a sharp turn at a normal rate of speed."

Once again, Sergeant Davies paused to take another drag on his cigarette before he continued and said, "Now you know why I'm worried that Ross is gonna want you boys to help him steal whatever he can get his hands on, so he can pay back his girlfriend. To get you to agree, he'll promise you boys a piece of the action, so you can go home from this war with some money in your pocket."

When Cal asked if the other drivers were helping to pay off his debt, Sergeant Davies took one last drag from his cigarette, before he answered the question like a man who was telling the truth. "As far as I know, the other drivers started working for the Top before I came to this unit. While they're making money hand over fist, I'm still pay'in off my debt by letting the Top use me and my truck as a way to do his stealing."

After hearing what Sergeant Davies had to say, Cal paused to light his cigar before he did his best to sound like a true blue friend when he said, "I say we take the rest of the night to plan our next move. We'll meet the First Sergeant when we're ready and not before and if he gives you any shit for not showing up tonight, you tell him to talk to me."

After saying his peace, Cal put his arm around the Sergeant's back and guided him along, as he and Benny walked away from The Café Liege under the watchful eyes of Captain Lorenz and Sergeant Bill Hayes.

During their brief stay near the Rhine River Camp, Jim had Al Parker and the men from CIC conduct a number of interrogations of wounded and sick German POWs, before and after they received treatment from Doc Keller and an Army Doctor. While some of what they documented would be passed on to Army Intelligence, most of the information they gathered about German intentions in Southern Germany was based on propaganda broadcasts.

The one kernel of seemingly credible intelligence about pro Nazi guerrilla operations in Southern Germany came from a wounded senior non-commissioned officer who developed an infection and dysentery. As a member of a railway transportation company, this German NCO was privy to information that involved the use of trains to ship military personnel, Allied POWs and equipment to various locations in Europe. Because he was tired of the war and grateful for the care that he was receiving, Sergeant Rolf Bender told his interrogators about a shipment of weapons, ammunition and other supplies that was sent by train to Southern Germany.

While providing details of this shipment to Al Parker and Captain Barnes, Sergeant Bender mentioned that a contingent of SS troops under the command of a highly decorated major boarded this train before it headed south. After the train left the station, Bender's commanding officer expressed his disbelief, that such a large amount of war material was being sent into the countryside of Southern Germany, when these supplies could have been put to better use defending major cities in other parts of The Fatherland.

Once they were satisfied with the results of their interrogations, Al Parker and Captain Billy Barnes reported their findings to their commanding officer. After being briefed, Jim Beauregard instructed his men to break camp and be prepared to head south in an hour.

As soon as everyone was ready to go, Al Parker assembled the men around the lead Jeep. With the entire contingent standing by, Jim handed Hans and his son two envelopes as he spoke up and said, "Before we left that sorry excuse for a prisoner of war camp, I took the liberty of using Major Hampton's typewriter to prepare discharge papers for you and your son. In addition, I included two sets of orders that identify Hans Sigmann and Peter Sigmann as civilian German policemen assigned to this unit. These orders are co-signed by Captain Barnes from the Counter Intelligence Corps and authorize the two of you to be issued sidearms for personal protection. We're able to make these appointments, because one of the missions of the Allied armies will be to help stabilize Germany, by establishing a working civilian government that is not under Nazi control. This includes the hiring of all types of government officials, including policemen."

When Jim finished addressing Hans and his son, he turned to Al Parker and said, "Go ahead, Al." As soon as Al acknowledged the order and he issued a pair of 9mm German P38 Pistols with one spare magazine to Hans and his son, Jim continued and said, "I'd keep those pistols out'a sight as much as possible. I also want you and Peter to wear your helmets at all times." Jim then faced Peter Sigmann and said, "Sergeant Blair will stick to you like glue. Never leave his side when we're in the presence of other Allied troops. If for any reason Sergeant Blair isn't by your side, someone else from this unit will always be close by. One of us will also be with your father at all times."

Once again, it seemed quite evident that Hans Sigmann and his wife raised a very respectful younger son when Peter responded and said, "Yes, Sir."

When Jim continued, he patted the young German aviator on the top of his shoulder and said, "You ready to go home, Lieutenant?"

"Yes, herr Oberst," responded Peter. While Jim Beauregard continued to address the mixed contingent of CID Agents, CIC Agents, MPs and their two passengers, he finished his remarks by saying, "Mount up."

Jim then handed Al Parker his map and said, "Mind if I drive while you navigate?"

Once again, Al proved that he had an excellent sense of humor when he sat in the passenger seat of the lead Jeep and looked at Hans as he climbed into the back seat and said, "Hey, Hans, which way is Germany?"

Ever since that day they met during the Ardennes Offensive, Hans felt very comfortable around his American military law enforcement counterparts. Today was no different and Hans proved it when he pointed off to the east and said, "As the cowboys like to say in the American western films, Germany is that'a way."

After taking a walk away from his company area, Cal Parker spotted the Jeep that had the initials DL written in chalk near the front passenger side of the vehicle. Once he spotted Captain Don Lorenz and Agent Bill Hayes off in the distance, Cal made sure no one else was around, before he removed a box of matches and a small notebook from his right hand pant's pocket.

While Cal leaned up against the left side of the Jeep, he casually dropped the notebook that contained a hand written report, on the passenger side floorboard of the parked vehicle. Cal then used a wooden match to light his cigar and let his back up team know that the drop was made. Once again, Cal casually looked around to make sure the coast was clear, before he started walking back to his company area. After stopping by a parked 2 ½ ton 6x6 cargo truck, Cal waited until Captain Lorenz and Bill Hayes recovered his notebook and drove off in their Jeep, before he returned to his quarters.

After receiving Cal's handwritten report, Captain Lorenz, Sergeant Hayes and the local police chief payed a late night visit on Camille Anholts, the prostitute who was reportedly involved in blackmailing Sergeant Davies. To let this young girl know the seriousness of the situation, the local police chief advised the prostitute, that if she misrepresented one fact, she would be immediately taken into custody.

Once the Captain Lorenz explained that CID would rather have her be a witness than a defendant, Camille decided that it was in her best interest to cooperate. A few minutes later, Captain Lorenz and Sergeant Hayes had a signed sworn statement that further implicated First Sergeant Steven Ross, several truck drivers and the widowed owner of The Café Liege in a thriving black market and blackmail operation.

In order to keep Camile from alerting anyone about CID's interest in black market activities in town, arrangements were made to have the young prostitute call the owner of the Cafe Leige, to say that she was leaving for Brussels in the morning. Once this call was made, Captain Lorenz had Camile transported under guard to Brussels.

After making their next run, Sergeant Davies took Cal and Benny to have a drink with First Sergeant Ross. The good news was that Sergeant Davies was a lot less nervous about meeting the First Sergeant, now that he had Private Al Carter and Private Benjamin Redman willing to help him deal with the crooked senior NCO at Q179.

Just as they expected, First Sergeant Ross wasted no time in recruiting Cal and Benny into his black market operation. The First Sergeant began making his recruiting speech when he remarked, "I heard you boys had some trouble in Paris and have no love for MPs?"

As soon as Cal removed the cigar from the corner of his mouth and said, "You heard right, Top," First Sergeant Ross explained how once he paid off the rest of Sergeant Davies debt, all three of them would be making some serious money, by skimming a little off the top from the mountain of supplies that were constantly moving through Q179.

When Cal asked how much was needed to pay off the Sergeant's debt, First Sergeant Ross responded and said, "Four hundred bucks and he's home free. In fact, the way I hear it, the whore who threatened to file charges against him, is on her way to Brussels with the pile of cash that we paid her to keep her mouth shut. Worse yet, as soon as she was paid off, the bitch told one of the other prostitutes who's friends with my girlfriend, that Sergeant Davies never raped her, or threatened her in any way. The way she tells the story, the good sergeant left the room when he saw how young she was. That means it cost me and him two thousand bucks plus interest and he never even got laid."

By the time they finished their first round of drinks, Cal and Benny agreed to work for the First Sergeant and his black market operation, as a way to help Sergeant Davies pay off his debt and make money that they could put in their own pockets. After celebrating their business arrangement with the crooked supply sergeant, Cal and Benny left The Café Liege with Sergeant Davies. On their way back to camp, Sergeant Davies thanked Cal and Benny for going along and meeting with the First Sergeant.

While Cal drove the Jeep back to camp, Sergeant Davies paused to light a cigarette, before he sat sideways in the front passenger seat and said, "Now that you boys are my witnesses and you know that I'm telling the truth, I decided to go to the MPs and tell 'em all about the First Sergeant."

When Benny leaned forward and asked if he was sure he wanted to turn himself in, Sergeant Davies responded and said, "I like this man's army and want'a stay in it, even if I lose my stripes for letting that whore blackmail me and letting the First Sergeant use me the way he did."

While Cal Parker slowed their Jeep down, when they got behind a truck convoy that was returning to the company area, he looked at Sergeant Davies and said, "Don't worry, Sarge. Even though me and Benny have no love for the MPs, we'll go with you when you tell 'em what's been going on here in Liege. After all, having us as witnesses makes it three against one, if the First Sergeant tries to deny that he's been running a black market operation at Q179."

Just like he promised Cal and Bennie, Sergeant Davies turned himself and made an initial statement that emphasized, that at no time did he personally steal any Army supplies, even though he knew that First Sergeant

Ross was using him and his truck to do so. As soon as Sergeant Davies finished making a detailed statement to Major Brickel and the two men from CID, Captain Lorenz informed the Army truck driver that Camille Anholts confessed to blackmailing him, on behalf of First Sergeant Ross and the owner of The Café Liege. Even though Sergeant Davies wasn't an educated man, he was streetwise enough to figure out that if CID obtained a full confession from Camille, the Army Agents were well informed about his dealings with First Sergeant Ross and his Belgian girlfriend.

As soon as Sergeant Davies remarked, "I guess that means you and the Major know I'm telling the truth, Captain," the street cop from New Haven, Connecticut, who was now serving in CID responded and said, "Based on what we know so far that's correct. We also know that you send the bulk of your pay home to take care of your wife and kids, that you don't gamble and that you've been a good soldier ever since you joined the Army."

As soon as Captain Lorenz finished speaking, Bill Hayes sounded like another Army cop who had no ax to grind with Sergeant Davies when he said, "Thanks to you, we also know a lot more about the men at the POL Dump and the other drivers who've been helping the First Sergeant steal Army gas and supplies."

After hearing Sergeant Davies remark, "I just hope the Army will let me go back to driving my truck when this is all over, Sir," Captain Lorenz looked across the table at Bill Hayes and said, "Bring 'em in, Bill."

As soon as Cal Parker and Benny Greene entered the room, Sergeant Davies stood up and began defending the two new men in his unit. "Excuse me, Captain, but these boys are good soldiers. All they did was try to help me out by meeting with the Top Sergeant, so the Army would believe my story. They ain't done nothing wrong, except talk."

After telling Sergeant Davies to sit down, Captain Lorenz remarked, "You're right. These men are good soldiers. In fact, it's because of them, that we've been able to wrap this case up a lot sooner than expected."

As soon as Captain Lorenz handed the two undercover agents their leather badge cases, Cal and Benny identified themselves as U.S. Army CID Agents. Initially, Sergeant Davies was speechless. "You boys are with the Army Police?" remarked a shocked Sergeant Davies.

As soon as Cal turned to his undercover partner and said, "Go ahead,

Bennie. Tell him," the youngest man in the Paris based CID unit sounded as proud as ever, when he responded and said, "That's right. Me and Sergeant Parker are with Army CID."

After picking up some Army rations, fuel and fresh water from an engineer unit in Remagen, Jim Beauregard and his men made their way to Liege, Belgium. Once they checked in with Captain Lorenz, Jim and his men planned to pick up additional provisions at Q179 before they linked up with the French Army in Speyr, Germany.[7] As long as their undercover services were no longer needed, Cal Parker and Benny Greene would be allowed to join the expedition into Southern Germany.

CHAPTER 3

IN HARM'S WAY

Now that First Sergeant Ross was in custody, Captain Lorenz, Sergeant Bill Hayes, MP Major Brickel and his MPs were busy rounding up the other American GIs and local civilians, who were involved in black market activities in and around the supply depot known as Q179. After notifying General Tremble that they successfully completed their mission in Belgium, Jim and his men prepared to rendezvous with the French Army. As soon as their vehicles were refueled and loaded with all the supplies that they could carry, Al Parker walked over to where Jim Beauregard was reviewing a map and said, "We're ready to go, Jim."

"OK, Al. Load 'em up," responded Jim as he folded his map and slipped it into his field jacket pocket, while he and the recently promoted Captain Parker walked over to the cargo truck that was parked nearby. As soon as they approached the truck, Jim called out, "I've got something to give you, Bennie."

While Corporal Benny Greene stood by the front bumper of the truck at a comfortable attention, Jim spoke as he approached the youngest man in his unit and handed him several sets of sergeant stripes. "Congratulations, Sergeant. You can sew these on when we make camp tonight."

After taking a second to admire the buck sergeant stripes, an excited Benny Greene snapped to attention and saluted his commanding officer and said, "Thank you, Sir. I mean it, Colonel. Thanks a lot, Sir."

As soon as Jim returned the salute, he shook the newly promoted sergeant's hand and said, "You're welcome, Bennie. Enjoy the promotion. You deserve it."

While smiling wide, Al Parker also stepped forward and shook Bennie's hand as he congratulated his son's undercover partner on being promoted.

Benny Greene was a very respectful young man, who appreciated the fact that he was given a second chance, after he made the terrible mistake of going AWOL and working for a brief period of time in Sergeant Moffet's black market operation. After saluting Al Parker and saying, "Thanks Captain," Benny remarked, "I can't wait to write my folks and tell 'em I got promoted."

After hearing what Benny Greene just said, Jim Beauregard cracked a smile before he addressed the newly promoted buck sergeant in a friendly tone of voice and said, "Mount up, Sergeant, we're moving out."

"Yes, Sir," said Benny as he slipped the sergeant stripes in his field jacket pocket and sat in the driver's seat of the Army cargo truck.

After hearing the Colonel say, "Hold on, Cal. I've got something for you too," Cal stood by the open passenger side door of the truck, while his commanding officer handed him six sets of Technical Sergeant's stripes and said, "Congratulations, Cal. General Tremble personally approved your promotion and wanted your father and I to hand you these tech sergeant stripes before we left Liege."

"Thanks, Colonel," responded Cal Parker as he accepted the stripes with his left hand, while he shook hands with his commanding officer.

"You and Benny both deserve to be promoted," remarked the Colonel as a smiling Al Parker shook hands with his youngest son and said, "I'm proud of you, son." "Thanks Dad," said Cal, who continued as he slipped the Technical Sergeant stripes in his field jacket pocket, "The extra pay that comes with that extra stripe will come in handy now that I'm a married man."

"You're right about that," responded Al.

After checking his watch, Jim looked at Cal then over to Benny and said, "Even though we shouldn't run into any trouble until we cross the Rhine, I want you men to stay sharp at all times. I also want you to position yourselves behind the number one half track. I'll tell Hank to let you get in front of him once we get rolling."

While responding in unison, Cal and Benny called out, "Yes, Sir," as their commanding officer and Cal's father went to check on the rest of the men in their unit.

After walking over to the last M3 half track in their convoy, Jim leaned closer to the open driver's side window and addressed Sam Carubba.

"Ready, Sam?"

"Yes, Sir," responded the former MP turned CID Agent.

Jim then looked up at Sergeant Mulligan and called out, "Ready, Mike?"

While the XXL size Mike Mulligan manned the M2 .50 caliber belt fed machine gun, that was mounted in the back of the number two half track, the former paratrooper turned CID Agent responded and said, "We're right behind you, Colonel."

"We'll see you at the next stop," said Jim.

As soon as Jim Beauregard and Al Parker walked over to the number five Jeep in their convoy, Jim addressed Peter Sigmann in a very friendly tone of voice. "You're looking better every day, Peter."

"Thank you, herr Oberst," responded the former Luftwaffe pilot, who was now carrying orders that identified him as a civilian German policeman assigned to a U.S. Army Liaison Unit.

After joking around with Hank Blair and his passenger by saying, "No stopping to talk to pretty girls," Jim instructed Sergeant Blair to let Benny Greene pull their supply truck in front of his Jeep once they started moving.

While Hank Blair responded and said, "Will do, Sir," Jim and Al walked over to the other M3 that was also towing a trailer that was filled with supplies for the trip.

As Jim looked up at Sergeant Janowski from CIC, who was standing by the belt fed M2 machine gun that was mounted on the number one half track, he called out, "Hang onto that 50 cal, Fred, because we might need it where we're going."

"She's loaded and ready to go, Colonel," responded the Sergeant from CIC, who survived the Battle of the Bulge with Captain Barnes and Lieutenant Kelly, by manning a .30 caliber machine gun when they found themselves cut off and surrounded by German troops.

"That's the spirit," responded Jim as he and Al stopped by the cab of the lead M3 and spoke briefly to MP Sergeants Dalton and Morgan, before they made their way to the MP Jeep that was occupied by MP Lieutenant Carl Miller and MP Corporal Thomas Baines. After asking MP Lieutenant Miller if he and Corporal Baines were ready to go, the MP Officer who commanded the detail of military policemen responded and said, "We're ready, Colonel."

While Jim and Al walked to the next vehicle in line, Jim looked back at the MP Corporal who was serving as Lieutenant Miller's driver and joked, "Don't drive too fast, Tommy. We don't want'a get in trouble with any MPs." Corporal Thomas Baines was selected for this trip because he was another military policeman who saw some combat when Paris was liberated in August of 1944. While Jim and Al walked to the next vehicle in line, the MP Corporal started the engine to Lieutenant Miller's Jeep as he called out, "The MPs got'a catch us first, Sir."

After hearing the young MP's comeback, Jim turned and gave Corporal Baines the thumbs up, before he looked at Al and said, "That kid has some sense of humor. I'm glad we brought him along." Al Parker agreed and quickly added, "I heard Lieutenant Miller and Corporal Baines were decorated by the French for rescuing a wounded resistance leader under fire and killing a German sniper during the liberation of Paris. After the French kissed them on both cheeks, our Army gave 'em the Bronze Star and a promotion."

"That's one reason why we're taking them with us," said Jim, who went on to say, "All the MPs who are coming with us on this trip are tough cookies and will come in handy if we get in a fight with the Germans." After stopping by to check on Lieutenant Miller and Corporal Baines, Jim and Al walked up to the next Jeep in line to have a few words with Sergeants Angelone and Coppola.

"You boys ready?" asked Jim.

While Sergeant Coppola sat sideways in the driver's seat of the number three Jeep in the convoy, he turned to his partner and said, "Go ahead, Ange. Tell the Colonel what we were just talking about."

As Sergeant Angelone faced Lt. Colonel Beauregard and Captain Parker, the young CID Agent who was known to be outspoken said, "Sal and I are worried about you and the Captain taking point, Sir. With all due respect, Sir. We would like to volunteer to lead the way....you know, Sir, just in case we run into any Krauts. After all, Sir, you're our CO and the Captain is your number two from CID on this trip."

Both Jim and Al were deeply appreciative of the level of enthusiasm and concern that two of their most aggressive and colorful agents had for them. In every respect, Sergeant Anthony Angelone and Sergeant Sal Coppola were was a lot like their fathers; two veteran law enforcement officers who served with Jim and Al in the New York CID Task Force. Rather than dampen their enthusiasm, or appear ungrateful, Jim responded and said, "Once we cross the Rhine, we'll be looking for a few volunteers who are full of piss and vinegar to take point. Until then you boys sit tight and enjoy the ride, OK?"

Immediately after the two sergeants responded and said, "Yes, Sir," Jim and Al moved to the next Jeep in line. Just before they reached the next Jeep, Al turned to Jim and said, "Ange and Sal are good kids."

"That they are and they're also a lot like their fathers," responded Jim, who went on to comment, "Police work is definitely in their blood."

Once Jim reached the second Jeep in line, the Colonel from CID looked at Captain Barnes and Lieutenant Dan Kelly and said, "We're all set in the back. Are you and the Lieutenant ready to do put some miles on that Jeep?"

"Yes, Sir," responded the Captain from the Counter Intelligence Corps.

Even Lieutenant Kelly seemed in good spirits when he spoke up and said, "You know what they say, Sir. Home alive in 45." As Jim Beauregard responded and said, "From your lips to God's ears, Dan," he walked up to the lead Jeep in their convoy and took his seat next to Al Parker.

When Jim turned sideways in his seat, he looked at Hans Sigmann and asked if he was comfortable sitting in the back of the Jeep?"

"If I have this much room in heaven, I'll be a lucky man," responded Hans.

While Al started the engine and put their Jeep in gear, Jim continued looking at Hans as he cracked a smile then said, "Ain't that the truth," before he turned around in his seat and remarked, "You're in charge, Al. 42nd and Broadway here we come."

In an effort to cut back on the number of cigarettes that he smoked, Jim decided to take up smoking a pipe. To plan for this transition, Jim purchased a Three Star Deluxe Dunhill pipe from the PX in Paris. As soon as Jim removed his new pipe from his trench coat pocket, he reached into the musette bag that he used to carry some extra ammunition and a few personal items. After feeling his way past a few packs of Lucky Strikes, three Hershey Bars, two 50 round boxes of .30 caliber Carbine ammunition and several packs of chewing gum, Jim found what he was looking for.

As soon as Jim removed a pouch of Half and Half Tobacco from the bag, he did his best to fill the bowl of his Dunhill in a moving Jeep. Since Al and Jim were as close as Army buddies could be, Al decided to tease Jim by saying, "Do you want me to pull over, so you can load that pipe without spilling half of your tobacco all over the interior of this Jeep?"

"I'll get the hang of it. Just give me time," responded Jim as he finished packing the bowl of his Dunhill and proceeded to brush the excess tobacco off his Army Officer's Trench Coat. After putting his pouch of tobacco away, Jim used his Zippo to light his brand new pipe for the first time. As Jim puffed away, he turned to face Al and grinned like a kid who was playing with a new toy, when he remarked, "How do I look?"

While Al continued driving the lead Jeep, he did his best to sound serious, as he glanced to his right and said, "Distinguished, Jim. Very Distinguished."

Even Hans contributed to the exchange, as he leaned forward in his seat and remarked, "And that tobacco smells great too."

"You're right, Hans. It does smell pretty good," said Jim, who quickly added, "I should'a started smoking a pipe a long time ago."

After arriving a day ahead of schedule, Jim Beauregard along with Al Parker, Captain Barnes and Sergeant Sam Carubba met with Colonel Reynald at the French Army command post in Speyr, Germany. Even though the French had no love for the Germans, Colonel Reynald knew that the day was coming, when a pro Allied civilian government would need to be installed to govern Germany. As a result, Colonel Reynald had no problem with the presence of two recently discharged "friendly" German soldiers, who were appointed to serve as civilian policemen, being assigned to the American Liaison Unit.

Colonel Reynald also understood the concept of returning a favor. Once the Colonel heard how Hans Sigmann enabled Jim Beauregard and Al Parker to capture an American glider pilot who was a wanted fugitive, he understood why the Americans went to such lengths to locate and help the German MP, who assisted them during the Ardennes Offensive. The fact that Hans Sigmann's son was taken along and put to work to further the Allied cause, was also agreeable to the French Colonel.

While the 3rd Algerian Regiment crossed the Rhine at Speyer on March 31st, Jim and his men were told would make the crossing with Colonel Reynald's intelligence unit and the French 9th Colonial Infantry Division further south at Leimercheim on April 2nd. Once the initial assault was made by troops in rubber boats, French combat engineers would build pontoon bridges across the Rhine, that would support the weight of their vehicles.[8]

In the early morning hours of April 2, 1945, Jim and his men watched as troops from the 9th Colonial Infantry crossed the Rhine, to begin the second phase of the French invasion of Southern Germany. While the French troops made the initial crossing, Jim addressed the men under his command. as they assembled around the lead Jeep in their convoy.

"OK, men, listen up. Once the French engineers get us across the Rhine, we'll be following Colonel Reynald's Intelligence Unit and a mechanized infantry and armored column through Southern Germany. That means that we'll be covering their rear, as the French Army drives through Southern Germany into Austria. Even though the French will likely end up doing the brunt of any fighting that takes place, we have to be prepared to defend ourselves and assist our French Allies as needed. This includes when this war is over, because Nazi resistance fighters known as Werwolves, are expected to continue to launch attacks on Allied personnel and installations, as well as on law abiding Germans."

After pausing to light his pipe, the Commanding Officer of the U.S. CID/CIC/MP Liaison Unit added, "One more thing. In the last few days, each of you have had the opportunity to get to know Hans Sigmann and his son Peter. As you all know, these men are recently discharged German military personnel, who are now serving as civilian policemen assigned to this unit. We're lucky to have them with us for more reasons than one. Seek their advice and assistance whenever you think they can help. Whenever we have contact with the German people, Captain Parker, Hans and Peter will serve as our translators. If we take prisoners, Captain Barnes, Lieutenant Kelly and Sergeant Janowski will be in charge of all interrogations, with Captain Parker, Hans and Peter serving as their interpreters. Lieutenant Miller and his detail of MPs will be in charge of security for this unit and will establish a schedule for guard duty that will be augmented by men from CID and CIC. Lieutenant Miller and his MPs will also take charge of any prisoners who fall into our custody. The rest of us will give our MP detail a hand as needed. Last but not least, Lieutenant Kelly will serve as our communications officer and Sergeant Carubba will serve as our liaison agent to the French Army. Any questions?"

When Sergeant Angelone raised his hand and asked if they were still planning to go all the way to Berlin, Jim responded and said, "Unless things change, one of the reasons we were assigned this mission, is so we can be escorted through Germany for the purposes of establishing the first CID Office in Berlin and based on what we were told, we can expect to have lots of work to do once we get there."

When no one else had any other questions, Jim checked his watch before he looked at the men under his command and said, "This might be a good time to check your equipment again and standby your vehicle. We'll be moving out soon."

After providing some instruction to his newest recruits, SS Major Gunther Kessler divided his ambush element into two main elements. While the bulk of his men were assigned to conduct ambush operations, along the road that ran through the Black Forest, SS Captain Gerhardt Schneider was tasked with the responsibility of organizing resistance cadres, to operate in the alpine passes of Southern Germany.

According to SS Major Kessler's plan, SS Captain Schneider would use the Nazi training school in Sonthofen, Germany and the Werwolf training camp at Langenwang, near Oberstdorf, Germany as his initial bases of operation. The Nazi training school in Sonthofen and the training camp at Langenwang were selected for Schneider's part of their mission, because a large amount of critical supplies were stockpiled at these location, for use by the Werwolf resistance movement. Once Captain Schneider's contingent was ready to go operational, Kessler's second in command would position his personnel in clandestine bases that were located in alpine passes and trails near Oberstdorf.

Immediately after Captain Schneider and his team left to begin their mission, Major Kessler began preparing his group to operate in the Black Forest. While regular German military units were assigned to defend the major cities, SS Major Kessler began to familiarize his ambush teams with the first location that he selected in the Black Forest, that would be used to execute attacks on Allied personnel.

After assigning SS Lieutenant Wolfgang Weber to command the two Hitler Youth/Werwolf volunteers and the eight volunteers from different Army and Luftwaffe units, SS Major Kessler led his twenty four enlisted SS troops on a patrol to familiarize them with the first ambush site. Once both units became familiar with their assigned positions, Major Kessler and his men met for lunch, before they spent the rest of the day training to execute guerrilla operations in the area.

After completing several days of ambush training in the Black Forest, SS Major Kessler began instructing his men how they would carry on the fight, once the Allies advanced further into Southern Germany. To prepare the men who survived their ambush operations to carry on, SS Major Kessler had his personnel reposition a portion of their supplies in a series if secret equipment caches in remote locations. If Major Kessler was killed, or their unit sustained significant casualties, the survivors were instructed to join up with SS Captain Gerhardt Schneider at the designated rendezvous points.

While assisting French troops to mop up the last elements of resistance during the battle to capture the City of Pforzheim, Jim Beauregard and Captain Barnes met with Colonel Reynald, to discuss the next phase of the Invasion of Southern Germany. As a mixed contingent of Jim's men and French soldiers disarmed and searched a group of recently captured German soldiers, Colonel Reynald opened his map case and showed the two American officers where they were going next.

After accepting a light from Jim, the French Army Intelligence Officer, exhaled cigarette smoke, as he pointed to his map and said, "Now that we have taken Karlsruhe and Pforzheim we'll be moving into the Black Forest."

As Colonel Reynald continued, he looked at Jim Beauregard and said, "Up until now we've been fighting regular German soldiers. Once we enter the Black Forest, we must be prepared to engage regular German military personnel, as well as the Werwolf resistance fighters that we believe will be active in this area. The ones who are wearing uniforms will be treated according to the Geneva Convention. Anyone we capture who is not wearing a uniform will be executed on the spot. We will also not tolerate attacks on our troops by anyone after Germany is forced to surrender."[9]

Jim Beauregard and the men under his command knew, that they were about to experience an ugly side of the war, one that their French Allies became familiar with when their country was occupied by the Germans. Under the circumstances, the Americans who were assigned to serve with the Free French Forces were not about to argue with Colonel Reynald. This war needed to end and end fast. As a result, the rules of war would be strictly enforced.

While Colonel Reynald closed his map case, Jim remarked, "Do you still want my men to bring up the rear?"

While participating in the battle to take the City of Karlsruhe, Colonel Reynald and his men fought alongside the American Liaison Unit that was commanded by Lt. Colonel James Beauregard. Even though French armored units and dismounted infantry handled the bulk of the fighting, the Americans who were assigned to the French Army proved to be an aggressive bunch. In addition to participating in urban combat, that included clearing buildings, Jim and his men assisted the French in rounding up and guarding German prisoners. The same level of cooperation existed during the three days of fighting to take Pforzheim. Even Doc Keller put his talents to work, by providing medical aid to wounded French troops and captured enemy personnel.[10]

After taking another drag on his cigarette, the French Army Intelligence Officer responded and said, "Having you and your men positioned at the rear of our column seems to be working out well for us."

"Then it's settled," said Jim, who quickly added, "You're in charge, Andre.

If you need us, just holler."

As Andre Reynald presented Jim with a casual salute, Captain Al Parker approached the French Intelligence Officer's Jeep and spoke as he addressed Colonel Reynald. "We're ready to go, Colonel. The last of the Germans we captured were just loaded into the truck that's heading to the rear with some of your MPs."

"Thank you, Captain," responded Colonel Reynald. When Jim asked Al if any of the Germans had anything worthwhile to say, Al responded and said, "Whenever I asked the Germans we interrogated if they knew anything about these Werwolf fighters, the few who were willing to talk said that everyone in Germany has heard of them. The only prisoner who would comment more than that, suggested that we should be real careful if we planned on traveling any deeper into Germany."

"That sounds like good advice," remarked Captain Barnes.

"I agree," said Jim, who went on to say, "OK, Al, load 'em up. We'll be following Colonel Reynald and his men to the next stop as soon as they're ready to go."

"Yes, Sir," responded Al, before he turned and walked back to where the American contingent was waiting by their vehicles.

The night before they entered the Black Forest Jim and his men spent the night on the outskirts of a small German village. In order to provide some additional security to the rear of the column, Colonel Reynald assigned a French Army Sherman M4 tank to the American Liaison Unit.

While using an empty building on the edge of the village as their bivouac area, the men who made up the American Liaison Unit wrote letters, sipped hot coffee and checked their equipment, before getting some sleep. As Jim put his canteen cup down and stood up, he looked at Al Parker and said, "Why don't we have a look around before we hit the sack." "Good idea," responded Al as he picked up his M3 Grease Gun and followed Jim out of the building.

After making the rounds and speaking to the MPs who were pulling guard, Jim stopped by the line of American vehicles that were parked in front of their makeshift campsite and said, "Hold it up, Al."

Al Parker had worked with Jim Beauregard long enough to know, that he was feeling the burden of being in command of soldiers who were serving in combat. Even though Jim Beauregard was an outstanding leader of men and an excellent military tactician, Al Parker knew that even the best commander had to be prepared to lose men in battle. As soon as Jim looked at Al, he sounded like a man who had something on his mind when he remarked, "I got that feeling again, Al."

"You mean the one that keeps good Army Officers awake at night?" said Al.

After nodding his head in agreement, Jim remarked, "That's the one."

"I don't know what else you can do, Jim. You've made all the right calls ever since we crossed the Rhine and the men know it," responded Al.

While standing next to one of the M3 half tracks, Jim continued expressing his concerns in a low tone of voice. "We're both in the same boat, Al. I say that, because I saw the look on your face when Cal and Benny took off with Ange and Sal, to flank that MG42 gun crew that had us pinned down back in Brotzingen."

"You're right, Jim. That was tough for you and me to watch," responded Al, who quickly added, "That place was a hell hole. We were damn lucky, but I lost count of the number of Algerian and Moroccan troops who were killed and wounded during the fighting in that section of Pforzheim."[11]

"I definitely lost a few years off the tail end of my life as well, when I saw what those crazy kids did," said Jim. Then, after pausing for a split second Jim added, "In fact, I'm damn proud of all the men. They fight well."

Now that it was Al's turn to respond, he tried to sound as reassuring as possible, when he continued and said, "You're right, Jim. All the men are good soldiers. They've done everything that we've asked them to do and more without any gripes or bitching."

After looking around to make sure that they were still alone, Jim faced Al as he continued and said, "What concerns me is that starting tomorrow we'll be going into an unknown battlefield, where any civilian could turn out to be a Nazi fanatic, who wants this war to drag on long after The Third Reich surrenders."

In an effort to help Jim understand that what he was feeling was normal,

Al responded as he pointed his right index finger at Peter Sigmann, who was having his bandages changed by Doc Keller in the back of their supply truck. "Before he was shot down, Lieutenant Peter Sigmann flew a number of missions against the 8th Air Force in a ME (Messerschmitt) 109. The American P51 fighters that he engaged on a number of those missions had red painted tail sections. Those aircraft belong to my son Jack's squadron. That means, that not that long ago, young Peter Sigmann just might'a shot at my son Jack and my son Jack might'a shot at him."

After hearing what Al had to say, Jim remarked, "I guess what you're telling me, is that the best thing we can do for these kids and for this world, is to end this stinking war as soon as possible and get as many of these boys home in one piece."

"That's how I see it," responded Al.

Jim never sounded more appreciative then when he looked directly at his good friend and said, "Thank, Al."

"The feeling is mutual," said Al, who couldn't resist the opportunity to joke around when he added, "After all, if it wasn't for you and General Tremble, I'd be back in New York City chasing crooks, drinking Irish Whiskey laced coffee and getting fat on Mary's home cooking."

Seeing Jim smile, was exactly what Al was hoping to achieve. They were back on track and it felt good. While Jim started to walk back to camp with Al, he seemed like a man who was in better spirits, when he patted his friend on the back and said, "Let's talk to Hans and Peter before we hit the sack. Up until now we've been keeping them on the sidelines. All that changes tomorrow when we enter the Black Forest.

CHAPTER 4

THE BLACK FOREST

As soon as the French Army column was spotted heading their way, SS Major Kessler instructed his men to take their positions just as they had rehearsed. Thanks to the terrain features, SS Major Kessler decided to launch a four pronged attack in rapid succession.

The initial attack would consist of three squads of Kessler's SS troops, who would ambush the lead elements of the French column from three different positions on the left side of the road. The first squad would launch their attack at an offset angle and concentrate their fire directly into the lead vehicles of the Allied column.

Once the first squad opened fire, the second squad of SS troops would lunch their attack from inside the treeline along the left side of the road. A split second after the second SS squad opened fire, Kessler's third squad was assigned to ambush the middle of the enemy column from the left side of the road. A fourth element, that was under the command of SS Lieutenant Wolfgang Weber, included an MG42 machine gun team, several men armed with MP44s and MP40s, as well as two teams consisting of a Panzerfaust gunner and an ammo bearer. In order to complete the ferocity of the ambush, SS Lieutenant Weber's section was assigned to attack the tail end of the Allied column from the right side of the road.

As far as SS Major Kessler was concerned, the level of fear associated with being ambushed from different vantage points would increase even more, once vehicles in the Allied column were destroyed and set ablaze. Attacking a vehicle column from four different vantage points, on both sides of a narrow forest road, would also make it considerably more difficult for the enemy to launch a counter attack. Since Kessler and his men were unable to call in air attacks or an artillery strike, their plan was to open fire from different positions and do as much damage as possible in a relatively brief period of time, before withdrawing from contact. If everything worked out as planned, Kessler and his men would regroup at a designated location and continue on their mission, to launch attacks on Allied units that ventured deeper into Southern Germany.

While briefing his mixed contingent of troops, who had different levels of experience, including no combat experience, Major Kessler went on to say, "For those of you who never served with me before, understand that my men and I have successfully used this tactic in the past. However, you must remember that the purpose of these ambush operations are to kill and wound as many of the enemy as possible, while destroying or damaging as many of their vehicles as possible, in the shortest amount of time. Ambushing an enemy column from different positions on both sides of the road should also make the Allied troops feel extremely vulnerable and will likely cause some of their troops to panic. We must exploit both of these points to our advantage, before we withdraw from contact with the enemy."

After pausing for a second, SS Major Kessler added, "You must also not deviate from how you have been trained to execute these ambush operations. Doing so, will enable us to strike hard and live to fight another day. Remember, Germany needs live soldiers not casualties, so do not press your attack after it's time to withdraw, unless you are directed to do so and there is a clear cut opportunity to use the element of surprise to your advantage. It is also imperative to remember, that the primary targets for the Panzerfaust gunners are enemy armored vehicles and fuel trucks. Everyone else should concentrate on engaging enemy personnel and other vehicles, such as Allied supply trucks and Jeeps."

While SS Major Kessler looked at the mismatched group of troops under his command, he continued and said, "While I command the first squad, Sergeant Mueller will command the second, Corporal Krebs the third and Lieutenant Weber the fourth."

In order for SS Major Kessler to insure the success of each ambush, he assigned his more experienced troops to conduct the attacks from the front and left side of the road, while the mixed contingent of less experienced men, were tasked with attacking the rear of the enemy column, from the right side of the road. Because they had no combat experience, the two Hitler Youth volunteers were assigned to carry extra Panzerfaust rockets, for the two designated Panzerfaust gunners in Lieutenant Weber's section.

Just before they entered the Black Forest, Jim Beauregard changed the order in which his men would proceed, as they traveled deeper into Southern Germany. According to Jim's plan, if they came under attack, he would make his way to the rear of the column, providing that it was possible to do so.

As Jim explained to his men, doing so would enable him to evaluate the severity of the situation and direct them accordingly. This left Captain Parker to command the front of their column and Captain Barnes to command the middle of the column. Should Jim not be able to reposition himself, Captain Barnes was tasked with the responsibility to direct the men stationed in the second half of the American Liaison Unit.

When Jim continued to explain how he wanted everyone to react to an attack, he instructed Sergeant Mike Mulligan to train his M2 .50 caliber machine gun toward the right side of the road, while Sergeant Janowski was instructed to cover the left side of the road with his belt fed M2. The rest of the men were instructed to cover fields of fire from all possible directions as they made their way through the Black Forest. To add to their firepower, Colonel Reynald continued to assign the same French Army M4 Sherman tank, that protected Jim and his men the night before, at the rear of the American column. Doing so, placed the American Liaison Unit in between the last French M3 half track in Colonel Reynald's column and a French Armored Division Sherman Tank.

As Jim finished his briefing, he turned to Sam Carubba and said, "If we come under attack, I want you to do what you can to protect the French Tank crew. Hank and Mike will do what they can to help."

Immediately after Sam Carubba acknowledged the order, Jim asked Doc Keller how Peter Sigmann was doing. "He still has a slight fever, Sir. His thigh wound is also starting to swell. If I had to guess, Sir, I'd say a small piece of shrapnel is keeping the Lieutenant's wound infected."

When Jim asked Doc Keller what he recommended, the experienced combat medic responded and said, "I spoke to the French Army Surgeon,

Sir, and he's agreed to take a look at Peter as soon as we make camp. In the meantime, I'm pumping him full of penicillin and covering his wounds with sulfur powder and fresh bandages."

After nodding his head, Jim remarked, "OK, Doc. Make Peter as comfortable as possible in the back of the number two half track. In the meantime, you can ride with Hank in the number five Jeep."

Once his briefing was over, Jim told his men to mount up and get ready to move out. While his men took their positions, Jim stood by the passenger side of the lead Jeep in the American column and addressed Hans Sigmann while he sat in the back seat. "Don't worry, Hans. We'll get Peter the medical attention that he needs as soon as we stop for the night."

"Your medic is right, Jim. Even a tiny piece of shrapnel that is barely visible to the naked eye, can cause a wound to remain infected and cause a man to get a fever," remarked Hans.

Al also contributed to their exchange when he added, "I'm sure the conditions in that sorry excuse for a prison camp didn't help."

"You're both right," responded Jim, as the French troops in front of their position climbed into their vehicles and prepared to proceed into the Black Forest. As Jim sat in the front passenger seat of the lead Jeep, he glanced back at Hans and said, "Hey Hans, when was the last time you were in this neck of the woods?"

"Before the war, Jim," responded Hans, who quickly added, "As much as I would like our ride through the Black Forest to be just as peaceful today as it was then, I have to warn you and Al, that the terrain in these woods are ideally suited for executing ambush style attacks."

As Jim responded and said, "I figured that," he faced forward while Al made the sign of the cross before he started their Jeep. Once the vehicles in front of their position began to drive away, Al worked his way through the gears, while he followed behind the last vehicle in the French column.

Even though they were driving into the unknown in time of war, Jim and Al had been through enough as cops and soldiers, to know how important it was to keep their sense of humor. Hans Sigmann was no different and helped to pass the time, by providing Jim and Al with more information about the terrain in this part of Germany.

After traveling deeper into the forest, Jim turned to Al and said, "I see you've done this before?" As a veteran combat soldier, Hans knew exactly what Jim was referring too, when he saw how Al Parker was keeping the right amount of separation between their vehicle and the French half track, that was positioned at the tail end of Colonel Reynald's intelligence unit.

"If it wasn't for the fact that we have to worry about coming under attack, this is a lot like driving through Central Park," joked Al as he continued to follow the French convoy. A split second later, all hell broke loose, when the Allied column came under attack from both sides of the road. As soon as Al brought their Jeep to a stop, the three occupants took cover behind the back of the vehicle. The second they did so, Hans pointed off to the right at a 45 degree angle as he called out, "Panzerfaust!"

By the time Jim and Al spotted the well camouflaged Panzerfaust gunner, the rocket left the tube and was streaking across an opening in the tree line. Even though Jim and Al managed to kill the Pankerfaust gunner and his ammunition bearer, the projectile impacted the French half track in front of their position with devastating results.

As the French half track exploded in a huge ball of flames, Jim got up in a slight crouch as he called out, "OK, Al, you know the drill. We'll meet up once things quiet down." Jim then turned to Hans and said, "This isn't your fight, Hans. I'll see you later."

The moment Jim went to turn around and take off, Hans spoke up and said, "With your permission, Jim, I'd like to check on my son."

As the enemy continued to unleash holy hell on the Allied column, Jim thought fast and remarked, "OK, Hans. You're with me, but stay low!"

While Al provided covering fire with his .45 caliber M3 Grease Gun, Jim and Hans took off running in a low crouch and stopped to take cover behind the next Jeep in line. As Sergeants Coppola and Angelone fired their Thompson submachine guns into the treeline, Jim called out, "Keep an eye on, Captain Parker for me!"

"Will do, Sir," responded Sergeant Angelone as he stopped to reload another thirty round magazine into his Tommy Gun.

"You boys be careful. That's an order," said Jim as he patted Sergeant Angelone on the back, before he and Hans took off again in a low crouch.

As soon as Jim and Hans arrived behind the third Jeep in the American convoy, they found MP Lieutenant Carl Miller sprinkling sulfur powder on the leg wound, that Corporal Baines sustained when the enemy opened fire. Immediately after the MP Lieutenant reported that Corporal Baines would be OK, Jim and Hans moved on to the next Jeep in the convoy. There they found Captain Billy Barnes doing an excellent job of directing the men in his section.

As soon as Captain Barnes finished directing the two military police sergeants, who were returning fire from their positions in and around the number one half track, the CIC Agent ran back to where Lieutenant Kelly, Lt. Colonel Beauregard and Hans Sigmann had taken cover behind his Jeep.

While Lieutenant Kelly fired his Tommy Gun and Jim Beauregard reloaded his M1 Carbine, Captain Barnes reported that the men in his section were holding their own in the fight.

As Jim cycled a round into the chamber of his M1A1 Paratrooper Model M1 Carbine, he spoke loud enough to be heard over the sound of gunfire and said, "Hold the fort, Billy. We'll be back."

The second Captain Barnes responded and said, "Will do, Sir," Jim and Hans took off in a low crouch toward the next vehicle in line.

Once they reached the number one half track, Jim and Hans took cover with the two MPs who were returning fire into the woods from keeling positions by the front of the M3. "It looks like we drove into a hornet's nest, Colonel," remarked MP Sergeant Rusty Morgan while he reloaded his M1 Garand Rifle with a fresh eight round clip of ammunition.

As sporadic incoming fire stuck the ground and half track near their position, Jim fired three rounds from his M1 Carbine into the treeline before he called out, "It sounds like our French Allies are getting hit a lot worse than us."

While MP Sergeant Rusty Morgan provided covering fire with his M1 Garand, MP Sergeant Dalton stopped to reload his M1 Rifle as he called out, "I guess we should count our blessings, Colonel!"

After telling the two MP Sergeants to be careful, Jim motioned Hans to follow him, as he took off toward the position in the column, that was being held by Cal Parker and Benny Greene. As Jim ran by, the half track he looked up and gave Sergeant Janowski the thumbs up signal as the CIC Agent reloaded his M2 machine gun with another belt of ammunition.

As soon as they reached the position that was being held by Cal Parker and Benny Greene, Jim saw that his two best undercover agents were behind good cover, on the side of the road, along the edge of the tree line. While armed with the two remaining M3 Grease Guns in their unit, Cal and Benny were blazing away at the muzzle flashes and brief glimpses of the enemy troops who were firing at the American column from the right size of the road. Before leaving their position, Jim patted Cal on the back and said, "You men be careful and that's an order."

While a confident looking Cal Parker called out, "Will do, Colonel," before he continued firing his Grease Gun, Benny Greene looked at their commanding officer, while he reloaded his submachine gun and said, "You be careful too, Sir."

After remarking, "You have my word on that, Bennie," Jim led the way as he and Hans took off again in a slight crouch, while they made their way to the Jeep that was being driven by Sergeant Hank Blair.

When Hank stopped to reload his Thompson Submachine Gun, Jim provided covering fire with his M1 Carbine and ended up killing one of the Whermacht troops, as he reloaded his 9mm MP40 Maschinepistole also known as a Schmeisser. Once Hank was back in the fight, Jim called out, "Watch your ass, Hank. We'll be back," before he and Hans moved on.

While Jim and his men returned fire using small arms and belt fed machine guns, the French M4 Sherman Tank that was positioned at the rear of the American column, fired shell after shell into the woods on the right side of the forest road. When Jim and Hans reached the end of the column, they found Sam Carubba providing security for the French tank crew, while Sergeant Mike Mulligan raked the nearby forest with a steady stream of .50 caliber Armor Piercing and Incendiary (Tracer) ammunition.

After seeing his MG42 gun crew get killed by a high explosive tank round, SS Lieutenant Weber's section was down to three men, including a wounded Wehrmacht Corporal, his remaining Panzerfaust gunner and the Hitler Youth volunteer who carried an additional Panzerfaust. As the enemy continued to pour a steady stream of small arms fire, heavy machine gun fire and tank shells into the forest, SS Lieutenant Weber instructed his remaining Panzerfaust gunner and ammo bearer to withdraw from contact and take the wounded Corporal with them, while he remained behind to provide covering fire.

When the Luftwaffe Private who volunteered to operate the Panzerfaust responded and said, "But Lieutenant we haven't fired any rockets," SS Lieutenant Weber reached out and grabbed the Panzerfaust as he relayed a direct order to the Luftwaffe Private. "Take the little one with you and withdraw. Just make sure you pick up Corporal Fischer on the way. Once the enemy believes the attack is over, I'll move closer to the road and destroy that tank, providing of course that I can do so without getting myself killed in the process."

"Shouldn't we stay and cover you, Lieutenant?" asked the young Hitler Youth volunteer.

As much as he appreciated the concern that the young teenager had for his safety, Lieutenant Weber had no time to explain himself and limited his response to saying, "Good soldiers do as they are told. Now go."

"You heard the Lieutenant," remarked the Luftwaffe Private as he reached out and grabbed the fourteen year old Hitler Youth volunteer by the arm, while they withdrew from the ambush site.

When the firing on both sides of the road died down and eventually stopped, Hans climbed up into the back of the last M3 half track in the American column to check on his son. "It sounds like they're pulling back," said Hans as he checked on Peter, while Mike Mulligan reloaded the M2 .50 caliber machine gun with another belt of ammunition.

After developing a fever again, Peter was kept warm and positioned in between ammo cans and crates of supplies for his protection. Until the French Army stopped for the night, their surgeon would not be able to investigate the cause of Peter's infection. In the meantime, Peter was made as comfortable as possible. After patting Peter on the top of his right shoulder, Hans remarked, "Rest easy, son. We should be moving again in a few minutes.

Once they reached Corporal Fischer's position, the Luftwaffe Private handed the Corporal's 9mm MP40 Submachine Gun to the Hitler Youth volunteer, while he helped the wounded man make his way to safety. As the fourteen year old boy continued to look back to where they left SS Lieutenant Weber, the Hitler Youth Volunteer took off in the direction of the ambush site. Under the circumstances, there was nothing that the Luftwaffe Private or Corporal Fischer could do, as they watched the foolish young kid heading back to where SS Lieutenant Weber was located.

The last thing that SS Lieutenant Weber expected to see, was the Hitler Youth volunteer crawling up behind him with an MP40 submachine gun slung across his back and a Panzerfaust rocket in hand. "I gave you an order," whispered Lieutenant Weber as he pulled the young kid closer to the felled tree that he was hiding behind.

While speaking with all of the innocence of a child, the young teenager lifted the spare Panzerfaust 100 off the ground, as he responded in a very respectful albeit low tone of voice and said, "I thought you could use the extra Panzerfaust, Lieutenant."

If there was one thing that the SS appreciated, it was the devotion to their cause that the younger Germans possessed. While SS Lieutenant Weber continued to lay next to the youngest "soldier" that he ever commanded in battle, he shook his head then whispered, "You remind me of my younger brother. He never listened to me either."

As soon as his young assistant pointed forward and whispered, "The enemy is coming, Lieutenant," SS Lieutenant Weber faced forward and watched as a small number of enemy soldiers began to search the edge of the treeline along the forest road. Off to their right, other enemy troops searched the woods and checked the dead Germans who were killed in the exchange of fire.

While SS Lieutenant Weber and the youngest fighter in his unit continued to take cover behind a fallen tree, the enemy troops began to return to their vehicles. Now that they were alone, Lieutenant Weber debated in his mind whether they should leave the area unscathed, or launch an attack, now that the enemy was acting as if the threat of being ambushed was over.

After considering his options, Lieutenant Weber turned to his fourteen year old assistant from the Hitler Youth as he spoke just above a whisper and said, "You are to do as I say or face being court martialed in the field. While I advance to launch my attack, you will cover me from here. If anything happens to me, I am ordering you to withdraw and report back to Major Kessler. Do you understand?"

As the young teenager who dreamed of the day when he would be decorated by the Fuhrer for heroism acknowledged the order, SS Lieutenant Weber slowly placed the sling from his MP44 Sturmgewehr assault rifle over his shoulder. Once that was done, Lieutenant Weber reached out and took the extra Panzerfaust from the Hitler Youth volunteer as he whispered, "Remember, if you must provide covering fire, once you empty your weapon you are to withdraw from this position without delay."

After hearing the teenager acknowledge the order, Lieutenant Weber slowly advanced at an angle, toward the position on forest road where the enemy tank was located. While the Hitler Youth volunteer pointed the 9mm MP40 in the direction of the enemy and retracted the bolt, he watched the brave SS Officer move closer to the road to find the right firing position. The fact that SS Lieutenant Weber was able to advance without having to worry about incoming fire, insured the success of a surprise attack.

As soon as the shooting stopped, Hans stood up and joined the others as they cautiously looked around to see if it was safe to proceed. When Jim called out to the men who were standing in the back of the number two half track and said, "See anything?" Mike Mulligan responded and said, "Nothing, Sir."

While Jim reloaded his M1 Carbine, he looked up again and asked Hans how his son was doing. As Hans stood in the back of the half track, he called down to Jim and said, "He still has a fever. Otherwise, he's OK."

While Jim stood with Sam Carubba in between the back of the half track and the front of the French Army M4 Tank, he looked up at Hans again and said, "Tell Peter to hang on. Once we stop for the night, the French Surgeon will take a look at his leg."

As Hans remained standing in the back of the half track, he sounded as appreciative as any other father would sound under similar circumstances when he responded and said, "Thank you, Jim."

Now that the shooting stopped and Al spotted French troops returning to the column after conducting a search of the forest, he decided to check on the rest of the men and meet with Jim at the rear of the formation. As soon as Al Parker stopped to check on Sergeants Angelone and Coppola, he found his fellow New Yorkers kneeling behind their Jeep with their Tommy Guns pointed toward the treeline.

When Al asked if they were OK, Sergeant Angelone responded while he kept his Thompson Submachine Gun pointed at the nearby treeline. "We're OK, Sir, which is more than I can say for the French troops who were in that half track that got blown to bits."

"You're right about that, Ange," said Al, who quickly added, "The French definitely got hit a lot worse than we did."

After surviving such a brutal attack, Sal Coppola only had one thing on his mind when he faced Captain Parker and said, "The question, Sir, is how many more of these ambushes are we gonna have go through before we get through this forest?"

While Al got up in a slight crouch, he patted Sergeant Coppola on the top of his right shoulder and said, "I wish I knew, Sal. In the meantime, I want you and Ange to be ready in case the Germans launch a counter attack. Remember, anything can happen at any time, so sit tight and don't move from this position."

While Anthony Angelone continued to hold his Thompson at the ready, he spoke up again while he remained focused on the nearby treeline. "Don't worry, Captain. You can count on me and Sal."

"I know I can," said Al as he cracked a friendly grin and tapped Sergeant Angelone on his helmet, before he moved on to the next Jeep in line.

As soon as Al reached the third Jeep in the convoy, he found MP Lieutenant Carl Miller and Corporal Baines in a kneeling position by the back of their vehicle.

When Al spotted the bloody bandage that was wrapped around Tommy Baines's left leg and he asked the young MP how he was doing, the Corporal responded and said, "I'll be OK, Captain. It's just a scratch, Sir."

After turning to face Lieutenant Miller, the MP Officer filled Captain Parker in by saying, "The Corporal got hit as soon as the Krauts opened fire and we took cover behind our Jeep. He's one hell of a soldier, Sir. I actually had to had to order him to sit still while I bandaged his leg. As far as I'm concerned, the Corporal deserves a medal for how he handled himself today."

"Write it up and give it to the Colonel," said Al, who quickly added, "I'm sure he'll approve it on your say so, Carl."

"I will, Sir," responded the MP Officer, who was no stranger to working with the Negro Captain from CID.

While the Military Police Lieutenant held his M1 Carbine at the ready, Captain Parker looked into the nearby woods and said, "Sit tight, Carl. We should be moving out soon."

As soon as MP Lieutenant Miller remarked, "Will do, Captain," Al looked at the wounded MP Corporal, who was kneeling nearby with his M1 Garand rifle in hand and said, "Stay sharp, Tommy, we're not out'a the woods yet."

Without looking back, the young MP Corporal called out, "I sure will, Captain."

After tossing MP Lieutenant Miller a casual salute, Al left to inspect the next position in the convoy. By the time Al reached the next Jeep, Doc Keller was securing a bandage around the gunshot wound that Captain Barnes sustained in his right shoulder.

"How you doing, Billy?" asked Al.

"I'll be OK, Al," responded the CIC Agent as he sat on the ground and leaned up against the front bumper of his Jeep, while their medic finished bandaging his wound.

"The bullet went clean through, Sir," remarked Doc Keller who quickly added, "How's everyone else doing, Captain?"

While Al scanned the treeline, he answered Doc Keller in a friendly and down to earth tone of voice. "We got away cheap up front, Doc. Unfortunately, our French Allies weren't as lucky."

Before Al moved on to the next vehicle, he stopped to visit with Lieutenant Kelly, who was kneeling by the rear passenger side tire of his Jeep. "How we doing, Dan?" "So far so good, Captain," responded the Lieutenant from the Counter Intelligence Corps, as he knelt by the spare tire that was mounted on the back of his Jeep with his Tommy Gun in hand.

"I'll be back," remarked Al as he moved on to check on the men who were assigned to the number one half track. As soon as Al arrived, he found Sergeant Janowski manning his M2 machine gun, while MP Sergeant Rusty Morgan secured a bandage around MP Sergeant Dalton's right ankle.

Before the Captain from CID could ask what happened, Rusty Morgan spoke up and said, "Steve got hit in the ankle just before the Krauts stopped shooting, Sir. It looks like the bone is chipped."

As Al reached out and grabbed Sergeant Dalton by his left arm, he spoke up and said, "Let me give you a hand getting Steve in the back of the half track."

"Thanks, Captain," responded Rusty as he and Al Parker helped the wounded MP Sergeant limp on one foot over to the back of the M3. Once MP Sergeant Dalton was resting comfortably in the back of the number one half track, MP Sergeant Morgan looked at Al Parker and said, "I'll be available if you need me, Sir."

"Thanks, Rusty," responded Al, before he moved on to check on his son Cal and Benny Greene. As soon as Al arrived by the passenger side of the cargo truck, he was grateful beyond belief that Cal and Benny were alive and well.

While Cal and Benny inspected the minor damage on their shot up truck, Al remarked, "Better that truck took a few hits than you boys." As Cal faced his father and asked how they made out in the front of the column, Al responded and said, "Captain Barnes took one in the shoulder, Corporal Baines got hit in the leg and Sergeant Dalton got it in the ankle."

While Cal turned and look toward the tail end of their formation, he added, "I guess everyone in the back of the column is OK. If someone was hit they'd be calling for our medic."

As soon as Benny Greene spotted the empty Grease Gun magazines, that littered the ground where they took cover, he spoke up and said, "Excuse me, Captain, but I better pick up our empty magazines so we can reload 'em. We'll sure need 'em if we run into more Krauts."

Immediately after Cal thanked Benny for retrieving his empty magazines, Al Parker remarked, "Good thinking, Bennie," as the young Negro soldier walked over to the edge of the treeline and picked up the six empty magazines that he and Cal dropped on the ground, when they reloaded their weapons while engaging the enemy.

As soon as Al Parker said goodbye to Cal and Benny and he walked to the back of the column, Cal walked over to the edge of the treeline, just as Benny picked up the last empty Grease Gun magazine.

"Here you go, Cal," said Bennie, as he handed three empty 30 round magazines to his buddy. While Cal thanked Benny and he placed the empty magazines in the shoulder bag that was designed to hold six Grease Gun magazines, something caught Bennie's eye as he faced the forest.

While SS Lieutenant Weber slowly advanced toward the rear of the enemy column, the Hitler Youth volunteer spotted a Negro enemy soldier looking into the forest, from a position along the edge of the treeline. As best as the young German teenager could tell, this was one of the same two Negro enemy soldiers, who kept him and the Luftwaffe Private pinned down and unable to move, while the enemy tank began lobbing high explosive shells all around their position.

The moment the young German became convinced that SS Lieutenant Weber was spotted, he decided that he had to provide covering fire for his superior officer. After standing up and advancing through the forest, the Hitler Youth volunteer leveled the 9mm MP40 in the direction of the Negro enemy soldier. The second SS Lieutenant Weber heard the sound of movement from behind his position and he looked back, there was little that he could do to put off the inevitable.

As soon as Cal spotted the expression on his buddy's face, as he looked into the forest, all he was able to say was, "What's wrong, Bennie?" before all hell broke loose. In the time that it took for Benny to turn and say, "Look out, Cal!" as he pushed his buddy of the line of fire, Sergeant Greene's body was riddled with a burst of 9mm bullets. In his zeal to serve the Fatherland and provide covering fire for SS Lieutenant Weber, the Hitler Youth volunteer acted like a fearless soldier, as he fired burst after burst from the MP40, while he advanced toward the forest road.

As soon as Cal Parker recovered from being hit in the right side of his torso and he scrambled to make his Grease Gun ready to fire, Hans Sigmann opened fire with his Walther P38 pistol from his position in the back of the number two half track.

By the time Cal fired a short burst from his Grease Gun, the Hitler Youth volunteer was falling over dead, after being shot several times in the head, shoulder and chest. SS Lieutenant Weber was also killed when Jim Beauregard, Al Parker, Sam Carubba, Hank Blair and Mike Mulligan opened fire and filled the right side of the forest with a deluge of bullets in various calibers. Reacting the way they did, prevented SS Lieutenant Weber from firing a Panzerfaust projectile at the French Sherman Tank.

While Jim Beauregard ordered Mike Mulligan, Sam Carubba and Hank Blair to check the forest, he ran to see what happened with Al Parker by his side. As Cal knelt over Benny Greene and called for their medic, Doc Keller was already on the way with his medical bag in hand.

Once he arrived by his patient's side, Doc Keller inspected Bennie's multiple gunshot wounds, while the mortally wounded CID Agent looked up and asked if his buddy was OK. "You saved my life, Bennie," responded Cal as he held his friend's head off the ground and told him to hang on, while Doc Keller did his best to try and stop the bleeding.

While MP Sergeant Morgan knelt down facing the woods to provide security, MP Lieutenant Miller, followed by the wounded Corporal Baines, also arrived to see if they could provide assistance.

As Jim Beauregard knelt next to Benny Greene, he looked up at MP Lieutenant Miller and said, "Give the men searching the woods a hand. I also want every dead German searched for anything that might prove useful to us, as far as intelligence information is concerned."

As soon as MP Lieutenant Miller acknowledged the order and entered the treeline, Jim looked up at Corporal Baines and said, "Get over to the number two half track and make sure that nothing happens to Hans Sigmann and his son."

As disappointed as he was that he was not participating in the search, Corporal Baines responded like a good soldier and said, "Yes, Sir," as he limped over to the last M3 half track in the American column.

All his life Jim Beauregard wanted to be a policeman and a soldier. Once Jim had the chance to serve under officers like General Black Jack Pershing and a young George Patton during the Punitive Expedition in Mexico, he believed that he was destined to lead men in battle. While Jim looked down at Benny Greene, he remembered the day that he watched MP Lieutenant Chester Wright leave this world, after being horribly wounded during the pursuit to capture Ivan Larson and Francis Shorty Mc Ghee.

While Cal cradled Bennie's head in his arms, Doc Keller removed a morphine syrette from his medical bag and said, "You'll be feeling better in no time Benny once this morphine takes effect."

As the tears streamed down Cal's face, Benny looked up and said, "Bye, Cal. You take care of yourself."

"Please, Benny hang on," said Cal.

After seeing his son plead with Benny to hang on, Al Parker turned to their medic and said, "Doc?"

While Doc Keller injected Benny Greene with a morphine syrette, he limited his response to saying, "I'm sorry, Sir."

As soon as Cal looked at his father and Jim Beauregard and he explained how Benny spotted the German armed with a Schmeisser and that he pushed him out of the line of fire, Benny remarked, "You'd do the same thing for me."

While Cal fought back the tears, he did his best to smile, before he responded and said, "You know I would."

Both Al Parker and Jim Beauregard were just as choked up at the sight of such a nice kid dying before his time. When Benny looked up at his commanding officer and asked if he would write his mother and father and tell them that he made sergeant, Jim responded and said, "In addition to writing your folks, Captain Parker and I will visit them when we get back to the states, so we can give them the medal you earned, for saving Cal's life and alerting us about another enemy attack."

After being injected with morphine, Benny found it hard to hold on and was about to close his eyes for the last time when he whispered, "I can't believe I'm gonna get a medal....Thanks, Colonel."

The moment the recently promoted Sergeant Benny Greene passed away, Cal Parker broke down as he held onto the best friend he had in the Army. While Al Parker patted his son on the back, he did his best to comfort him. "I'm sorry, son. We all liked Bennie. He was a good kid."

When Jim spotted blood on the right side of Cal's field jacket, he tried to sound as calm as possible when he said, "Doc, you better take a look at Cal. I think he's been hit."

While Al instinctively grabbed his son by the left arm and said, "Easy son," Doc Keller got up and moved around to Cal's right side. "I've got him, Sir," said Doc Keller as he unbuckled Cal's pistol belt, while Al Parker removed the shoulder bag that contained his son's extra Grease Gun magazines.

While Doc Keller inspected the wound that sliced open the right side of Cal's torso, after penetrating the top section of his heavy cotton pistol belt, Jim asked, "What's the story, Doc?"

"Cal's a lucky man, Sir. It looks like his pistol belt absorbed the force of the bullet before it took a chunk out'a his side," responded the experienced medic as he sprinkled sulfur powder on the young CID Agent's wound. Once he was finished, Doc Keller placed a clean bandage over the wound and instructed his patient to put some pressure on the wound, before he continued filing his report. "As soon as I get Cal bandaged up, we should put him in the back of one of the half tracks and make him as comfortable as possible, Sir. Once we make camp, we can ask the French Army Surgeon to take a look at Cal and the other men who are wounded." As Jim stood up and remarked, "I'll make room in the lead half track," Cal asked his CO if Benny could ride with him"

"Sure thing, Cal," responded Jim Beauregard as he stood over Al's youngest son, while Doc Keller finished bandaging his patient's wound.

While Jim walked over to the back of the number one half track, Al remained next to Cal and said, "We'll hold a service for Benny as soon as we make camp for the night."

As soon as Cal thanked his father, Lieutenant Miller and the other men finished conducting their search of the woods. While Lieutenant Miller stood nearby, he filed his report to Captain Parker. "We found five dead, Sir, including an MG42 machine gun crew that got turned into mince meat by a tank round from our French escort. The SS Officer who was carrying the Panzerfaust was also chopped to pieces. Another Kraut armed with a machine pistol was killed with small arms fire. The one who killed Benny took a few in the head, chest and shoulder. He was only a kid, Sir."

As Lieutenant Miller continued, he held onto a captured map case and a German helmet that was filled with folded maps, wallets, personal mail and a notebook. "We took this stuff off the dead Krauts, Sir. The map case, the brown wallet and the notebook belonged to the SS Lieutenant who was armed with an MP44 and a Panzerfaust. The other maps, wallets and papers were taken off the other dead Germans."

Immediately after Captain Parker complimented him for a job well done, Lieutenant Miller went on to say, "Rather than leave anything behind that could be used to attack our troops, I had the captured weapons that were still serviceable put in the back of the number two half track."

Once again Al said, "Good work, Carl," before he added, "That means we got seven of 'em, if you count the two we killed who attacked the tail end of Colonel Reynald's Intelligence Unit." When Lieutenant Miller asked Captain Parker if he would like him to search the other two dead Germans for intel, Al responded and said, "Good idea, Carl, but take Sergeants Angelone and Coppola with you when you check 'em out. And do me a favor and put this intel and anything that you find on the other dead Germans in the back of the Colonel's Jeep."

"You got it, Captain," responded Carl, before he headed to the front of their column. Once Doc Keller was finished caring for Cal, Al Parker helped his son to stand up, while he asked Doc Keller, Sergeant Morgan and Hank Blair to put Bennie's body in the back of the number one half track.

"Yes, Sir," said Doc Keller, as he along with Sergeant Morgan and Hank Blair picked up Benny Greene lifeless body up and carried it over to the back of the lead half track.

Immediately after Al Parker, Jim Beauregard and Sergeant Janowski helped Cal get comfortable and covered him with a blanket, Benny Greene's body was placed inside the same vehicle and covered with a blanket. When Doc Keller suggested that Captain Barnes ride with Peter Sigmann, Jim agreed and had his medic bring the wounded CIC Agent over to the back of the number two half track.

Just as Jim and Al jumped out of the lead half track, Colonel Reynald walked over to meet with his American Liaison Unit. As the French Army Intelligence Officer looked into the back of the number one American half track, he looked at Jim and said, "I came to check on you and your men before we move out. I see you have sustained casualties as well."

"We had three men wounded and one killed in action, Colonel," responded Jim, who quickly added, "How bad was it for you and your men?"

"Three dead and one wounded in my unit and several wounded when the vehicles leading our column were ambushed," said Colonel Reynald who quickly added, "Three of our vehicles were also destroyed in the attack."

While Colonel Reynald removed a cigarette from the pack that he carried in his field jacket pocket, he accepted a light from his American counterpart, while Jim continued and said, "We also found some maps, a notebook and other personal effects on the Germans that we killed during the attack."

"Excellent work, Jim," responded Colonel Reynald, who wasted no time in asking the American Colonel if Captain Parker could examine the captured items and report his findings as soon as possible."

"Captain Parker will be happy to do so, Sir" responded Jim, who decided to use the opportunity to explain the contribution that Hans Sigmann made during the ambush. "I think you should know, Colonel, that Hans Sigmann alerted us to the presence of the Panzerfaust gunner who destroyed the half track, that was bringing up the rear of your column. Unfortunately, Captain Parker and I were unable to engage the Panzerfaust gunner and his ammo bearer until after he fired his rocket. Hans also saved Sergeant Parker's life, when he killed a member of the enemy ambush team who was responsible for killing Sergeant Greene. The German that Hans killed was covering an SS Lieutenant armed with a Panzerfaust, who was also killed, as he advanced on the Sherman, that you positioned at the end of our column."

And how did your German policeman accomplish this?" asked the French Colonel.

"With the pistol that we issued him," responded Jim.

As much as Colonel Reynald had no love for Germans, he knew the day was coming when the war would be over and Germany would need to be stabilized. If men like Hans Sigmann could help the Allies transform Germany into a peaceful European nation, men like Colonel Andre Reynald would have to welcome their participation in the process. In an effort to start the process of mending fences, with the recently discharged enemy soldier, who was now serving as a civilian German policeman, Colonel Reynald asked where he could find Hans Sigmann.

"He's with his son in the number two half track, Sir," responded Al.

"Is his son still sick with fever?" asked the Colonel.

"Yes he is, Andre," responded Jim, who quickly added, "Our medic thinks Peter Sigmann might have a small fragment of shrapnel in his thigh wound that's causing an infection."

Without saying a word, Colonel Reynald walked over to the passenger side of the M3 Half Track, that was positioned in front of the French M4 Sherman Tank. As the French Intelligence Officer looked up and made eye contact with Hans, he did his best to sound sincere when he said, "I know it wasn't easy for you to do what you did, but I am grateful that you were able to save the life of Captain Parker's son."

When Hans Sigmann responded, he sounded like a man who found no pleasure in killing a teenage boy, who was brainwashed by the Nazis to believe that it made sense to continue to fight. "It was something that had to be done, Colonel."

After nodding his head ever so slightly in agreement, Colonel Reynald continued and said, "Hopefully, we'll be successful in our mission to put an end to this war as quickly as possible." Then, as the French Army Intelligence Officer started to walk away, he stopped, turned around and looked up at Hans Sigmann and said, "After we make camp I will have our surgeon tend to your son, before we hold services for the men who were killed in action."

Immediately after Hans thanked the French Colonel, the two men exchanged casual salutes.

As soon as they stopped for the night, Doc Keller helped the French Army Surgeon care for their casualties, which included having the French Doctor investigate the cause of Peter Sigmann's fever. While the casualties were being treated, Jim Beauregard had Lieutenant Kelly send a message to General Tremble, to request that Major Billy Davis fly in supplies and a few replacements, before evacuating the wounded. While the men were checking vehicles and going over their equipment, Lieutenant Kelly received confirmation, that a C47 would be landing at their location with a fighter escort at 0800 hours the next day. Once Jim notified Colonel Reynald about the resupply and medical evacuation that was scheduled for the morning, the decision was made to hold a service for the men who were killed in action.

With a contingent of French troops providing security, the first to speak was Colonel Reynald. Once Colonel Reynald and a French Army Chaplain finished their end of the ceremony, Jim Beauregard stepped forward and spoke over the grave that was prepared for Sergeant Benny Greene. Even though Jim had some experience speaking at the funerals for policemen, this ceremony was different, because he was burying a young soldier, who was killed in action while serving under his command.

While Jim faced his men, as well as a contingent of French troops, he held his Bible in hand while he spoke from the heart and said, "We are assembled in a foreign land in time of war, to bury the men who were killed in action earlier today. It is befitting of the circumstances of what transpired, that we bury Sergeant Benjamin Greene next to our French Allies, because all of these brave soldiers died while fighting in the same battle."

After pausing for a split second, Jim continued with his eulogy. "As a man of faith, I'd like to believe that these brave souls are witnessing us pay tribute to them before they are laid to rest. Once it is possible to do so, our Graves Registration Units will have the bodies of the soldiers who fell in battle today moved to a military cemetery elsewhere in Europe." Once again, Jim paused before he continued and said, "On a personal note I'd like to say, that Sergeant Greene was one of the nicest and most respectful young men that I have had the pleasure to meet and serve with. Even though he came to work with us under unusual circumstances, Benny proved to be an outstanding undercover agent and one hell of a soldier. It was my honor to be his commanding officer."

As soon as Jim opened his Bible, he began reading the 23rd Psalm (23: 1-6). When he did so, tears streamed down his face, as well as Cal Parker's face and his father's face. "The Lord is my shepherd; I shall not want. He maketh me to lie down in green pastures: he leadeth me beside still waters. He restoreth my soul: he leadeth me in the paths of righteousness for his name's sake. Yea, though I walk through the valley of the shadow of death, I will fear no evil: for thou art with me; thy rod and thy staff they comfort me. Thou preparest a table before me in the presence of mine enemies; thou anointest my head with oil; my cup runneth over. Surely goodness and mercy shall follow me all the days of my life: and I will dwell in the house of the Lord for ever."

When Jim finished and he closed his Bible, Al Parker stepped forward and relayed the command, "Present arms! Hand salute!" On that command, the men who carried sidearms presented a snappy salute, while the other men raised their rifles, carbines and submachine guns in the appropriate fashion to comply with the order to present arms. Since they were still operating behind enemy lines, there would be no bugle call, or twenty one gun salute for the men who fell in battle. Those honors would be carried out, once the bodies were moved to a military cemetery in the European Theater of Operations.

When the ceremony was over and the men were dismissed, Jim Beauregard walked over and did his best to comfort Cal Parker and the other men in his unit. After asking Doc Keller and Sam Carubba to take the wounded men who attended the ceremony back to the medical tent, Jim invited the men in his unit, as well as Colonel Reynald and the men in his intelligence unit, to join him for a drink, to honor of the soldiers who were killed and wounded during the ambush.

In their first engagement with the enemy, SS Major Kessler lost SS Lieutenant Weber and all but two of the new men. Fortunately, of the four men who were wounded, Corporal Fisher was the only one who would not be able to return to full duty any time soon. One of the biggest problems that Kessler and his men faced, while fighting in the wooded terrain of the Black Forest, was the lack of combat experience by the men in SS Lieutenant Weber's squad. The other problem that Kessler and his men faced, was the fact that the enemy column was comprised of experienced troops, who were well armed and properly led. Instead of panicking when the ambush was initiated, the enemy reacted with ferocity, when they unleashed every weapon at their disposal with tremendous accuracy. The fact that the enemy column included a number of tanks and half tracks, also made it possible for the Allied troops to effectively defend their column during the attack.

As soon as Kessler's remaining troops met at a location that was deep in the Black Forest, the decision was made to recruit assistance from the local civilian population and round up other troops who were filtering through the area. The good news for Major Kessler, was that the French Army was moving through Southern Germany at such a quick pace, they were not taking the time to search the wilderness areas for the German military personnel, who were purposely staying off the main roads. If Kessler and his second in command were able to organize these stragglers into a cohesive fighting force, they would be more effective in making life miserable for the invading Allied armies.[12] Kessler also believed that more pressure needed to be placed on the civilian population to resist the Allied invaders. If this could be accomplished, the pro Nazi guerrilla movement would have a real chance of being successful. This would be equally as critical once SS Major Kessler continued traveling east, to organize and command resistance units that were intended to operate in the German Alps.

Later that night after the funeral service, Jim sat in the command tent and wrote a letter to his wife Bea. The moment Al Parker entered the tent he looked at Jim and said, "I can hear you thinking to yourself all the way on the other side of the camp."

As Jim looked up at Al, he sounded like a man who had a very long and difficult day when he said, "After I finished writing a letter to Bennie's folks, I decided to write one to my wife to tell her about my day." "Don't forget to tell Bea that I said hi," said Al.

While Jim put pen to paper, he repeated what he wrote and said, "Al just walked in and asked me to give you his regards."

The next time Jim looked up and he asked how Cal and the other men were doing, Al wasted no time in saying, "The French Doctor gave him a shot to help him sleep. The other men are also asleep." You'll also be happy to know, that Doc Keller was right about the cause of Peter's fever. The French surgeon found a tiny piece of shrapnel buried deep in his thigh wound that was causing an infection. Now that it's out, he should be OK in a few days."

"That's good news," remarked Jim.

As Al removed a cigar from his field jacket pocket, he continued and said, "You also need to know that before he hit the sack, Corporal Baines asked if he could remain with the column. I told him that you'd be the one to make that decision, after your spoke to Doc Keller about his leg wound."

"Did you talk to the Doc about him?" asked Jim.

"Yes I did," said Al, who went on to say, "According to Doc Keller, Tommy Baines has a nasty leg wound that qualifies him to be classified under the text book definition of walking wounded, or in his case, as limping wounded."

After rubbing his tired face, Jim looked at Al and said, "He's a good kid and he's gonna do his best to convince me to let him stay."

"You're right. Tommy Baines is a good kid. They're all good kids," responded Al, who quickly added, "If he stays and he survives this war, you'll feel like you make the right call. If God forbid something were to happen to him, you'd never forgive yourself for not forcing Tommy Baines to be evacuated, when you had the chance to get him the hell out of this war."

After nodding his head in agreement, Jim remarked, "You're right on all counts."

In an effort to help Jim cope with the pressures of being in command, Al quickly lit his cigar before he continued and said, "Would you like to hear my opinion on this subject?"

"Shoot," said Jim.

As Al looked at the man who was his friend and his commanding, he spoke like an Army Officer who was just as concerned about their men as Jim was when he said, "If Billy Davis is bringing us a few replacements, we can afford to send Tommy Baines back with the other wounded men."

While Jim packed his pipe with a fresh bowl of tobacco, he agreed with Al. "You're right. Sending our gung ho MP Corporal back to France is the right thing to do." After using his Zippo to light his pipe, Jim went on to say, "At least Cal and the other men are out of this war for a while."

When Al asked if they should send Peter Sigmann back to Paris with the other wounded, Jim sounded as if he had already given this matter some thought when he responded and said, "I thought about sending him back, but I'm afraid if we do, he'll only end up in another prison camp." Then, after pausing for a split second, Jim went on to say, "As long as Doc Keller and that French Surgeon say he can travel, Peter will stay with us. Besides, unless we run into any more trouble, we should be able to get Hans and his son home in a few days."

As soon as Al picked up the bottle of scotch that was resting on the top of a foot locker, he looked at Jim and said, "How 'bout a night cap before we hit the sack?"

After putting his pipe down on the makeshift table, Jim responded as he placed two metal canteen cups closer to Al. "As long as you're buying, make mine a double."

After arriving at the local Burgermeister's home, SS Major Kessler instructed SS Sergeant Mueller to take two squads and secure the area, while he took the rest of the men, including the wounded with him, when he met with the highest ranking civilian official in the town. As soon as Sergeant Mueller acknowledged the order, the veteran NCO motioned the men from the first and second squads, as well as the Luftwaffe Private from Lieutenant Weber's ambush team, to follow him as he said, "You heard the Major."

While the battle tested non commissioned officer posted sentries around the building, SS Major Kessler knocked on the door. Due to the late night hour, it took a bit longer for the door to be opened.

The last thing that the Burgermeister expected to see at his door at this hour, was a highly decorated SS Major with a squad of heavily armed SS troops, along with three SS soldiers who had minor wounds and the regular German soldier who was more seriously wounded. After introducing himself, Major Kessler wasted no time in saying, "I have four wounded men who need medical attention. My men and I also need something to eat and a safe place to stay for the night."

As soon as the Burgermeister invited the SS Officer and his men into his home, he stepped aside while Major Kessler motioned his men to enter the residence. Once the last of his men were inside, Kessler addressed the Burgermeister as he stepped into the home. "I also have men securing the area who will need something to eat as well."

Under the circumstances, the Burgermeister had no choice but to comply and offered the SS Major and his men some bread, cheese, boiled potatoes, hot ersatz coffee and homemade schnapps. "It isn't much, but this is all that I have at the moment," said the chief official of the town.

While Major Kessler had his wounded men brought into another room, he sat at the table in the small kitchen and said, "What about a doctor? Do you have one who can treat my wounded?"

"Yes, I can get him as soon as I get your men something to eat," responded the Burgermeister, as he began placing food and two bottles of schnapps on the table.

When SS Major Kessler asked if he knew if any German troops were filtering through the area, the Burgermeister responded and said, "Yes, Major. Many of our soldiers have been passing through in different size groups. When they ask for food we share what we have. Then they move on, but I have no idea where they go from here, other than to say they tend to stay off the roads."[13]

Once the food was on the table and a pot of water was heated up, Major Kessler instructed Corporal Ernest Krebs to escort the Burgermeister to the town doctor's house and make sure he returned with whatever was needed to treat their wounded. As soon as the Corporal left with the Burgermeister,

Major Kessler instructed SS Private Derek Grueber and SS Private Stephan Schultz to distribute some black bread, cheese and schnapps to the wounded men. Once the two enlisted men acknowledged the order and carried a tray of cheese and bread to the wounded men, Major Kessler removed a map from his uniform jacket pocket and laid it out on the table.

After pouring some schnapps into a glass, Major Kessler lit one of his cigarettes while he examined his map. As soon as the Major looked around to make sure that he was still alone, he drank some of the strong fruit brandy, before he spoke just above a whisper and said, "If I only had more men."

When SS Private Derek Grueber returned to retrieve the bottle of schnapps and a tray filled with small glasses, Major Kessler remarked, "Be generous with the schnapps, Derek. It will help the men who are in pain from their wounds."

While Private Grueber held the bottle of homemade fruit brandy in his right hand and a small tray of shot glasses in his left, he responded in a respectful tone of voice and said, "Yes, Sir."

As the decorated Private started to walk away, Kessler called out, "You and Schultzy deserve some schnapps as well and that's an order."

"Yes, Sir. Thank you, Sir," responded the Private as he reached the entrance to the other room where the wounded were being treated.

While MP Corporal Thomas Baines stood at a comfortable attention in the French Army medical unit tent, Jim addressed the young man while he stood next to Doc Keller. "What's this I hear about you refusing to be evacuated with the other wounded?"

"Like I told Captain Parker, Sir, all I have is a scratch," responded the young military policeman.

"According to Doc Keller, it's one hell of a scratch," remarked Jim, before he continued and said, "Regardless, you're going back to Paris with a recommendation from me that you be promoted and assigned to CID. CID is short handed and can always use a good man like you. As a result, I'm sending a letter back on the plane that directs Major Savino to get you transferred to CID as soon as you're cleared by an Army Doctor to report for duty."

After hearing what Lt. Colonel James Beauregard just said, Corporal Baines had no objections to getting on the C47. "Yes, Sir, thank you, Sir," was all the young man said as he smiled and saluted the Colonel from CID.

As soon as Jim returned the salute, he turned to Doc Keller and said, "Get the wounded ready to go, Doc. Billy Davis should be here in a few minutes."

While Doc Keller responded and said, "Yes, Sir," the Colonel walked over to visit with the other wounded men. After visiting with Captain Barnes and Sergeant Dalton, Jim stopped to visit Cal Parker. As Jim stood over Al Parker's youngest son, he sounded more like a friend than a superior officer when he asked Cal how he was feeling.

"I'm OK, Sir. I just wish I was staying with the column so I could see Berlin," responded Cal. "Don't worry, Cal, you'll get there. Berlin's not going anywhere, at least what's left of it," said Jim, before he relayed more important information to Cal. "I thought you'd like to know that I sent a message to Major Savino and asked him to bring Michelle out to the plane when you land. This way you can see your wife before you get transported to the hospital."

After hearing the news Cal Parker smiled for the first time since Benny Greene was killed.

"Thanks Colonel," said Cal.

As Jim Beauregard returned the smile, he pointed his right index finger at Cal as he remarked, "You get better and that's an order."

In order to provide security for the American C47, Lt. Colonel Jim Beauregard and Colonel Andre Reynald stationed armored vehicles and dismounted troops along the edge of the improvised landing zone, that was adjacent to the location that was used as their makeshift camp for the night. In the air above the LZ, a pair of American P51 fighter planes circled overhead, to protect the aerial resupply and evacuation mission.

Once Jim used a hand held radio to let Billy Davis know that the coast was clear, the C47 that had the name Six Gun stenciled on the front of the nose section came in low over the edge of the treeline and landed in the open pasture. By the time Billy Davis had his aircraft turned around and brought to a stop, his crew chief had the cargo door open and was deploying the ladder. With the engines still turning and the two P51s circling overhead, Jim Beauregard was surprised to see Captain Don Lorenz and a Chinese American Army Officer disembark the C47, while Sergeant Chris Jacko, Sergeant Mike Butler and the crew chief helped a long line of American and French troops unload supplies from the plane.

As soon as Jim Beauregard and Captain Lorenz exchanged pleasantries, the CID Agent from the Paris Office spoke loud enough to be heard over the noise that was produced by the engines on the C47. "When General Tremble called Major Savino and said you could use some help, every man in the office placed their dog tags in a helmet. Chris Jacko, Mike Butler and yours truly were the lucky ones Sir."

Captain Lorenz then introduced Lt. Colonel Jim Beauregard to the Chinese American Army Officer who volunteered to come along and said, "Sir, this is Captain John Lew, Stanford University Class of 41. Captain Lew is a language expert from the Counter Intelligence Corps, who speaks fluent German and Chinese, as well as some Russian. He just transferred to the ETO from the CIB."

When Jim extended his hand and said, "We're glad to have you with us, Captain," the Chinese American Officer from Southern California responded and said, "I'm glad to be here, Sir."

While an American Jeep and a French M3 half track delivered the American and French wounded over to the plane, Al Parker walked over and shook hands with Captain Lorenz as he welcomed him to the column. "It's good to see you, Don. I see you're brought us some help."

After shaking hands with Al Parker, Captain Lorenz introduced Al to Captain Lew.

As soon as Al welcomed Captain Lew to their unit, he turned to Jim Beauregard and said, "If we want'a say hi to Billy Davis, we better do so now, Sir."

"We'll be right back," said Jim, as he excused himself and walked with Al over to the cargo door of the C47. After stopping for a second to greet

Sergeant Jacko and Sergeant Butler, Jim and Al climbed on board and walked past the wounded men on their way into the cramped cockpit. Both Jim Beauregard and Al Parker were all smiles when they greeted the Army pilot who helped them capture Ivan Larson. "Thanks for stopping by, Billy," said Jim, while he shook hands with the young Army aviator as he sat in the pilot seat of his aircraft.

"My pleasure, Sir," responded Billy Davis.

"We'll see you at Gabby's place when we get back to Paris," added Jim. "Dinner and drinks on us," commented Al. "That sounds like a plan," responded Billy, who continued as he removed a cotton canvass shoulder bag from the back of the pilot's seat and handed it to Lt. Colonel Beauregard. "Before I forget, Sir. Here's that box of cigars, some extra smokes and the pipe tobacco that you asked for."

As soon as Jim accepted the khaki green colored shoulder bag, he responded and said, "Thanks, Billy. Put the tobacco on our bill."

"Will do, Sir," responded Billy Davis.

After saying goodbye to their favorite C47 pilot, Jim and Al left the cockpit and said goodbye to the wounded before they disembarked the aircraft. As soon as Al Parker knelt down next to Cal, he looked at his youngest son, while he spoke loud enough to be heard over the hum of radial engines and said, "Give Michelle a big hug for me and don't forget to write your mother and your brother. Once she receives the telegram that you've been wounded, she'll be worried sick. The sooner you let her know you're OK, the better off she'll be."

When Jim leaned over and patted Al and the back, he said goodbye to Cal, before he added, "Come on, Al. It's time to go."

As Cal reached out and shook hands with his father, he sounded dead serious when he said, "Promise me that you and the Colonel will be careful. No hero stuff, OK Dad? The same goes for the other men."

"Don't worry, son. We'll take care of each other," said Al, as he stood up and took one last look at his youngest son, before he and the Jim Beauregard left the aircraft.

Once Jim and Al walked clear of the plane, Billy Davis applied full power and piloted his plane into the air. As the C47 flew back to France with two P51s flying top cover, Jim turned to Al and said, "It's time to get back on the road

CHAPTER 5

THE NAZI RESISTANCE CONTINUES

After a few other incidents when French Forces and their American Liaison Unit were sniped at, a much larger engagement was fought, when French troops and Colonial Moroccan soldiers came under fire when they entered the Town of Freudenstadt. This battle erupted when the German troops who took refuge in a building inside the town square refused to surrender. Even though it made no sense to resist the presence of a heavily armed French column, several dozen German troops did their best to go down fighting, rather than capitulate.[14]

As soon as the fighting broke out, Jim Beauregard directed his men to pull their vehicles over to the side of the road and take defensive positions, in preparation of repelling an attack. Due to the size of the French column, Jim and his men could hear the exchange of gunfire, but were not in a position to observe the battle that was taking place up ahead.

The moment Jim spotted Colonel Reynald signaling his men to return to their vehicles, he turned to Al and said, "Load 'em up, Al. We're moving out."

While Al Parker relayed the order to mount up, Jim made eye contact with Colonel Reynald and exchanged waves, as the French Army Intelligence Unit and their American Liaison Unit prepared to enter Freudenstadt, Germany. As they did so, it was obvious that the French and Colonial Moroccan troops who were leading the column, were still heavily engaged.

After being asked by Colonel Reynald to secure the rear of the column, Jim instructed Hank Blair to take Hans and his son into an empty shop, while Mike Mulligan and Fred Janowski manned the machine guns on the two half tracks and the rest of his men took positions on both sides of the street. In order to get some eyes on any potential threats, Al Parker suggested that they put some men on the second floor of a nearby building, that commanded a view of the intersection.

"Good idea," responded Jim, before he turned to Captain Lorenz and said, "Don, take Mike and Chris and cover our position from the second floor of the corner building on our left."

"We're on the way, Colonel," remarked Captain Lorenz, who quickly turned to the two CID Agents who volunteered to come on this mission and said, "Chris you're on me...Mike you bring up the rear."

As soon as Don Lorenz and his two man detail took off, Jim turned to Al and said, "Captain Lew and I are going to the corner to have a look. You're in charge until we get back."

Even though Al wanted to get closer to the action, he understood why Jim wanted to take the Captain from CIC with him, when he went to see what was going on up ahead. As soon as Jim turned to Captain Lew and said, "Ready, John," the highly educated Chinese American Army Officer, who served in the China India Burma Theater of Operation, before being transferred to the ETO, reacted with enthusiasm and said, "I'll take point, Sir,"

After hearing the CIC Agent volunteer to take the lead, Jim knew that General Tremble sent him a good man to replace Captain Billy Barnes. "I'm right behind you," responded Jim, as the two Army Officers made their way to the corner. As soon as they stopped and took cover, in the doorway of the building on the right side of the street, Lt. Colonel Jim Beauregard and Captain John Lew had a front row seat to the action.

"The French are really pouring it on, Sir," remarked Captain Lew, as he watched a French bazooka team fire a 2.36 inch rocket into the building, that was being used by a group of heavily armed German soldiers to resist the Allied advance.

"It looks like they don't have a choice," responded Jim, who quickly added, "God, I wish this damn war would end."

Once the firing stopped and the French troops moved in to take prisoners, Colonel Reynald walked over to meet with Jim Beauregard and the Captain from the Counter Intelligence Corps. As the three men met on the corner, a frustrated Colonel Reynald remarked, "This was unnecessary. All they had to do was surrender and they would have been taken prisoner."

While flanked by his SS troops, Major Kessler stood in front of the assembly of civilian volunteers on the other side of Freudenstadt and said, "My men and I have provided you with the means to resist the Allied invasion of our homeland. The time has come for all Germans to serve the Fatherland, before everything we have left is taken from us."

While the formation of armed Werwolf fighters and Volkstrum militia remained silent, Major Kessler continued and said, "My men and I will be moving on to organize other resistance units from here to the Alps. Our mission is to make the Allies pay such a heavy price for their invasion of the Fatherland, they will agree to peace terms, that will enable us to focus our full attention on fighting the Russians." With nothing else to say, Major Kessler raised his right hand in the air, as he presented the Nazi salute and said, "Heil Hitler!"

Once the group of resistance fighters returned the Nazi salute with enthusiasm, they began to leave the assembly area on the outskirts of town, in order to launch their attack on the French invaders. While the others left to launch their attack, one of the younger German fighters remained behind and approached SS Major Kessler.

While the Major examined a map, a thirteen year old boy wearing civilian clothes and a Panzer crewman's black cap, who carried a belt of MG42 machine gun ammunition draped over his shoulder and a can of machine gun ammunition in his left hand, approached the SS Officer and said, "Excuse me, herr Major, but I would like to volunteer to go with you."

Had Major Kessler's only son survived the bombing of his hometown, he would be about the same age of the boy who was standing before him. Even though Gunther Kessler was a tough son of a bitch, he was deeply moved by the offer that was just made to him, by a young German teenager, who wasn't much older than the son he lost, during an Allied bombing raid on Mannheim.

While the last of the towns defense force vanished from sight, Major Kessler gripped the boy's right shoulder as he said, "What's your name?"

Even though he was weighed down by MG42 machine gun ammunition, the young boy did his best to stand up straight as he identified himself.

"Rudolf Kraft, Sir."

"And how old are you?" asked Kessler.

As tempted as he was to lie about his age, Rudy sounded like most young boys, who couldn't wait for their next birthday when he answered the question. "I'll be fourteen in August, Sir."

Even though Major Kessler had work to do, he took the time to ask the boy where he got the Panzer crewman's cap. While responding with pride, Rudy remarked, "It belonged to my older brother Johan, heir Major. His commanding officer sent it to me when he was killed at Kursk."

After nodding his head ever so slightly, Major Kessler went on to say, "All of us including your brother are very proud of you, for serving Germany in our moment of need." Major Kessler then tapped the boy's black panzer crewman's cap in a friendly fashion and added, "Remember, Rudy, without ammunition bearers like you, our machine gunners would be useless. Besides, with young men like you fighting here in Freudenstadt, those of us who assume positions in the mountain passes of the Alps won't have much to do."

The moment he saw the look of disappointment on the young boys face, SS Major Kessler saluted the teenager then said, "You better join the others, because they will surely need the ammunition that you are carrying before this day is over."

While young Rudy Kraft stood as erect as possible, he returned the salute and left the forested position on the outskirts of town, to join the other fighters. Even though they didn't have any real chance of preventing the Allies from occupying Freudenstadt, they went anyway, because they believed it the right thing to do.

As the boy walked away, Major Kessler turned to SS Sergeant Bruno Mueller and the SS troops under his command and said, "Our work is finished here. While I take our wounded men with me, so I can help Captain Schneider finalize our plans to move into the Alpine passes near Oberstdorf, you men know what to do. No matter what happens, you must remain one step ahead of the Allied invasion force. Your written orders will allow you to pass all checkpoints. We'll meet at the training school at Sonthofen no later than the 25th. From there, we'll be moving to the Werwolf training camp at Langenwang, then to the outskirts of Oberstdorf, where we'll operate from various clandestine bases in nearby Alpine passes." Then, after wishing his men good luck, SS Major Kessler got into a civilian truck and left with the three SS solders who were still recovering from minor wounds.[15]

As soon as Colonel Reynald finished making his comment, more firing broke out, as a heavily armed group of Germans wearing civilian clothes and an assortment of military caps, helmets and jackets attacked the Allied troops. The moment this attack was launched, Captain Lorenz and the two men who were with him opened fire and engaged the enemy from their elevated position across the street.

Immediately after Jim motioned Sergeants Angelone and Coppola to join him on the corner, he instructed Captain Lew to bring up the number two half track. While the Captain from CIC left to get the M3, Jim Beauregard, along with Sergeants Angelone and Coppola, assisted Colonel Reynald and his men engage the enemy with small arms fire. When the enemy attack force started firing several Panzerfaust weapons at the Allied invaders, the French responded by having two of their tanks, send round after round of high explosive shells at various enemy fighting positions. Immediately after a French tank was hit by a German Panzerfaust projectile, several other Panzerfaust projectiles were fired at Allied vehicles. As the fighting intensified, additional French and Colonial Moroccan troops arrived on scene, to assist Colonel Reynald's men and their American allies to repel the attack. At the same time, Captain Lorenz and his two man detail arrived on the corner.

As soon as a pair of French Sherman Tanks, followed by French and Colonial troops, advanced toward the several dozen pro Nazi partisan fighters, Jim Beauregard called out, "Hold your fire!" A split second later, the number two American half track arrived on the corner, with Mike Mulligan manning the M2 .50 caliber machine gun and Captain Lew by his side. While speaking in a raised voice, so he could be heard over the sound of battle, Jim turned to Colonel Reynald and said, "With your permission, Andre, my men and I will be happy to lend a hand and clean this mess up."

"Thank you, Jim," responded Colonel Reynald, before he turned to the men in his intelligence unit and said, "Let's go! Fall in behind the American half track." While the men in the French Intelligence Unit moved into position, Jim leaned into the cab of the number two half track and instructed Sam Carubba to follow the French troops.

"Yes, Sir," responded Sam, as the CID Agent put the M3 half track in gear and started to follow the French soldiers, who were walking behind a pair of French Sherman Tanks.

Jim then turned to Chris Jacko and relayed an order as if they had no time to waste, "Tell Captain Parker to bring up the rest of the men and the other half track! And be careful doing so, Chris."

"Yes, Sir," responded Sergeant Jacko, as he took off to relay the message to Captain Parker.

Once again, Colonel Reynald was impressed with the fighting spirit of his American Allies. While the American half track drove off, Colonel Reynald and the men in his intelligence unit joined forces with their American Allies in the mopping up operation. Even though the sound of gunfire was dying down, there were still a few armed German civilians, including a number who were wearing Volkssturm armbands and various pieces of military clothing and equipment putting up resistance. When several armed German civilian fighters opened fire from different rooms on the second floor of a building across the street, Jim turned to Colonel Reynald and said, "We'll take this one, Andre."

"We'll cover you," responded the French Intelligence Officer as the mixed contingent of French and American troops returned fire, using an assortment of smalls arms and the M2 .50 caliber machine gun that was mounted in the number one half track.

Once the raiding party reached the front door, Sergeant Angelone stepped in front of Lt. Colonel Jim Beauregard and said, "Excuse me, Sir, but this is a job for me and Sal. After nodding his head in agreement, Jim stepped aside, as Sal Coppola kicked the door in and his partner led the way with his Thompson Submachine Gun at the ready. The second Sergeant's Angelone and Coppola entered the building, Captain Lorenz remarked, "Excuse us, Sir," as he and Captain Lew followed by Sergeant Mike Butler filed past their commanding officer. As much as Jim wanted to go in first, he knew that his job was to direct his men and let them be good soldiers.

Now that the raiding party entered the building, Mike Mulligan and the other troops providing covering fire stopped shooting to avoid hitting any of Allied soldiers.

By the time Jim followed Sergeant Butler into the building, Sergeant Angelone shot and killed a German resistance fighter as he reloaded his submachine gun, while he sat on the floor in a room that overlooked the street. A split second later, Sergeant Coppola stepped into the room and shot another badly wounded German, when he attempted to retrieve a hand-grenade from the body of a fallen comrade. Further down the hallway, Captain Lorenz and Captain Lew traded shots with a young German fighter armed with a bolt action K98 rifle.

As soon as the enemy resistance fighter was seriously wounded and fell to the floor, the two American Army officers entered the room and secured the prisoner. At the same time, Lt. Colonel Jim Beauregard and Sergeant Mike Butler engaged a wounded German Werwolf fighter armed with a Sauer 38H .32 caliber pistol, when he burst out of a closet in a small room off to their left.

Under the circumstances, it was blatantly obvious that the Germans they were running into were a determined lot, who were willing to go down fighting rather than surrender. While Mike Butler tucked the captured pistol in his belt, Jim called out to his men, "Let's go over this place with a fine tooth comb and be careful!"

After advancing further down the hallway behind his commanding officer, Mike Butler provided security, while Jim Beauregard kicked open a closed door and fired two rounds from his M1 Carbine, as he called out, "Grenade!" and quickly backed out of the room. Even though the German Volkstrum fighter was already mortally wounded, he had enough life left in him to detonate a hand- grenade, at the sight of an American officer coming his way. Fortunately, the Volkstrum fighter dropped the grenade in his lap, after two of Jim's .30 caliber bullets took the rest of the life from his body.

As the sound from the blast dissipated, Sergeant Butler remarked,

"That was close, Colonel."

"Better him than us," responded the Colonel as he led the way toward the other side of the second floor.

Just as the Colonel made his way to the staircase, Captain Lorenz stepped out into the hallway and said, "We have a live one in here, Sir, but he's hit pretty bad." "Good job, Don. I'll be right there," said Jim, before he turned to Sergeant Butler and said, "Tell Captain Parker that we captured a badly wounded prisoner and we need him, Doc Keller and Hans up here as soon as possible. Also, ask the Captain to let Colonel Reynald know what we're up too."

While Mike Butler acknowledged the order, he stepped passed the Colonel and went down the stairs at a fast pace. By the time Sergeant Butler made his way out into the street, Captain Parker was holding a captured German sniper rifle as he exited a building on the other side of the street, with Chris Jacko, a prisoner and two of Colonel Reynald's men. As soon as Sergeant Butler relayed the Colonel's message to Captain Parker, Al handed Sergeant Butler the captured German sniper rifle and asked him to put it in the lead half track, before he turned to Chris Jacko and said, "Get Doc Keller and Hans and tell Hank to stay in a safe place with Peter Sigmann."

Once Chris Jacko acknowledged the order and he ran off to bring up the men who were wanted by the Colonel, Al Parker turned to Sergeant Butler and said, "Come on, Mike. Let's tell Colonel Reynald about this wounded German prisoner."

As soon as Al Parker and Sergeant Butler walked over to the lead American half track where the French Intelligence Officer was standing, Al spoke up and said, "Excuse me, Sir, but Sergeant Butler just advised me, that Colonel Beauregard and the men who hit the house across the street have a wounded prisoner up on the second floor. He's in pretty bad shape, Sir, so we sent for our medic to take a look at him, while he's being interrogated."

While the battle raged on a few streets over from their present position, the sound of incoming artillery sounded like freight trains streaking over-head, as the French Army began bombarding the enemy into submission. The moment another round of French artillery shells landed in a nearby section of Freudenstadt, Colonel Reynald faced Al Parker and Mike Butler and said, "We've had enough of this resistance. As long as the Germans continue to wage war, so will we." After telling another French Intelligence Officer to take charge of the prisoners, Colonel Reynald turned to Al Parker again and said, "Come Captain. Let's go and see what this wounded German has to say."

Just as Al and the French Colonel made their way across the street, Chris Jacko returned with Doc Keller and Hans Sigmann. Before they entered the building, Al instructed Sergeants Jacko and Butler to provide security outside. While Colonel Reynald and Doc Keller entered the building, Al sounded more like a concerned father than a superior officer when he faced Sergeants Jacko and Butler and said, "And for God's sake be careful, because Lord knows who else is running around this town with a gun in hand who doesn't want this war to end."

Both Chris Jacko and Mike Butler appreciated the concern that Captain Parker had for them and the other men in their unit. Whenever they made camp, both Captain Parker and Lt. Colonel Beauregard made sure they were always well fed, warm and safe. Captain Parker and the Colonel were also famous for showing up in the middle of the night with a canteen cup of hot coffee for the men on guard duty. Both Captain Parker and Lt. Colonel Beauregard were also very personable and made sure the men took the time to write letters and check their equipment.

Captain Parker also made sure that all of the vehicles in their convoy were properly maintained. In fact, it wasn't unusual for Captain Parker to be found checking tires, refilling gas tanks and adding engine oil to the vehicles in the convoy. Even when the men in charge of that vehicle came over to assume that responsibility, Captain Parker would continue to help out, while he described how much he missed working on cars and trucks back home. When an engine was running rough, Captain Parker seemed to show up out of nowhere and after a minute or two under the hood, he had the soldier's vehicle purring like a kitten.

It was also blatantly obvious, that losing Benny Greene and seeing the other men, including Cal Parker, get wounded, had a profound affect on Captain Parker and Lt. Colonel Beauregard. Once their unit sustained casualties, both Al Parker and Jim Beauregard seemed to age a bit and were often observed sitting alone, or together, as if they were consumed by concern for the troops under their command.

After hearing Captain Parker express concern for their safety, the two CID Agents acknowledged the order and stood guard in front of the building. As soon as Captain Parker and Hans Sigmann went to enter the building, Chris Jacko called out, "Don't worry, Sir, we'll be careful."

Once he arrived upstairs, Doc Keller did his best to keep the badly wounded prisoner alive, while Captain Lew continued interrogating the young Nazi partisan. After looking up at Lt. Colonel Beauregard and Colonel Reynald, the Captain from CIC said, "This kid is one hell of a believer, Sir. In addition to saying, that he's grateful that he was given the chance to serve the Fatherland, his only regret, is that he didn't take more of us with him, before he was badly wounded."

When Jim asked Captain Lew how old the kid was, the CIC Agent asked the prisoner his age. As soon as the proud German teenager, who wore an armband that identified him as a member of the Volkssturm responded, Jim understood enough German to repeat his age in English. "Thirteen.... unbelievable."

After turning to Hans, Jim spoke in a friendly tone of voice when he said, "You want'a take a crack at this kid and see what you can find out?"

Even though the Nazi run German armed forces had not yet surrendered, it was clear to men like Hans Sigmann that there was no future in continuing the war. As far as Hans was concerned, the last thing that Germany needed was more casualties, or another city and town that was turned into rubble.

Now that he was officially discharged and serving as a civilian German policeman, Hans had no reason to honor the oath that he took to Adolf Hitler, when he was inducted into the German Army. Once Hans agreed to see what he could find out, Captain Lew stepped aside as Hans knelt beside the prisoner. While Doc Keller continued tending the prisoner's multiple gunshot wounds, Hans pointed to the ceiling as he looked at the 13 year old fanatic and said, "Do you hear that? That is the sound of this beautiful old German town being destroyed by French artillery, because you and your friends decided to open fire on Allied tanks and troops."

When the young teenager responded, he sneered, then said, "I'd rather see Germany destroyed, than be captured and occupied by the Americans, the British, or the French."

"You should be real proud of yourself, because that is exactly what is happening," remarked Hans, before he played a long shot and said, "Your commanding officer wasn't as brave as you. When we captured him he was running away from the battle."

The thirteen year old prisoner was no match for an experienced policeman like Hans Sigmann, when he thought he was defending the honor of the man who sent him and the others on this mission.

As the angry young teenager lifted his head off the floor, he responded in a raised tone of voice and said, "That's a lie! Major Kessler is a highly decorated SS Officer. He would never surrender. Besides, he wasn't running away. He was leaving Freudenstadt to plan more attacks in other parts of Germany." Then, as the young teenager continued, he seemed to be enjoying the moment, when he remarked, "After what the Major and his men did in the Black Forest and in other parts of Germany, the Allies will lose so many soldiers, they will sue for peace rather than continue this war. You'll see."

As soon as Hans relayed what the young kid just said, Jim remarked, "Good job, Hans. Now we know who's behind these attacks. Why don't you thank the kid for helping us out. I'm sure it'll make him feel real good, when you let him know that you tricked him into identifying SS Major Kessler."

Once Hans told the young Nazi what he did, the kid became furious and pushed Doc Keller aside and ripped off his bandages while he called Hans a traitor. The moment he did so, Hans grabbed the young Nazi fighter by the throat and pinned him against the wall as he let his feelings about the war be known. "I served Germany in two world wars and have six decorations for bravery and for being wounded in battle. How long have you served and how many decorations do you have?"

The moment Hans heard Al Parker speaking in German and say, "Easy Hans," Hans loosened his grip on the teenager's throat as he continued and said, "My oldest son died for nothing on the Eastern Front because we had a corporal instead of a general giving the orders. The proof that I am right is evident by the fact that the Russian Army is closing in on Berlin, while other Allied armies are pushing east and have already captured many of our major cities." Then, after calming down a bit, Hans continued to sound every bit as sarcastic as he did before when he said, "The super weapons and the new divisions of well equipped German soldiers, that are supposed to turn the tide of this war, are not coming because they don't exist. Instead, the SS is relying on thirteen year old boys to do their bidding."

"That's another lie," screamed the badly wounded teenager.

While doing his best to control his emotions, Hans looked at the young resistance fighter and said, "I know it's hard for you to understand, but whether you like it or not, we have all been lied too. If you wish to live, you need to tell us what we want to know, so we can stop the rest of Germany from being destroyed."

As soon as the wounded prisoner yelled, "Go to hell," Hans stood up and faced the Allied Officers and said, "The Nazis own his mind. He would rather die that cooperate."

When Jim asked Doc Keller for a prognosis, the experienced Army Air Corps medic looked up and said, "He's shot up pretty bad, Sir. I doubt he'll make it through the night."

After hearing all that was said, Colonel Reynald turned to Jim and said, "Once again, you and your men have been of great help."

"That's what we're here for, Colonel," said Jim.

As the French Colonel continued, he turned to Hans and said, "I would like to invite you to assist Captain Parker and Captain Lew in interrogating the men in this village, who will be rounded up to see if we can put an end to this unnecessary bloodshed."

Under the circumstances, Hans agreed to help with the interrogations. As soon as he did so, Colonel Reynald told Jim that he would send two French medics with a stretcher to pick up the mortally wounded prisoner.

While Jim folded the metal wire stock on his paratrooper model M1 Carbine, he faced the French Colonel and said, "I'll have Doc Keller and two of my men stay with the prisoner until your medics arrive."

"Thank you, Jim," responded Colonel Reynald.

After instructing Sergeants Angelone and Coppola to stay with Doc Keller and the wounded prisoner, Jim and the rest of his men left the building with Colonel Reynald.

By the time Jim and his men, along with Colonel Reynald made their way down to the street, the air was filled with smoke as the Town of Freudenstadt was engulfed in flames. Now that the French artillery barrage was over, the only sound that was heard was the crackling of burning embers and the collapsing of destroyed wooden structures. While Captain Lew watched a wooden structure down the street collapse, after being destroyed by the out of control fire, he looked at Lt. Colonel Beauregard and said, "One thing's for sure, Colonel. If this fire continues to spread, the whole town's gonna go up in smoke."

While Jim watched several wooden buildings engulfed in flames, he agreed with the Captain's assessment, then added, "As far as I'm concerned, the townspeople can blame the Nazis for this fire, not the French Army." As sad as it was to see the bulk of an historic town on fire, the French had every right to defend themselves. Unfortunately, the wooden construction of the old buildings made it easy for fires to spread out of control and destroy a number of locations that were not involved in the fighting. Fortunately, for the French, their American allies were able to refute allegations, that the French Army destroyed the town on purpose and without cause.[16]

In order to prevent any further attacks, the French rounded up every person in the town who might pose a threat to the Allied occupation of Freudenstadt. Once the prisoners were placed under guard in an encampment, a number of interrogations were conducted. Only one of the men who was rounded up had anything of substance to say, when he was interrogated by Al Parker and Hans Sigmann. As the father of one of the young teenagers who volunteered to serve in the defense of Freudenstadt, the German civilian, who was one of the men rounded up by the French, lost an eye and an arm in an Allied air raid, while serving as a fireman in Hamburg. After being forced to retire, Mr. Kraft brought his family south, to live in the town where his wife was from.

As a parent who lost his oldest son in the war, Mr. Kraft understood why his youngest son Rudy ran off to join the Nazi resistance movement. "The Nazis have been brainwashing my sons and all of the other children, ever since they came to power," said the disabled fireman. When he continued, Mr. Kraft sounded like a man who was telling the truth, as he looked at his interrogators and said, "Then again, who am I to talk. We all wanted to believe in the Thousand Year Reich, which makes all of us responsible for what has happened to Germany."

When Mr. Kraft continued, he explained how according to his son, an SS Major by the name of Kessler, was recruiting Werwolf resistance fighters, to help SS troops and regular German military personnel to fight the Allies. As Mr. Kraft continued, he described how this SS Major had his youngest son and others convinced, that the war weary Americans, British and French would make peace with Germany, if they inflicted enough casualties on their armies. Once that happened, Germany would be able to focus all of its resources on fighting the Russians.

While Al Parker offered Mr. Kraft a cup of American coffee and Hans gave the disabled fireman an American cigarette, he went on to tell his interrogators, that according to his youngest son, he planned to join the men, who were organizing in a wooded area on the edge of town, so they could continue to defend Freudenstadt from the Allied invaders."

Once again, Mr. Kraft paused before he continued and said, "When I told Rudy that the war was lost and that ten thousand boys his age could not change the outcome, he got angry with me and ran out of the house. Shortly after I started looking for him, I heard the shooting and knew that it was too late for me to prevent my youngest son from participating in the attack."

Immediately after Mr. Kraft paused to take a sip of coffee and a quick drag on his cigarette, he went on to say, "When I found Rudy he was barely alive. Based on what he told me, he was on his way to retrieve more ammunition for the older men, when he was mortally wounded."

Once again, Mr. Kraft took another drag on the unfiltered American cigarette, before he continued. "Before Rudy died, he told me how he volunteered to serve with this SS Major, in the resistance unit that he was organizing in the German Alps. Rudy never looked more proud, when he said that this Major Kessler treated him like a real soldier and explained, that while he was needed to serve here in Freudenstadt, other brave Germans would be serving throughout the Fatherland, including in the mountain passes of the Alps."

Once again, the disabled fireman paused, before he looked at his interrogators and added, "When my son asked if I was proud of him for what he did, he died before I was able to respond."

Because they were fathers themselves, both Al and Hans knew that Mr. Kraft was a broken man when he went on to say, "When the French soldiers arrested me, I was carrying my youngest son's dead body away from where the fighting was taking place."

After finishing the rest of his coffee, Mr. Kraft spoke in a low somber tone of voice, when he finished his remarks by saying. "Most of Germany is tired of the war and will not resist the Allies. Unfortunately, there are still some among us who believe that it is their duty to fight on, even though all is lost. Until you deal with this SS Major and the others like him, the Allies and the German people who have had enough of this war, will be in danger. That is all that I have to say."

After thanking Mr. Kraft, Captain Parker and Hans Sigmann left the room that was being used to conduct interrogations, to file their report with Lt. Colonel Beauregard and Colonel Reynald. Based on the request that was made by Al Parker, the French Colonel ordered the release of Mr. Kraft. The others who were being held remained in custody.

After completing their last interrogation, Al Parker and Hans Sigmann finished examining the items, that were taken from the dead Germans troops who ambushed their column in the Black Forest. Once they completed their review, they reported their findings to Jim Beauregard, when he returned to where they were standing by the lead Jeep.

"I think we're on to something, Jim," said Al, as he pointed to the maps that were laid out on the hood of their Jeep. "If you look at SS Lieutenant Weber's map, you'll notice that it has no markings on it. If you look at the maps that were taken from three of the regular soldiers, you'll notice that their maps have the same locations marked."

After giving Jim some time to examine the maps, Hans leaned forward and presented Jim with the notebook that was taken from the dead SS Lieutenant. "The SS Lieutenant who was killed was obviously more disciplined than the regular Wehrmacht and Luftwaffe troops, when it came to keeping potential useful intelligence information from falling into enemy hands."

While Jim compared the captured maps, he continued and said, "Two of the locations marked on these maps are between Freudenstadt and the German Austrian Border. The three other locations that are circled are small towns in the southern most part of Germany, in and around the Allgau section of the German Alps. The name Captain Schneider is also written on the maps that were taken from the bodies of the regular Wehrmacht and Luftwaffe troops." Then, as Jim leaned closer to the map, he added, "In fact, SS Captain Schneider's name is written in pencil just above the town of Sonthofen."

As an excited Al Parker patted Hans on the back, he seemed very proud of Jim when he remarked, "I told you he'd see that clue."

"So I'm right. There is some significance to the town of Sonthofen?" responded Jim.

"That's correct, Jim" said Hans, who quickly added, "The reason this could be significant is because there's a Nazi training school in Sonthofen."

As soon as Hans finished making his comment, Al perked up again and said, "There's more, Jim. Tell him Hans."

Immediately after Hans pointed to another marking on the captured map, he removed a cigarette from the pack that he carried in his field jacket pocket, as he continued and said, "This map also indicates that there is a Werwolf training camp in the small village of Langenwang. As you can see, Langenwang is just south of Sonthofen and is a few kilometers north of Oberstdorf. This is significant, because Oberstdorf is the southern most town in Germany and is within a dozen or so kilometers away from various Alpine trails and passes."[17]

After accepting a light from Jim's Zippo, Hans went on to say, "As I told Al. I know this area well. After I was wounded in the Great War, I met my wife while she was working as a nurse, in the hospital where I was being treated. As crowded as that hospital was, my wife Anna cared for me as if I was her only patient. When I asked her to marry me and she said yes, I was lucky to find work with my father as a Customs Official. Unfortunately, my new job sent us in different directions, because Anna had a job waiting for her back home in Oberstdorf, where she worked as a nurse in her grandfather's medical practice. Since it was almost impossible to find a good job in

Germany after the war, we decided to postpone getting married, until we could afford to do so."

After Hans took a quick drag from his cigarette, he went on to say, "Needless to say, I took all of my leave in Oberstdorf, so I could spend time with Anna and her family. Once we saved enough money and we got married, my father's older brother helped me get a position with the Munich Police. I enlisted in the Army again to serve in this war, when it became too difficult for me to be a policeman in the birthplace of National Socialism. I guess you can say, I wanted to get as far away from Munich as I could, even though I served the same master."

"Is that when your wife moved back home to Oberstdorf?" asked Jim.

"That's correct, Jim," said Hans, who took another quick drag on his cigarette before we continued. "My wife's father is the Police Chief in Oberstdorf. All of her closest relatives live there as well. They're very religious people and have no use for the Nazis.[18] That's one of the reasons why I had my wife move back to Oberstdorf when I joined the Army again. The other reason was because I knew the day would come, when the Allies would get around to bombing Munich."

"I heard Munich got hit pretty hard from the air," responded Jim.

After nodding his head in agreement, Hans remarked, "Much of the city, including the home that we lived in, has been destroyed." Once again Hans paused for a split second to take a drag on his American cigarette. When Hans continued, he spoke in a very confident tone of voice when he said, "Once I get to Oberstdorf, I intend to make a new life for me and my wife in this beautiful alpine town. Our son Peter will also have to make a new life for himself as well."

Both Jim and Al could tell, that it wasn't easy for Hans to talk about the impact that the war had on his personal life, on his family and on his country. Rather than push the issue, they opted to continue their discussion about intelligence matters, when Hans changed the subject and said, "Shall we get back to work."

Once Hans retrieved the dead SS Lieutenant's wallet from the hood of the Jeep, he removed a black and white photograph and showed it to Jim, while Al handed Jim the SS Officers Soldbuck, that contained a photo of SS Lieutenant Weber. While Jim compared the two photographs, Hans continued with his end of the briefing. "According to the names that are written on the back of this photograph, this is a picture of SS Lieutenant Wolfgang Weber, SS Lieutenant Gehard Schneider and an SS Captain by the name of Gunther Kessler. As you can see, they are standing in front of a destroyed Russian tank, which means, these men served together on the Eastern Front before being reassigned."

While Jim examined the front and the back of the black and white photograph, Hans quickly added, "Based on the other intelligence information that we gathered, it's seems logical to believe, that Kessler and Schneider were both promoted at some point after this photograph was taken."

As soon as Jim handed the photograph and the SS Lieutenant's Soldbuck back to Hans, he removed his pipe from his pant's pocket and used the stem as a pointer, while he examined the locations on the maps that were circled. After checking the maps that contained specific markings, Jim looked at Al and Hans and said, "Based on what we know so far, I'd say it's in our best interest to stop SS Major Kessler and everyone he's working with from prolonging this war. The fact that we have a photograph of Kessler and Schneider should help us hunt these bastards down."

"That's the good news," responded Al, who quickly added, "The bad news is, it won't be easy to find two German SS Officers, while Germany is filled with troops who haven't surrendered, or been captured."

Jim agreed. Al was right. Pursuing Kessler and his men would not be an easy task, even though they had some worthwhile leads to follow. Jim also knew that they would need to secure authorization from SHAFE, before they would be allowed to leave the French column, in order to pursue SS Major Kessler and his men. When Jim raised this issue, Al spoke up and said, "Do you think General Tremble will give us the green light?"

"I don't see why not," responded Jim, who went on to say, that once they briefed Colonel Reynald and the other men, he would draft a detailed message that Lieutenant Kelly could send to SHAFE after they stopped for the night.

While Al and Hans retrieved the intelligence information from the hood of their Jeep, Jim added, "We also need to find out if our French Allies recovered any intelligence information from the ambush site that can add to what you two found."

As Al and Hans stood holding the intelligence information that they just evaluated, Al remarked, "We're ready, Jim."

"OK, let's fill everyone else in on what you and Hans found," responded Jim, as he led the way to brief the others.

As soon as Jim, Al and Hans briefed Colonel Reynald, Captain Lorenz, Captain Lew, Captain Garnier, Lieutenant Kelly and MP Lieutenant Miller, the senior French Intelligence Officer explained, that no intelligence information of any value was found on the two SS troops who were killed by French soldiers, during the recent ambush in the Black Forest. Colonel Reynald also stated, that regardless of whether the circled locations were places where enemy resistance personnel planned to meet, where enemy supplies were stored, or where they planned to launch attacks, the French column would continue to drive through Southern Germany into Austria.

When Colonel Reynald continued, he pointed to one of the maps that contained various markings and said, "That said, I agree that we need to pass this intelligence information along to SHAFE, so other Allied units can be made aware of potential threats and locations where Nazi resistance groups may be storing supplies or operating from. Naturally, we will do our best to eliminate any threats that we encounter, as we continue on our mission."

Colonel Reynald then faced Jim and said, "I also have no problem with you taking some of your men, along with Captain Garnier and one of our tanks, to see if you can capture this SS Major and his men. The rest of us will eventually meet up with you in Oberstdorf." When Colonel Reynald concluded his remarks, he thanked Jim, Captain Parker and Hans Sigmann, for the detailed briefing.

After making camp on the outskirts of Freudenstadt, Al Parker sat in the command tent and read the letters that he received from his wife Mary and his oldest son Jack. While Mary had a lot to say about Cal getting married and deciding to live in Paris after the war, Captain John Jack Parker reported that after attending his brother's wedding, he shot down another enemy plane.

Once Al finished reading his mail, he decided to write Mary and his oldest son to report what happened on their trip through the Black Forest. Under the circumstances, this was not an easy letter for Al to write.

Jim Beauregard also had some mail to read. After reading a letter from his wife Bea, Jim read the two letters that he received from his oldest son Peter and his youngest son Michael. The boys were doing well and had plenty to report. While Michael was serving as an instructor at Ft. Bragg and was dating a local girl that he met at a Red Cross dance, Peter was serving on a destroyer escort in the Pacific. The fact that the boys included a few recent photographs, gave Jim the opportunity to see how much they both changed since they became fighting men.

As grateful as Jim was that his youngest son was stationed to a stateside post of duty, he had good reason to be worried about Peter. This was the case, because the Armed Forces Radio Network was constantly broadcasting reports about the fighting that was taking place in all theaters of operation, including the Pacific. Knowing that the Pacific War was also Navy War, meant that Peter Beauregard would be in harms way for as long as the Japanese continued to fight.

After walking into the command tent and approaching Al, as he finished reading his mail, Jim spoke up and said, "Good news I hope?"

As Al placed the two letters in the inside pocket of his field jacket, he looked at Jim and said, "Mary's elated that Cal met a nice girl and got married, but she's concerned about his decision to make a new life in Paris after the war. She also misses him and asked me if I would consider retiring from the police department, so we could spend more time visiting Cal and Michelle once the war is over. She's also concerned about our son Jack's decision to make a career in the Army Air Forces."

"It sounds like Mary is being a good mother who misses her sons," remarked Jim, who held up one of his letters as he added, "Bea's going through the same thing."

"Maybe I should retire when the war is over," said Al.

"The same thought crossed my mind as well," responded Jim, who went on to say, "After all we've done, maybe it's time for us to kick back and take it easy. Besides, if we're lucky and we become grandpars, we'll be able to spoil our grandchildren, then hand them back to their parents to raise."

"That sounds like fun," said Al.

As Jim sat next to Al in their command tent, he got serious and said, "Thanks for coming with me, Al. Being here wouldn't be the same without you."

"I wouldn't have missed this for all the tea in China," remarked Al.

After reaching into his inside field jacket pocket, Jim removed the message that he intended to send to General Tremble. As Jim handed the message to Al, he continued and said, "Take a look at this and let me know what you think."

While Al put on his glasses and he began reading the message, Jim remarked, "The information that you and Hans picked up from the father of that dead kid sealed it as far as I'm concerned. Even though we're being opposed by relatively small numbers of German troops and armed civilian fighters, their continued resistance is proving to be royal pain in the ass. In addition to killing and wounding Allied troops when this war is almost over, these Nazi fanatics are also hurting their own people by continuing to fight."

As soon as Al finished reading the message, he removed his glasses, before he handed the report back to Jim and said, "You certainly hit the nail on the head. The question is, what will General Tremble want us to do about it."

"All we can do is pass along the intelligence," responded Jim, who quickly added, "Personally, I believe the General is gonna approve our plan, especially since Colonel Reynald has agreed to allow us to pursue SS Major Kessler and his men. Besides, all we're really doing, is serving as an advanced patrol for the French forces, that plan on occupying the southern most part of Germany all the way to the Alps."

"Good point," said Al, who continued as he removed a cigar from his field jacket pocket. "Hopefully, we can pick up some good intel along the way, when we take Hans and his son back to Oberstdorf. We'll also have two good scouts with us who are familiar with the area."

"At least we won't get lost," joked Jim, as he leaned closer to Al and offered him a light from his Zippo.

After cracking a grin, Al covered his mouth as he recovered from a smokers cough, before he said, "I gotta tell ya, Jim. I really believe that it was no accident, that we ran into Hans last December and that we were able to find him in that hell hole of a prison camp."

After taking two quick puffs on his cigar, Al quickly added, "Ever since I was a kid my old man's been telling me, that if it's meant to be, it'll happen."

"I know what you mean," said Jim, who continued while he added some tobacco into the bowl of his pipe. "You're right. Too many good things have happened since we met Hans for this to be a coincidence."

Immediately after Al agreed, he became dead serious when he added, "In addition to making it possible for us to capture Ivan Larson, he saved Cal's life with that fancy shooting of his and with a pistol no less. Hans also turned out to be an excellent guide through Southern Germany. He also knows how to get information from people, especially from Nazi troublemakers."

As soon as Jim finished lighting his pipe, he slipped his Zippo lighter in his pant's pocket, as he responded to Al's last remark. "Hans and his son are living proof that not all Germans are Nazis. Even Colonel Reynald seems to have accepted Hans and his son."

After hearing what Jim had to say, Al snickered a bit, before he responded in a low tone of voice and said, "For a minute there I thought Colonel Reynald was gonna kiss Hans on both cheeks and give him a medal, when he saw the way he got that badly wounded German kid to identify SS Major Kessler."

As Jim became more serious, he looked at the man who had become his close friend and a professional colleague and said, "You know, Al. There's hope for this world yet when a Frenchman and a German can get along."

Without hesitating, Al shot back with, "Ain't that the truth."

While traveling with Colonel Reynald's intelligence unit, the French First Armored Division and 4th Moroccan Division, the American composite liaison unit, under the command of Lt. Colonel James Beauregard, continued traveling through Southern Germany toward Lake Constance. Along the way, the French troops under the command of General Bethouart and their American Allies experienced different levels of resistance, as they traveled toward the Swiss and Austrian borders.

While some of the attacks and acts of sabotage were relatively minor incidents of resistance, other events were more serious in size and scope. In addition to periodic incidents of sniping, Allied personnel were still being ambushed, roads were mined, bridges were blown, Allied vehicles and supply dumps were sabotaged and acts of retribution were carried out against German officials and civilians who were deemed to be disloyal in any way.

A number of these acts of resistance were carried out by young German males and females, including young teenagers, who were fanatically loyal to Adolf Hitler and the aims of National Socialism. In other instances, a number of armed encounters took place between the invading Allied armies and various size German military and SS units, as well as non German Axis forces. One non German para military unit, that was active in these last ditch acts of resistance, was comprised of pro Nazi/pro Vichy French Milice paramilitary personnel. Now that they were on the losing side of the war, members of the French Milice had good reason to be concerned, that they would face serious reprisals, for siding with the enemy of France.[19]

★ ★ ★

As soon as SS Major Kessler arrived in Sonthofen, he was immediately impressed with the success that Captain Schneider had in organizing resistance units in the surrounding area. The Major was even more impressed, when he learned that his second in command recruited some additional German troops, who had no intentions of surrendering to the Allies, especially to the French. As an added bonus, SS Captain Schneider also recruited a decorated Panzer Grenadier Lieutenant by the name Albert Emich to join their Nazi resistant unit. In addition to being in excellent physical condition, Lieutenant Emich grew up in the nearby Austrian Alps. This made Lieutenant Emich ideally suited, to help train the regular German troops in their new command, to operate in the higher elevations on a year round basis.

In order to prepare to begin operations as soon as the Major arrived,

Captain Schneider had seventy five troops from various branches of the service, escorted from Sonthofen to a remote camp near Spielmannsau, Germany. The arrival of SS Sergeant Mueller and his men expanded their capabilities even more. Even the three slightly wounded SS troops who arrived with Major Kessler, continued to prove useful and eagerly volunteered to return to full duty.

Once the Werwolf fighter who was serving as their lead scout, returned from another escort mission to Spielmannsau, SS Major Kessler gave the young man time to rest, before ordering his three squads of SS troops to move out. With their young Werwolf Scout leading the way, SS Major Kessler, SS Captain Schneider and their three squads of battle hardened SS soldiers left Sonthofen, to begin mounting operations in and around Oberstdorf, Germany.

After pausing to take a break and retrieve additional supplies at the Werwolf Training School at Langenwang, SS Major Kessler and his men traveled the rest of the fourteen miles to a location on the outskirts of Oberstdorf. Their next stop was a secluded location near Gruben, that was just under three kilometers south of Oberstdorf. This particular location was selected to serve as the closest clandestine base of operations to launch operations in Oberstdorf.

While their men stored several wooden crates filled with supplies at the camp near Gruben, SS Major Kessler turned to SS Captain Schneider and said, "We might as well send out our first patrol, while we join the rest of the men at our camp near Spielmannsau. Have Sergeant Mueller and his 3rd squad operate from this location, while they begin conducting a thorough reconnaissance of Oberstdorf. We'll return to this camp on the night of the 30th to conduct a debriefing. Once we know more about what's taking place in Oberstdorf, we'll begin conducing offensive operations in the early morning hours of May 1st."

As soon as SS Captain Schneider acknowledged his commanders instructions and he began to walk away, SS Major Kessler called out, "One more thing, Gerhardt."

Once the Captain turned and faced his commanding officer, Major Kessler continued and said, "Even though their objective is to gather intelligence information, Sergeant Mueller and his men are authorized to defend themselves and if necessary eliminate any disloyal Germans, or Allied troops they encounter. However, I want you to stress to Mueller and his men, that they should only take action, if they are confident that they can inflict casualties on the enemy and withdraw from contact, without being pursued to this location."

As soon as SS Captain Schneider acknowledged his commanders instructions, SS Major Kessler added, "Tell the men I said good luck and above all to be careful. We can't afford to lose anyone."

After acknowledging the order, SS Captain Schneider walked away from his commanding officer, to relay the instructions to Sergeant Mueller and the men in his squad.

With their young Werwolf scout leading the way, SS Major Kessler and his men traveled to their next clandestine camp along the Traufbach stream near Gottenried. After concealing some additional supplies at this location, Kessler and his men rested for an hour, before departing for their primary base camp near Spielmannsau.

Now that they had more freedom of movement, SS Captain Schneider suggested that the Major should inspect a famous resort called Kemptner Hutte, that was not being used at this time. The Captain made this recommendation, because this remote location was at an even higher altitude and might come in handy, if they had to evacuate their other camps, in order to evade detection.

When SS Major Kessler asked his second in command to tell him more about this place called Kemptner Hutte, Captain Schneider produced a map and showed his superior officer exactly were this very isolated alpine resort was located. As Captain Schneider continued his briefing, he used his pencil to draw a line, along the route that led from their camp near Spielmannsau to Kemptner Hutte. "As you can see, Sir, the terrain gets more demanding as we travel to the higher elevation."

"You're right, Gerhardt. This alpine resort is located on some very rugged terrain and we can certainly use that to our advantage," remarked the Major.

As soon as SS Major Kessler finished speaking, Captain Schneider continued and said, "Kemptner Hutte was built back in 1839 and was last renovated and made a bit larger in 1931. If the Allies or any disloyal Germans come looking for us, this old Alpine resort might just be the perfect place for us to fall back to. Besides, as the Americans like to say, taking the high ground is always the preferred course of action in a combat situation."

While SS Major Kessler took another look at the map, he remarked, "I'm curious, Gerhardt. how did you find this place, as well as the three camps that are ideally suited for our operations in this area?"

As SS Captain Schneider folded his map, he responded and said, "I was waiting until we had the chance to inspect the Alpine resort known as Kemptner Hutte, to tell you more about how I came to select these locations, Sir."

While the Captain continued, he pointed to their Werwolf Scout who was helping the men unpack supplies. "When our young Werwolf fighter heard that I was looking for remote locations where we could operate from, he volunteered his services and explained in detail, every possible location in the vicinity of Oberstdorf, where we might consider establishing different size bases."

After pausing for a split second while he faced his commanding officer, Captain Schneider added, "He just turned 15, Sir. Of all the young Germans I recruited into the Werwolf program, Walter Vogel proved to be the best candidate to serve as our scout. He also comes from a very good family. His father was a respected mechanic from Langenwang, who volunteered for service with the Luftwaffe early in the war. After his father survived serving in North Africa, he was killed by the Americans, when he was preparing one of our jet fighters to take off, so it could engage the enemy."

While SS Captain Schneider slipped his map into his coat pocket, SS Major Kessler remarked, "Your young assistant has certainly proven to be a valuable asset to our mission."

"Yes he has, Sir," responded SS Captain Schneider who went on to say, "As a boy growing up in Langenwang, Walter's father took him up and down these alpine trails and passes. They even stayed at Kemptner Hutte on several occasions." Then, after pausing briefly, SS Captain Schneider added, "Lieutenant Emich has also been extremely helpful. In fact, he commanded the first contingent that traveled with our Werwolf Scout and set up our primary camp near Spielmannsau."

After nodding his head in approval, SS Major Kessler remarked, "We had a long journey from Sonthofen. Once we get some rest, our Werwolf Scout can take us on a hike, so we can inspect this place called Kemptner Hutte. Manheimer and Gustav Lang will accompany us."

Even though they had been together since the early days of Operation Barbarossa, SS Captain Schneider always knew how to behave whenever he dealt with his commanding officer. Clearly, the two worked well together, which is why they remained an effective team. After nodding his head ever so slightly, the SS Captain tossed his commander a casual salute, as he acknowledged his orders and said, "I'll make sure the men are ready, Sir."

Captain Schneider didn't take three steps, when Major Kessler called out in a much more down to earth tone of voice, as he pointed to their young Werwolf Scout and said, "Make sure Mr. Vogel is well fed and given an extra blanket, so he'll be well rested when he takes us on our hike in the morning."

As usual, Captain Schneider responded in the appropriate fashion when he remarked, "I'll personally see to it, that he's well cared for, Sir."

After hearing Major Kessler say, "Carry on, Gerhardt," SS Captain Schneider used his left hand to motion the young Werewolf fighter to join him as he called out, "Kommen hier, Walter."

After eating a meager breakfast of Germany Army cheese spread, a slice of dark bread and washing it down with some ersatz coffee, SS Major Kessler, SS Captain Schneider, Walter Vogel and SS Private's Christian Manheimer and Gustav Lang left to inspect the resort known as Kemptner Hutte. While SS Major Kessler and SS Captain Schneider were off on their scouting mission, Lieutenant Emich led the non SS troops in their command on a training exercise, in one of the nearby Alpine passes. This was necessary to prepare the assembly of military personnel from different units, to operate as a cohesive unit in higher elevations.

The resort at Kemptner Hutte proved to be ideally suited, to accommodate SS Major Kessler, SS Captain Schneider and their three squads of SS troops. Once the Major completed his inspection, he turned to Walter Vogel in the presence of Captain Schneider and said, "You've done excellent work for us, Walter."

"Thank you, Sir," responded the young Werwolf Scout.

While SS Privates Christian Manheimer and Gustav Lang provided security, the two SS Officers and their Werwolf Scout stood in front of Kemptner Hutte and admired the alpine resort one last time, before returning to their primary base of operation. Clearly, the Major was impressed and agreed with his second in command, that this resort was an ideal location to use in an emergency as a fall back position.

As soon as SS Major Kessler faced Captain Schneider, he sounded as if he was in an exceptionally good mood when he said, "As soon as we get back to our camp near Spielmannsau, I want Mr. Vogel to lead the men from the first and second squad to this location. I want the men to transport enough supplies to this location, so all three of our squads can operate from Kemptner Hutte for a minimum of ten days."

When Captain Schneider asked about the personnel who were from various regular German Army, Navy and Air Force units, Kessler responded and said, "I have other plans for the men that Lieutenant Emich is in the process of training to function as a cohesive unit. When they're ready to go operational, we'll disperse some of our more experienced men in with the others. This will insure that they are properly led." SS Major Kessler then turned to Walter Vogel and gripped the top of his left shoulder, when he continued and said, "Only SS men and you are to know about this place. No one else. Do you understand?"

As soon as the enthusiastic young Werwolf fighter responded and said, "Yes, Sir," SS Major Kessler pointed to the trail head and said, "Lead the way, young man."

The second the Major made eye contact with the two SS Privates and said, "Move out," Christian Manheimer and Gustav Lang knew exactly what to do without being told and assumed positions at the front and rear of the column.

While Walter Vogel led the way back to their camp near Spielmannsau,

SS Major Kessler turned to SS Captain Schneider and said, "I wish we had a dozen more like him. Two dozen would be ever better."

The advance toward the Austrian border was delayed, when the French column met with armed German resistance when they entered Friedrichshafen. Situated on Lake Constance, Friesrichshafen was home to enough German military personnel to initially prevent the French Army from racing through the city toward the Austrian border.[20] After some brief street fighting, the city was secured and the French were able to proceed with their plans to cross over into Austria.

After defeating the German defenders of Friedrichshafen, the French column and their American liaison unit made their way to the border with Austria on April 29, 1945. Unfortunately, the French advance into Bregenz, Austria met with fierce resistance. Rather than continue to sustain casualties at this late stage of the war, the decision was made to issue an ultimatum to surrender or face the consequences. When the German defenders refused to meet these demands, the French proceeded to bombard the city into submission using aircraft and artillery. It took the destruction of Bregenz, to crush the fanatical defense of the Austrian city, that was never attacked up until this point in the war.[21]

When Lieutenant Dan Kelly received a priority radio message from General Tremble, he wasted no time in delivering the response to Lt. Colonel Beauregard. "A message from General Tremble, Sir."

"Thanks Dan," responded Jim, as he accepted the message and he began to read the contents. As soon as Jim finished reading the note, he handed the message to Al Parker as he remarked, "You're gonna love this, Al."

While reading the message out loud, Al spoke at a fast pace, "Request approved to have Captains Lorenz and Lew command the Liaison Unit, while you and your reconnaissance unit investigate Nazi resistance activities in the aforementioned locations." Once Al finished reading the message, he handed the note back to Jim and said, "This is good news. We got the green light to do whatever is necessary, to locate SS Major Kessler, SS Captain Schneider and any troops, or individuals who are serving under their command."

While Jim slipped the message into his Army Officer's trench coat pocket, he looked at Al as he responded and said, "Let's hope we're as good at finding SS Major Kessler and his men, as we were in locating Ivan Larson and Francis Shorty Mc Ghee."

"Thank God we ran into Hans when we did, or things might have been a lot different," responded Al.

"Hopefully, having him along for the ride, will increase our chances of being successful again," responded Jim.

When Al agreed that they made a good team, Jim added, "We certainly do."

Once they received orders from SHAFE, that authorized a portion of the American Liaison Unit to leave the French column to pursue SS Major Kessler and his men, Al turned to Jim and said, "Have you decided who we should take with us?"

"Like you said before, Al. They're all good men," remarked Jim, who quickly added, "Any suggestions?"

As soon as Jim asked Al to recommend who should go with them, Al felt the burden of command weigh heavily on his shoulders. While his thoughts were filled with the image of Benny Greene dying before his eyes, Al made a command decision and said, "How 'bout we take Ange and Sal with us. They've been hounding us to take point ever since we left Q179. Besides, I'm afraid if we leave them behind, they might go AWOL and follow us."

Seeing Jim crack a smile then say, "Good choice and you're right about them following us if we don't take them with us," reassured Al that he made the right selection.

"That's two volunteers," remarked Al.

When Jim continued, he sounded like a commander, who was 110% confident about how they should proceed. "In keeping with the composite nature of our unit, we should also take a CIC Agent and an MP with us."

"How 'bout Lieutenant Kelly and Lieutenant Miller," responded Al.

"You read my mind," said Jim, before he went on to say, "In addition to Captain Garnier, we'll also take Sam Carubba and Mike Mulligan and the number two half track with us. Between our Half Track and that French Sherman tank, we should have plenty of firepower at our disposal if we run into trouble."

"You want'a bring those captured German weapons along as well?" asked Al.

"Why not," said Jim, who quickly added, "I also think it makes sense to have Ange and Sal swap their Thompsons for two M1 Garands. Those rifles will be a lot more effective than a Tommy Gun if we have to operate in Alpine terrain." Then, after pausing for a split second, Jim added, "They can give Sergeant Morgan one of their Thompsons when they pickup his M1 and the rifle that Sergeant Dalton carried before he was wounded."

"You got it, Jim," responded Al.

As Jim removed a pack of gum from his field jacket pocket and offered a piece to Al, he continued and said. "Since the French have a surgeon and several medics attached to their column, Doc Keller can also come along for the ride. Hopefully, his services won't be needed, but I'd hate to have us run into trouble and not have him with us."

While Al removed the wrapper from the stick of gum, he responded and said, "I'll let the Doc know that he just volunteered for our side trip into the alpine region of Southern Germany."

Just before Jim and his men began their trip, General Tremble sent the following coded message to the American Liaison Unit, that was serving with the French Army. "Allied Intelligence just confirmed...SS Major Gunther Kessler and other unnamed members of his command are wanted for war crimes by two Allied nations. Good hunting! See you in Berlin.

Tremble."

When pro Allied Austrian partisans met with French Army commanders, to assist in the securing of Bregenz, this same group of anti Nazi fighters offered to provide assistance to Lt. Colonel James Beauregard and his
men. Jim welcomed their assistance, because there were still German troops
in Austria who were opposing the Allied invasion of the Fatherland. Rather
than wait for the bombardment of Bregenz to force the German defenders
into submission, Jim Beauregard and his men accepted the help of a heavily
armed group of pro Allied Austrian partisan fighters, who agreed to escort
the American column through Austria. Doing so would enable the Allied
contingent of CID Agents, Intelligence Officers and other personnel, to
continue their pursuit of SS Major Kessler and his men in a timely fashion.

After heading south to Dornbirn, Austria, the Allied column and their
Austrian escort unit traveled to the village of Hittisau, which is located in
the district of Bregenz, in the Austrian state of Voralberg. From Hittisau,
the pro Allied Austrian resistance unit known as 05 and the Allied composite unit traveled approximately 10 kilometers, to the small municipality
of Osterreich, Austria. After completing their escort duty, the members of
05 wished Lt. Colonel James Beauregard and his men good luck, as they
proceeded on their mission. As the detachment of Austrian 05 resistance
fighters returned to Bregenz, Jim and his men entered Germany and passed
through the small village of Balderschwang on their way to Oberstdorf.
(*see Footnote 21 for the actual historical references on the O5 Resistance
Organization.)

CHAPTER 6

ANOTHER MANHUNT

Before leaving the French column, Jim Beauregard asked Hans Sigmann to select a suitable location on the outskirts of Oberstdorf, that could be used to receive an air drop of supplies. After receiving confirmation that their resupply mission was approved, the composite unit that was led by Jim Beauregard proceeded to the drop zone near Oberstdorf, Germany. After traveling over 60 kilometers from Bregenz, Austria into Southern Germany, the American column arrived at the location that was selected for their resupply mission.

The last thing that Gunther Jager wanted to do at 64 years of age was fight his own people. Unfortunately, the Nazis had ruined his country and refused to see, that continued resistance to the Allied invasion of Germany was making a bad situation worse.

As the Police Chief in Oberstdorf, Gunther Jager was asked by the men who originally formed the town's home defense force to command their militia unit. Once Gunther accepted the position, he and his fellow resistance fighters began making plans, to arrest every Nazi official and all German military personnel stationed in Oberstdorf, including members of the SS. The decision was also made to post sentries on the outskirts of the town, before they started making arrests later that evening. Gunther Jager also recommended that once they posted sentries at key vantage points, that he should lead a patrol around the outskirts of Oberstdorf. This recommendation was made, because Gunther, along with his best friend Koenraad Berger and other members of their resistance unit, recently observed dozens of SS troops and regular soldiers, transporting supplies into the alpine trails and passes south of town.

From the moment that he took command of the local militia unit known as a Heimatshutz, Gunther Jager wondered how long his lightly armed citizens could hold out, before Allied units arrived to occupy the area.[22] As a decorated World War I veteran, who had a long police career, Gunther knew that fanatical members of the SS were organizing a last ditch effort, to resist the Allied occupation of Germany and prolong the war. The presence of German civilians in the surrounding area known as Werwolves, added another dimension to this threat, because these civilian Nazi resistance fighters operated out of uniform. This meant that Werwolf operatives could easily blend in and commit attacks using more covert means.

Gunther also knew that many of these Werwolves were impressionable young teenagers, who were brainwashed to do the bidding of the Nazis. As a result, Gunther's greatest fear, was that if this SS led Nazi resistance movement was even moderately successful, the Allies would deal very harshly with any individuals, or jurisdictions that assisted, or supported the aims of these fanatics. For all of these reasons, the citizens who made up the Oberstdorf defense force, were determined to secure their town at all cost. To do otherwise, would be foolish at this late stage of the war, especially for a community that was dominated by Bavarian Catholics, who came to believe that their country was hijacked by a sinister Nazi regime.[23]

The first phase of their operation, was to make sure that men from their town militia were secretly posted at key positions. This was done to prevent the escape of Nazi officials and military personnel once they began making arrests. These guard posts were also designed to make it more difficult for Werwolves, or SS led resistance units, to easily penetrate the town's defenses.

Once Gunther was satisfied, that the bulk of his militiamen were in position to take control of the town, he led four of the older men, who were World War 1 veterans, on an extended patrol of the area. Even though they were lightly armed, Gunther Jager and his militiamen had one advantage over anyone who tried to oppose their efforts. They knew the area, including the Alpine trails and passes, like the back of their hand.

★ ★ ★

After spotting an American cargo plane and two P51 fighters approaching the outskirts of Oberstdorf, Gunther turned to the men on his patrol and said, "The Allies must be close if one of their planes is dropping supplies nearby."

When one of his civilian volunteers, who lost an eye while fighting in World War I, remarked, "They could also be dropping Allied Fallschirmjager troops or commandos," Gunther looked through his binoculars before responding. "Either way, we should head in that direction. If I had to guess, I'd say they're using the pasture owned by our friend Erich Schafer for their drop." Then, as Gunther lowered his field glasses, he faced his men and added, "The road that leads to Oberstdorf runs right by that open pasture. If Allied troops are in this area, we need to warn them about the holdouts from the SS, the Werwolves and the stragglers from different military units, that we've observed moving into the nearby Alpine trails and passes."

As soon as SS Sergeant Bruno Mueller and his men heard the distinctive sound of aircraft approaching from the west, Corporal Ernest Krebs remarked, "Now that the illustrious Luftwaffe has been swept from the sky, that has to be the sound of Allied aircraft heading this way."

While the veteran SS Non Commissioned Officer stood on the high ground above the nearby alpine road, he corrected his subordinate, while he used his binoculars to get a better look at the approaching aircraft. "That's enough of that talk, Ernest. With or without the Luftwaffe, we have a mission to perform. Remember that."

"Yes, Sergeant," was all that the SS Corporal needed to say, to get back in the good graces of his squad leader. To prove that all was forgiven, SS Sergeant Mueller took his eyes off the approaching Allied aircraft long enough to face SS Corporal Krebs and say, "Move the men down this hill and position them inside the edge of the treeline, along the side of the road. I'll join you in a minute."

Immediately after the Corporal acknowledged the order and he directed the other members of their squad to follow him to their next position, SS

Sergeant Mueller continued looking through his binoculars. After observing two American P51 fighters circling at a higher altitude, a slower flying American cargo plane descended over an open field, that wasn't all that far from his squad's current position.

Even though Sergeant Mueller's primary concern was to conduct a reconnaissance mission in and around Oberstdorf, he was also instructed to engage any targets of opportunity, that could be easily overwhelmed by him and his men. While SS Sergeant Mueller made his way down the hill to join his troops, he decided to evaluate the size of the enemy force, before making the decision about executing an ambush. The fact that his orders allowed him to attack Allied troops, as well as disloyal Germans, gave him a free hand to use his discretion, when taking action against anyone who opposed the aims of National Socialism.

When it came to air dropping supplies to Allied troops on the ground, Billy Davis was on time and on target. While a pair of P51 fighter aircraft circled overhead, the C47 that was being flown by Billy Davis descended to an altitude of 300 feet and headed straight for the open pasture, that Hans Sigmann selected for their resupply mission. Meanwhile, on the ground, French Army Captain Charles Garnier, along with the French Army Sherman Tank crew, Sergeant Carubba, Lieutenant Kelly and MP Lieutenant Miller provided security, while Captain Al Parker and Sergeants Mulligan, Angelone, Coppola and Doc Keller stood by to retrieve the supplies. Hans and his son Peter were also standing by to lend a hand.

As soon as the C47 bearing the name Six Gun headed for the center of the DZ, Jim spoke into a SCR 536 handie talkie radio and said, "You're looking good, Billy." A split second later, the C47 flew over the edge of the field and headed straight for the line of U.S. Army vehicles, that were being used to identify the actual drop zone. Once the C47 approached the first parked vehicle, the crew chief and the radioman began pushing supply bundles out of the C47. In addition, two parapacks were also jettisoned from the bottom of the plane

By time the last package was floating down to the ground, the C47 was making a shallow climb to a higher altitude, before banking to the right. As the C47 headed back over the drop zone, Al Parker and the rest of the men, including Hans and his son, were almost finished retrieving the supply bundles from the open field.

While the C47 flew over the DZ, Jim and the others could see a smiling Billy Davis giving them the thumbs up signal, as he got back on the radio and said, "Don't hesitate to call if you need us, Colonel."

As soon as Jim tossed Billy and his crew a casual salute, he got back on the handie talkie radio while the C47 was still in range and said, "Thanks, Billy. That's two rounds of drinks that we owe you."

While the C47 started to climb back up to a higher altitude, Billy Davis was heard over the radio one last time as he remarked, "You and Al be careful, Sir. The same goes for the rest of your men."

A split second later, the two American P51 fighter planes flew over the DZ and followed the lumbering C47 back to its base in France.

As soon as the various parachute bundles were collected, Al Parker drove up in a Jeep that was laden with supplies and said, "We're all set, Jim."

While the other vehicles drove up and parked behind the Colonel's Jeep, Hans jumped out of the back of the M3 half track and walked over to where Jim was standing. "Your air drops were always an impressive sight to watch," remarked Hans, before he quickly added, "This one was no different."

As Al Parker cracked a smile, Jim addressed Hans, just as Sergeants Angelone and Coppola drove up and parked their Jeep in the lead position. "Lead the way, Hans."

"My pleasure," responded Hans, as he walked past the Colonel's Jeep and he climbed in the back of the Jeep, that was being driven by Sergeant Angelone.

While Hans sat in the middle of the back seat, he was surrounded by cans of U.S. Army small arms ammunition and a captured German MG42 machine gun with a spare barrel and a supply of ammunition. When Sergeant Angelone started the Jeep, Sergeant Coppola turned around in the front passenger seat and spoke in a friendly tone of voice, as he handed

Hans a captured German 9mm MP40 submachine gun and a black leather ammo pouch, that contained three loaded 30 round magazines. "The Colonel thought you should be armed with something more powerful than a pistol, not that you didn't impress the hell out'a us, when you used a P38 to shoot the kid who killed Benny Greene and wounded Cal."

As Hans took possession of the machine pistol and the extra ammunition, he remarked, "Thank you, Sergeant. Let's hope it won't be necessary to expend anymore ammunition."

When Sergeant Angelone glanced back and said, "Which way, Hans?" the former German Military Policeman, who was now serving as a deputized civilian German policeman, pointed off to the right and said, "Off to the right, Sergeant. Once we get back on the road turn left. Oberstdorf is a few kilometers down the road."

"You got it," remarked Sergeant Angelone, as he drove off and led the convoy out of the open pasture and back on the road to Oberstdorf.

CHAPTER 7

ENGAGING THE FORCES OF EVIL

A s soon as the convoy of Allied vehicles was heard approaching their position, SS Sergeant Muller held up his right hand, in preparation of giving his men the command to open fire. While Sergeant Mueller and his men prepared to execute the ambush, SS Corporal Krebs spotted a German policeman and four armed civilians coming their way. The fact that these men were wearing armbands, that displayed the white and blue colors of the Bavarian Flag, meant that they were members of the same town militia, that SS Sergeant Mueller and his men observed being posted around Oberstdorf earlier that afternoon.

After alerting the other men who were nearby, Corporal Krebs made his way to the position closer to the road, where their squad leader was preparing to direct the ambush. As soon as Corporal Krebs alerted his squad leader, of the presence of armed civilians coming their way, SS Sergeant Mueller turned to his Corporal and said, "Ernst, take the men across the road. "I'll be along shortly."

Just as Corporal Krebs acknowledged the order and motioned the men to go, several shots rang out, as the four man patrol from the Oberstdorf defense force opened fire on SS Sergeant Mueller and his men. As tempted as he was to remain behind, Corporal Krebs followed the order and called out, "Go, go, go!" while SS Sergeant Mueller returned fire with his 9mm MP40 submachine gun.

After firing a few quick bursts at the uniformed German policeman and the armed civilian militiamen, SS Sergeant Mueller withdrew and joined his men. Doing so, enabled SS Sergeant Mueller and his squad to vanish from sight, before the Allied patrol arrived in the area.

Once they knew they were not being pursued, SS Sergeant Mueller instructed Corporal Krebs to take the men back to their clandestine camp near Gruben, while he returned to the road, to see if he could gather any worthwhile intelligence information. Ernst Krebs was promoted to the rank of Corporal because he knew how to take an order. Krebs had also served with Sergeant Mueller long enough to grow fond of the seasoned veteran. As a result, it was easy for Sergeant Mueller to see the look of concern on his Corporal's face, when he acknowledged the order, as he shouldered his MP40.

While facing his subordinate, SS Sergeant Mueller remarked, "I'll be OK, Ernst. Now go."

As the patrol led by SS Corporal Krebs returned to their clandestine camp near Gruben, SS Sergeant Mueller made his way to a position near the side of the road. All Sergeant Mueller could think about, as he knelt down behind good cover to make his observations, was that the war was no longer a black and white conflict, that involved one side fighting the other. This became painfully evident, when SS Sergeant Mueller and his men were shot at by a German policeman and four armed German civilians. The fact that these Germans were wearing armbands that displayed the white and blue colors of the Bavarian flag, was a blatantly clear indication that they were not supporters of National Socialism.

While SS Sergeant Mueller watched the German policeman and the four armed civilians walking cautiously along the road, he thought to himself that a lot had changed, since the Allies crossed the Rhine River and advanced deeper into The Fatherland. A split second later, SS Sergeant Mueller heard what sounded like an American Jeep coming to a stop, before making the next turn in the road.

After hearing gunfire off in the distance, Sergeant Angelone brought their Jeep to a halt, before proceeding around the next turn in the road. While Hans jumped out of the back of the Jeep with his MP40 in hand, the two CID Agents exited the vehicle and aimed their M1 Garand rifles down the road. A split second later, Jim Beauregard and Al Parker, along with the other men in their convoy came to a stop behind the lead Jeep and exited their vehicles.

"See anything worth shooting at?" asked their Commanding Officer.

"No Sir, but it sounded like two different groups were firing at each other."

While Hans held the MP40 with the muzzle pointed safely off to the left, he looked at Jim and said, "Sergeant Angelone is correct, Jim. Those shots were definitely fired from two different groups, just beyond the next turn in the road."

"A perfect place for an ambush," remarked Al Parker.

"You're right, Al" said Jim, who looked at the men occupying the lead Jeep and said, "Let's take it slow. Once we make our way around this bend in the road, we'll dismount and check the area on foot before we proceed."

As soon as Sergeants Angelone and Coppola acknowledged the order, Jim looked at Hans and said, "Keep that MG42 ready to go, Hans. It might come in handy before this day is over."

After nodding his head once, Hans responded and said, "Yes Jim," as he climbed into the back of the Jeep and exchanged his 9mm submachine gun for the MG42, that was loaded with a 72 round drum of ammunition.

The moment Gunther Jager spotted the American vehicles driving slowly around the turn and coming to a stop, he instructed his men to shoulder their rifles and stand fast. Gunther then held up his right hand and waved, to let the approaching Allied troops know that he and his men were not a threat.

At the same time that Gunther held up his hand, Sal Coppola remarked, "We got company, Ange and one of them is wearing a uniform," as he instinctively aimed his M1 Garand rifle down the road, while his buddy stopped the Jeep and picked up his rifle.

As soon as the uniformed German policeman and the four armed German civilians cautiously approached the Allied convoy, an excited Hans Sigmann leaned forward and patted Sergeant Coppola on the top of his left shoulder and said, "Rest easy, Sergeant. I know the man who is waving at us. He's my wife's father. He is the Polizeichefin, or as you say in America, the Police Chief in Oberstdorf.

The second Hans put the MG42 down, he stood up in the back of the Jeep and began waving his right hand as he called out, "Gunther, it's me Hans."

Under the circumstances Gunther could not believe his eyes. It had been some time since his daughter heard from her husband, or her son Peter. By the time Hans jumped out of the back of the Jeep armed with his MP40, Gunther had already handed his rifle to one of his men and was walking toward the American vehicle. While Sergeants Angelone and Coppola stood guard and the other vehicles came to a stop, Hans was warmly greeted by his father in law. "It's good to see you, Hans. Anna has had such faith that you would come home to us."

The moment Hans saw Gunther notice the fact that he was wearing an American Army uniform, that displayed no rank, insignia or unit patches, Hans remarked, "After Peter and I were rescued from a prison camp by these Americans, we were given discharges and appointed civilian policemen to help stabilize Germany after the war." Hans then went on to say, "We're here to find an SS Major and his men, who intend to keep the war going for as long as possible."

"You and your American friends have come to the right place to continue your search," responded Gunther, who quickly added, "Because Oberstdorf is surrounded by Nazi troublemakers." As soon as the old man finished speaking, he was surprised again, when his grandson called out, "Grandfather," as the young man made his way to where he was standing.

Even though Gunther was a former soldier and a veteran policeman, his emotions began to get the best of him, when he embraced the young man who was his only surviving grandson. "Two surprises in the same day," remarked Gunther, as he gripped his grandson by the side of his left arm and said, "Your mother and I never lost hope that you and your father would return."

Due to the fact that a shooting just took place, Jim Beauregard wasted no time in turning to MP Lieutenant Miller and saying, "Carl, have the men secure this area, while the rest of us get introduced and find out who was doing the shooting and why."

As soon as the MP Lieutenant acknowledged the order, he directed Sergeants Carubba, Mulligan, Angelone and Coppola to fan out and keep an eye out for trouble. While the security team was posted along the road, Jim and the others approached Hans to learn more. As Hans turned to face the contingent of Allied Officers and Doc Keller, he introduced them to his father in law.

Once the introductions were made, Gunther presented the American Army Officers and the French Army Captain an American style salute, as he addressed Jim Beauregard in a very respectful tone of voice. "We are very glad to see you and your men, herr Oberst. As the Police Chief in Oberstdorf, I was asked to command the town's defense force. Once we heard that the Allies were advancing through Southern Germany and Austria, we decided it was time for us to act. We began operations to retake our town from Nazi control, by posting sentries at key locations around Oberstdorf to prevent their escape. As soon as we completed a patrol of the area, we intended to arrest every Nazi official and all military personnel stationed in Oberstdorf. This includes some SS men. There are also American Prisoners of War being held in Oberstdorf, who were forced to do manual labor in harsh weather conditions by the Nazis. These men will need to be cared for once their guards are taken into custody. You and your men should also know, herr Oberst, that all of my men can be identified by the armbands that they wear, that display the colors of the Bavarian Flag."[24]

When he continued, Gunther turned to his right and pointed to the position where he and his men observed a squad of SS troops positioned along the road, before he faced the American Colonel and filed the rest of his briefing. "While my men and I were finishing our patrol of the area, we spotted your planes coming this way. As we continued to move in this direction, we observed a squad of SS troops lined up along the edge of the road, just behind the treeline. At the time, I assumed they were waiting to ambush the Allied soldiers who were advancing toward Oberstdorf. Needless to say, my men and I could not let that happen, herr Oberst. After a brief exchange of gunfire, the SS troops fled to the south. That makes sense, because my men and I have been observing several well supplied groups of SS troops and other German military personnel, using carts and bicycles to establish camps in the remote mountain trails and passes. Our fear is that they intend to launch attacks from these positions, on Allied troops and any Germans who refuse to assist them."

As Gunther continued, he removed a map from his pocket and showed it to the American Army Colonel. "In addition to the Werwolf training camp in Langenwang, there is another Nazi training school located 14 miles north of Oberstdorf in Sonthofen."

While Gunther held the map in his left hand, he faced the American Army Colonel as he went on to say, "If our intelligence is correct, herr Oberst, you will find some of these troublemakers in both of these locations." Then, after pausing to accept an American cigarette and a light from Hans, Gunther added, "Once my men and I manage to secure our town, I am not sure how long we can hold out without help from the Allies."

After thanking the Oberstdorf Police Chief for the detailed briefing, Jim turned to Hans and said, "Hans, issue Chief Jager and his men all of the captured weapons and ammunition that we took with us, including the Schmeisser that you're carrying. I'll have Sergeant Coppola issue you the extra Thompson that we brought along."

While Hans responded and said, "Thank you, Jim," he handed his father-in-law the 9mm MP40 submachine gun and the leather pouch containing three spare 30 round magazines.

As soon Al Parker said, "I'll give you a hand, Hans," Al and Hans walked back to the M3 half track to retrieve the other captured weapons and ammunition.

As soon as they did so, Jim faced Gunther Jager again and said, "Hans and Captain Parker can give any of your men who might not be familiar with these weapons a quick lesson in how to put them to good use."

After nodding his head in a respectful fashion, Gunther responded and said, "Thank you, herr Oberst."

Jim then turned to Lieutenant Kelly and said, "Dan, I need you to get on the radio and let SHAFE know that we have confirmation that SS troops and other well supplied enemy personnel are operating in and around Oberstdorf, as well as in the nearby alpine passes. We also need to let General Tremble know, that we received a second report from the police chief in Obestdorf, about the presence of a Werwolf training camp in Langenwang and a Nazi training School in Sonthofen, Germany. Last but not least, advise General Tremble that the Police Chief and the civilian militia in Oberstdorf are assisting us in our efforts, to combat Nazi resistance in this section of Bavaria. Members of this civilian defense force are armed and can be identified by the armbands that they wear, that display the colors of the Bavarian Flag."

"I'm on it, Sir," responded the CIC Agent who were also serving as the communications officer for Lt. Colonel Beauregard's composite unit.

Jim then turned to Captain Garnier and said, "Charles, can you handle getting the same message to Colonel Reynald?"

After working with the Americans on the Mollet case, the former Paris policeman, who was now serving as a French Army Intelligence Officer, was very impressed with the level of courage and professionalism that was displayed by the U.S. Army Agents and MPs, who were serving under the command of Lt. Colonel James Beauregard. In addition to the fact that he appreciated being invited to attend Gunther Jager's briefing session, Captain Garnier was also grateful for having the needs of the French Army considered, especially since French troops were heading in the direction of Sonthofen and had the right to know what they might be facing in the way of enemy opposition. As a result, Captain Garnier was only to happy to relay the recently obtained intelligence information to Colonel Reynald.

Immediately after Captain Garnier enthusiastically remarked, "Oui, mon Colonel," and he walked over to the Jeep where their radio was located, Jim faced Chief Jager and said, "Chief, you can ride with me and Captain Parker in the number two jeep, while your men ride with your grandson in the back of our half track. Hans will lead the way with Sergeants Angelone and Coppola in the number one Jeep."

While Al Parker and Hans issued the captured weapons to the four town militiamen, Jim turned to his right and called out to MP Lieutenant Miller. "OK, Carl, we're getting this show back on the road."

As the men proving security returned to their vehicles and Sergeant Angelone noticed that the German civilians were more heavily armed than before, he turned to Sergeant Coppola and whispered, "What a war, Sal. Now were giving guns to the Germans."

"Only to the good ones, Ange," remarked Sergeant Coppola, as he patted his Army buddy on the back, while they returned to the lead Jeep in the convoy.

Once he finished making his observations, SS Sergeant Mueller was twice as convinced that their intelligence information about a growing anti Nazi resistance movement in Oberstdorf was correct. As soon as the German policeman and the four armed German civilians from Oberstdorf drove away with the Allied patrol, SS Sergeant Mueller decided to return to Oberstdorf, to get a closer look at what the Allies and these disloyal Germans planned to do next.

The moment Anna Sigmann saw Hans and Peter walk into her father's home, tears of joy streamed down her face, as she ran to embrace her husband and her only surviving son.

While being embraced by her husband, Anna kissed Hans several times in between repeating the words, "My prayers have been answered. You are both alive." Anna then turned to her son Peter and became even more emotional, when she placed her hands on both sides of his face and said. "My Peter…. I see you're limping. Are you hurt bad?"

"I'll be all right, mother. The Americans saved my life, when they got me and father out of a prison camp near Remagen. When my wound became infected, a French Army Surgeon also took care of me."

At that point in their reunion, Jim Beauregard and Al Parker were invited into Gunther Jager's home. Once Hans introduced Lt. Colonel James Beauregard and Captain Al Parker to his wife, he told Anna how he assisted the American military law enforcement authorities capture a fugitive, wanted for killing a New York City policeman, during the Ardennes Offensive. When Hans continued, he explained to his wife, how Colonel Beauregard and Captain Parker rescued him and Peter from a prisoner of war camp and made it possible for them to be discharged, appointed to serve as civilian German policemen and brought back to Oberstdorf.

No wife or mother in Germany was more grateful to her American guests than Anna Sigmann. While speaking in a very respectful tone of voice, Anna spoke almost perfect English when she thanked Jim and Al for what they did.

After Jim and Al thanked Anna for her kind words, she offered the two Americans and their men the hospitality of their home. As soon as she did so, Jim turned to Gunther Jager and asked if he would allow his men to bring in some of the extra supplies that they brought along, to share with Hans and his family. Because Jim knew that the Germans were proud people, he quickly added, "Please understand, Sir, that if it wasn't for Hans, my men and I would have been taken prisoner and a dangerous criminal who joined the U.S. Army to evade arrest, might have been able to escape justice. As a fellow policeman, I ask you to allow us to share what we have in the way of supplies, with you and your family and anyone else in your town, who is helping us to end this horrible war."

After hearing what the American Army Colonel had to say, Gunther Jager extended his hand in friendship and said, "You and your men are most welcome in my home and in the Town of Oberstdorf. With your permission, herr Oberst, Hans and I will help your men with the supplies that you wish to share with us. I will also find suitable accommodations for you, your men and your vehicles. Gunther then removed a list from his uniform coat pocket and said, "These are the Nazis who are being rounded up as we speak. Once we unload the supplies, you and your men can assist me and my men arrest anyone who is left on the list. In the process, we can make sure that the American POWs are well cared for, after we take their guards into custody."

By the time French tanks rolled into Sonthofen, SS Major Kessler and his 100 man unit were preparing to conduct ambushes, assassinations and other offensive actions in and around Oberstdorf. SS Major Kessler and his men were able to accomplish as much as they did, in such a relatively short period of time, due to the cooperation of a 15 year old Werwolf fighter by the name of Walter Vogel.

As a fully indoctrinated member of the Hitler Youth, Walter Vogel proved to be a valuable member of Major Kessler's team, because he was born and raised in Langenwang and was very familiar with the various trails, open valleys and Alpine passes in and around Oberstdorf. Having this local knowledge, enabled Walter Vogel to assist SS Major Kessler and his men, to establish a primary base camp near Spielmannsau and two smaller clandestine camps near Gottenreid and Gruben. In the process, Vogel escorted different size groups of German troops from Sonthofen to Langenwang, before taking them past Oberstdorf and on to Gruben, Gottenried and their final destination near Speilmannsau. Each time Walter Vogel delivered a contingent of German troops to their clandestine base near Speilmannsau, additional critical supplies were transported with them, to extend their ability to operate in the field, against Allied troops and disloyal Germans.

SS Major Kessler's plan, to establish a Nazi resistance movement in and around Oberstdorf, was complete, when he had critical supplies stored inside the vacant resort known as Kemptner Hutte. Once this was accomplished, SS Major Kessler had access to a more remote alpine location, that he and his SS troops could use in an emergency, to evade detection and mount future attacks.

After instructing Lieutenant Emich to continue training their contingent of non SS troops, Major Kessler, SS Captain Schneider and their Werwolf Scout Walter Vogel prepared to leave for their camp near Gruben. Just before they left, SS Major Kessler instructed his two remaining squads of SS troops, to reposition themselves to their camp near Gottenfried and report to the camp near Gruben at sunrise.

At 1800 hours on the night of April 30, 1945, Walter Vogel led SS Major Kessler and SS Captain Schneider to their clandestine camp near Gruben. When they arrived, they found two of SS Sergeant Mueller's men posted as sentries near the perimeter of their camp. After greeting his men, SS Major Kessler turned to Walter Vogel and said, "Get something warm to drink, while the Captain and I speak to Sergeant Mueller."

As soon as the respectful young man responded like a seasoned soldier and said, "Yes, Sir," SS Sergeant Muller extended his right hand toward the well camouflaged command tent and said, "After you, Sir."

Once inside, the two SS Officers and the senior NCO sat on ammo crates to discuss the results of the recent reconnaissance mission. After giving SS Major Kessler and SS Captain Schneider a brief run down of what he and his men observed during their extended scouting mission, SS Sergeant Mueller explained what occurred, when he and his men witnessed an Allied air drop on the outskirts of Oberstdorf. "Since we were in a perfect position to observe the road that led into Oberstdorf, I thought it made sense to remain in the area, to see if any Allied units were receiving supplies before moving into town. If this Allied unit was small enough for me and my eight men to handle, I planned to ambush the enemy personnel, before returning to our camp near Gruben. Unfortunately, before the Allied unit arrived at the ambush site, we were fired upon and were forced to engage a German police official and four armed German civilians. Rather than get caught in a cross fire, between these disloyal Germans and the approaching Allied unit, I provided covering fire, while my men made their way out of the immediate area." Then, after pausing briefly, the SS Sergeant added, "I couldn't believe it, Sir. They saw us as clear as day and had to know who we were, yet they fired on us as if we were the enemy. I also need to report, Sir, that these disloyal Germans were wearing armbands that displayed the colors of the Bavarian Flag."[25]

After being told to continue, SS Sergeant Mueller went on to say, "Once our efforts to ambush an Allied vehicle patrol was thwarted, by the actions of these disloyal Germans, I had my men return to this location, while I returned to the road to make additional observations. As soon I observed these disloyal Germans interacting with the Allied patrol on a friendly basis, I made my way back to Oberstdorf. While operating under the cover of darkness, I observed several dozen disloyal armed Germans civilians, working with the same policeman and a small number of Allied troops, as they arrested SS men, a few Wehrmach troops and even some of their own people. Additional armed civilians wearing the Bavarian colored armbands were also posted to strengthen the town's defenses."

Once large numbers of German units began capitulating, the job of fighting on was left to diehard Nazis like Gunther Kessler and his men. As the Allies advanced deeper into German held territory, they encountered local residents who provided different levels of support for National Socialism and the Nazi resistance movement, as well as citizens who had no desire to prolong the war. Included in this group, were Germans and Austrians who opposed the Nazis and cooperated with the Allies in various ways.[26]

German soldiers and civilians alike also had their preferences when it came time to surrender to Allied units. While no German willingly wanted anything to do with the Russians, their first choice was to surrender to the Americans and or the British, then the French. Even among the German armed forces, there were stark differences in the way in which some units continued to fight on, while others agreed to surrender. In some instances, splinter groups of German troops made every effort to continue to resist the Allied invaders, even when the units they belonged to capitulated, or were decimated.[27]

Between the intelligence information that was developed by SS Captain Schneider and his local Werwolf contacts and the observations that were made by SS Sergeant Muller, the Oberstdorf police chief and his civilian militiamen were accurately described as a group of anti Nazi Bavarian Catholics, who posed a real threat to their plan, to continue hostilities in this section of Germany.[28] As a result, SS Major Kessler was convinced, that something had to be done to nip this problem in the bud, before this anti Nazi sentiment in Oberstdorf spread to other areas.

After lighting a cigarette, SS Major Kessler faced Captain Schneider and said, "We've come too far and have accomplished too much, to have a few dozen traitors prevent us from achieving our objective." SS Major Kessler then asked Captain Schneider to have Walter Vogel brought into the command tent.

As soon as Vogel arrived by his side, SS Major Kessler wasted no time in saying, "Captain Schneider tells me that you have no love for some of the people from Oberstdorf, especially their police chief and some of his friends.

"That's correct, herr Major," responded the Werwolf fighter, who was serving as a scout for Kessler's SS led resistance unit.

When SS Major Kessler asked Walter Vogel to explain why he suspected the Oberstdorf police chief and some of his fellow citizens of being disloyal, the young Werwolf Scout remarked, "While growing up in Langenwang you hear things about people, herr Major. As soon as the Werwolf movement was created, we knew who we could trust and who we had to avoid. I am not the only loyal German who heard reports, that there was a resistance movement in Oberstdorf, that opposed the aims of National Socialism."

As Walter Vogel continued, he turned toward Captain Schneider and said, "As I told Captain Schneider, the some of the police chief's closest friends are suspected of being the founders of the local resistance unit. Based on what I heard, the police chief discounted the accusation as rumors, that were spread by nervous Germans, who were looking for traitors under every rock. The matter was dropped, because the police chief in Oberstdorf is a highly decorated former German soldier who served in the last war. In reality, the police chief used his standing in the community to protect his disloyal friends. That makes him just as guilty, as those who started this resistance movement, does it not, herr Major,"

After nodding his head ever so slightly in agreement, Major Kessler remarked, "Yes it does."

As soon as Major Kessler asked the young man to tell him more about this police chief, Walter Vogel answered immediately and said, "His name is Gunther Jager, herr Major. My father repaired two of the police chief's cars before he went to serve in the Luftwaffe. I even know where Gunther Jager lives, herr Major. I know this, because on two occasions I went with my father and one of his mechanics, when they delivered repaired vehicles to the police chief's home."

While SS Captain Schneider and SS Sergeant Muller stood by, SS Major Kessler continued questioning the young man. "Would this police chief have any way of knowing that you are serving the Fatherland as a Werewolf commando?"

"No, Sir," responded the young teenager.

"What makes you so confident?" asked Kessler.

After looking up at SS Captain Schneider, the young teenager faced SS Major Kessler as he answered the question in a very confident tone of voice. "Because Captain Schneider trained me well, Sir. My own mother doesn't even know that I joined the Werwolves. As far as she knows, I left home to get trained to become a fireman in Munich."

"What about your father? Did you tell him?" asked the Major.

"My father was killed a few weeks ago, when the Allies attacked the air base where he was stationed. He was loading ammunition into one of our fighters when an American P51 strafed the airfield. His commanding officer wrote my mother to let her know, that my father refused to leave his post, so the fighter he was arming could be launched to repel the attack. He was awarded the Iron Cross Second Class for heroism."

After nodding his head to show his approval, SS Major Kessler remarked, "Captain Schneider was right when he told me that you were the best Werwolf fighter in your unit. While the other Werwolves that you trained with serve elsewhere in Germany, it is a great honor to have you assigned to our command. Your father would also be proud of you, for the way that you are serving the Fatherland."

While sounding a bit less official, SS Major Kessler looked up at SS Sergeant Mueller and said, "Sergeant, see to it that our number one scout and the rest of your men are fully equipped and ready to leave at 0400 hours to execute our first mission in Oberstdorf. Captain Schneider will give you and your men a full briefing before you get some sleep."

Immediately after the veteran non commissioned officer acknowledged the order, he turned to Walter Vogel and said, "Follow me, son."

While SS Sergeant Mueller and their new recruit left the command tent, SS Major Kessler motioned Captain Schneider to join him at the makeshift table, as he continued with his briefing. "By 0530 hours I want you, Sergeant Mueller and the men in his squad, along with our young Werwolf volunteer, in position to carry out our first mission against disloyal Germans. Your mission will commence when you escort Corporal Krebs and our new recruit to a location where they can enter Oberstdorf undetected. While you and your men remain on the outskirts of town, Corporal Krebs and his young assistant will go to the home of the police chief and pay this traitor an early morning visit. If for some reason the police chief is not at home when they arrive, they are to make a reasonable effort to locate him and eliminate him. If they are unable to complete their mission, they are to rendezvous with you and your men. After you return to this camp, we'll try again tomorrow."

After pausing to refer to his map of the area, SS Major Kessler went on to say, "In order to insure that they will be able to complete their mission, Corporal Krebs and our Werwolf commando will take two bicycles with them, that they can use to get in and out of Oberstdorf as quickly as possible."

While SS Major Kessler removed the flask from his coat pocket, he continued as he unscrewed the top and handed the metal container to his second in command. "Once our two other squads join us in the morning, we will plan our next attack. Having all three squads at our immediate disposal, will also give us more than enough firepower, to deal with this disloyal group of Bavarian Catholics from Oberstdorf. We will also have more than enough men on hand, to give this lead element of Allied troops a beating that they will never forget."

Once Captain Schneider took a sip of schnapps and he handed the flask back to his commanding officer, SS Major Kessler took a quick sip and secured the top as he continued and said, "While we launch attacks against targets of opportunity in Oberstdorf, Lieutenant Emich will continue to train the rest of the men to operate in the higher alpine elevations. If anyone can turn these regular soldiers into mountain troops, it's a Panzer Grenadier Officer who grew up in the Austrian Alps."

While Major Kessler slipped the flask back into his coat pocket, Captain Schneider stood up and said, "I'll brief the men, Sir."

SS Major Kessler never sounded more serious when he looked up and remarked, "Assassinating this police chief will send a message to the other traitors, that we will not tolerate disloyalty among the German people."

"You're right about that, Sir," responded Captain Schneider, who quickly added, "We will never succeed in our mission, if we have to fight the Allies and some of our own people."

As Major Kessler continued to look up at his second in command, he sounded more like a concerned father than a strict disciplinarian when he added, "Remember, Gerhardt. Make sure the men dress appropriately in the early hours of the morning. Corporal Krebs should also wear one of the civilian coats that we brought with us over his uniform. Doing so will enable him to move more freely in and around Oberstdorf."

Once again SS Captain Gerhardt Schneider acknowledged his orders, only this time he presented his commanding officer with a casual salute, as he stood up and said, "Yes, Sir."

The moment his second in command went to leave the command tent, SS Major Kessler called out, "One more thing, Gerhardt. I want you to issue our Werwolf Scout a pistol and make sure he knows how to use it. Also, tell Mr. Vogel that I am assigning him with the responsibility to eliminate the police chief in Oberstdorf. Corporal Krebs will accompany him to provide security."

While Jim Beauregard sat in his room at the Hotel Mohren and sipped a class of local schnapps, Captain Gardnier knocked on the open door and said, "I have a message from Colonel Reynald, Sir."

"Come in Charles and join me for a night cap before we hit the sack," responded Jim as he poured some schnapps into another metal canteen cup. By the time Jim finished pouring a healthy shot of schnapps into the cup, the French Intelligence Officer approached the table where the Colonel was sitting.

"I'll trade you," said Jim, as he handed the canteen cup to the French Captain while he took possession of the message. After reading the message Jim looked up and said, "Pass the word to the men, that Colonel Reynald will be arriving tomorrow afternoon, with a column of French soldiers to officially occupy Oberstdorf and assist us as needed."

After raising his own canteen cup and saying, "Cheers," Jim took a sip of schnapps before he he continued and said, "That gives us plenty of time to return from our morning patrol and get cleaned up before he arrives."

As soon as he downed the rest of his drink, Captain Garnier responded while he placed the empty cup on the table. "It should be an interesting day, Sir."

"At the very least, we'll have a chance to walk off our breakfast," remarked Jim.

After saluting the American Army Colonel, the French Intelligence Officer went to leave when Jim spoke up again and said, "Do me a favor, Charles and tell the men to dress appropriately before we go out on patrol in the morning. It could get a little nippy once we make our way into the higher elevations."

As Captain Garnier stood by the open door to the American Colonel's quarters, he nodded his head once before he remarked, "I will relay your instructions to the men. Goodnight, Sir."

"Goodnight, Charles," responded Jim before he took one last sip of schnapps.

Once the French Army Captain closed the door as he left the room, Jim stood up and removed his pistol belt while he walked over to the bed. After placing his pistol belt on the floor next to his bed, Jim removed the .32 caliber Model 1903 Colt from the holster that he carried in his right side pant's pocket and placed the pistol under the pillow. Jim then shut the light, got in bed and pulled the woolen Army blanket over his bone tired body. In less than a minute Jim was sound asleep.

After getting out of a warm bed at 0445 hours in the morning, Jim slipped his .32 caliber Colt pistol in his pant's pocket, before he put his Army Officer's Trench Coat over his M65 Field Jacket. On his way to the bathroom, Jim grabbed his shaving kit that contained various toiletries.

By the time Jim was ready to start a new day, he needed a cup of hot coffee, before he went with Al and Hans, to check on the men from the town defense force, who were posted in and around Oberstdorf. After leaving the bathroom, Jim made his way into the kitchen of the hotel, that was being used to house him and his men, as well as a large number of children who were evacuated from Munich. Prior to being used to house refugees, the famous Hotel Mohron was used as a hospital and as a popular destination for Nazi officials. German military personnel also stayed at the hotel that was centrally located at Martplatz 6 in Oberstdorf.[29]

When Jim entered the kitchen, he found Al and Hans sitting at a table sipping hot coffee while dressed for a combat patrol. As Jim walked over to where they were sitting, Al sounded as if he was in a chipper mood when he spoke up and said, "You're just in time to join us, Jim. We just made a fresh pot of coffee. We can also thank a local farmer, who's friends with Gunther Jager, for providing us with some fresh milk."

"Coffee with milk and GI sugar. It doesn't get any better than that," remarked Jim as he sat at the table next to Hans. After checking his watch, Jim accepted a cup of coffee from Al and took a sip, before he looked at Hans and said, "This is just a suggestion, but maybe we should have your father-in- law remain behind with Captain Garnier to secure the town until the French Army arrives."

"Gunther has already agreed to do so," responded Hans.

When Hans removed a pack of American cigarettes from his pant's pocket, Jim continued and said, "Maybe I have no right to say this, but you just got home, Hans. You can sit this one out and no one in this town can criticize you for doing so."

After taking a drag on his cigarette, Hans responded in a friendly but matter of fact tone of voice. "I can't do that, Jim. You see, late last night Gunther was asked to become the Burgermeister, as you in America call the mayor. He agreed on the condition that I be made the police chief and my son Peter was appointed to serve as my assistant. That means that my son Peter and I cannot sit this one out as you say."

Under the circumstances, Jim knew that Hans was right. Rather than belabor the point, Jim decided to finish their discussion about the upcoming morning patrol. "If your father-in-law is staying behind, we can have Mr. Berger lead our patrol. Based on his knowledge of the terrain, we'd be crazy not to use him as our lead scout."

"I agree," said Hans, who went on to say, "I made arrangements for Mr. Berger to meet us here once we finish checking on the town's defenses. While we inspect the men on sentry duty here in town, my son Peter will be checking the guard posts in the more outlying areas of Oberstdorf."

Jim had gotten to know Hans Sigmann well enough by now to ask a personal question. "I know it's none of my business, but I'm curious what your wife had to say about all this? Like I said, you and Peter just got home."

Once again Hans responded without hesitation. "Anna knows that there can be no peace in Germany, until this war is over and the world is rid of the Nazis. If that means that her father and I, along with our son Peter must continue to serve in some capacity, then so be it," responded Hans.

"OK, Chief. It's your town," said Jim, who quickly added, "My men and I will back you up all the way."

After taking another drag on his cigarette, Hans confided in Jim and Al when he said, "I want you and Al to know, that while I would prefer to see the Americans or the British occupy this town, I anticipate no problems, if the French troops who remain in Oberstdorf, are commanded by officers like Colonel Reynald and Captain Garnier. Unfortunately, based on what I know, they will be moving on to Berlin and another French unit will administering occupied territory in Bavaria.

"Better the French than the Russians," remarked Jim.

"That is true," responded Hans, who quickly added, "But there is plenty of bad blood as they say, between our two countries and for good cause I might add."

"As my old man used to say, "Time heals all wounds," remarked Jim.

"Your father is a wise man," said Hans.

"Just a cop like us, only he was killed in the line of duty," responded Jim.

"Forgive me, Jim. I didn't know," said Hans.

"It happens, Hans" responded Jim, who did his best to change the subject by saying, "What's your plan for today?"

While Hans unfolded a map of the area, Jim and Al continued drinking hot coffee, as Hans placed the map on the table and began his briefing. "According to my father-in-law and his men, we need to focus our attention on the Iller Valley." As Hans continued, he ran his finger from the location on the map that was designated the Iller Valley through the nearby Alpine passes. "This is were my Gunther and some of the other members of the town militia, including Koenraad Berger and Mr. Feedler, the local Oberforstmeister, observed SS troops and mixed formations of Wehrmacht soldiers, Luftwaffe personnel and even some Kriegsmarine sailors, transporting crated supplies into the mountains."

As Al Parker refilled their canteen cups with more coffee, Jim remarked, "According to your father-in-law, if anyone knows what's going on in the mountains around Oberstdorf, it's Mr. Berger and Mr. Freedler."

"That's correct, Jim," remarked Hans, who quickly added, "Like I told you last night. Koenraad Berger has been a guide in the Alpine passes in the Allgau ever since he returned from the last war, after being wounded with Gunther in France. In addition to the fact that he is in better shape than any of us, he hates the Nazis for what they have done to Germany. The same is true for Oberforstmeister Johan Feedler. He also served with Gunther and Koenraad Berger in the trenches and has been working in the German Forest Service ever since he returned."

After hearing what Hans had to say, Jim paused to light his pipe, before he pointed to a position on the map and said, "This looks like a good spot for us to park our vehicles and begin our patrol on foot."

Without hesitation Hans responded and said, "I agree."

After checking his watch, Al remarked, "By the time we get back, the men should be up and getting ready to take an early morning walk in the countryside."

"We can brief 'em when we join 'em for breakfast," remarked Jim.

As Al grabbed his helmet and M3 Grease Gun off the table, he seemed to be in very good spirits when he agreed with Jim. "A briefing over chow sounds good to me, 'cause I'd hate to see us have to go looking for trouble without some food in our stomach."

As soon as Jim and Hans exchanged grins, Jim remarked, "I'll meet you two out front as soon as I grab my gear."

Using smaller clandestine camps near Gottenreid and Gruben enabled Major Kessler and his men, to position troops closer to Oberstdorf, before executing an operation in the area. The alternative was to make a more demanding trip on foot down mule trails and through wilderness areas, that would take a lot more time to complete, especially when the Major and his men traveled before sunrise and after sunset. Using their smaller camp near Gruben, also enabled the SS men and the regular troops under Major Kessler's command, to have a well equipped safe haven to return to, that was in relative close proximity to Oberstdorf.

If for any reason Captain Schneider and his men were pursued, they were instructed not to return to the camp near Gottenried, or the larger base camp near Spielmannsau, which was about nine kilometers from Oberstdorf. Having access to the seasonal resort known as Kemptner Hutte, also provided Kessler and his SS troops, with a well provisioned fallback position, that was situated about eight kilometers above Spielmannssau, in rugged mountainous terrain.

Even though it took more time to travel at night, Captain Schneider and his men reached the outskirts of Oberstdorf, in time to meet the 0530 insertion into their area of operation. After avoiding two civilian sentries who were huddled around a warm fire, Captain Schneider led his men to a more suitable vantage point, for Corporal Krebs and Walter Vogel to enter the town without being observed.

While Sergeant Mueller assigned four men to handle security, Captain Schneider rubbed his gloved hands together as he faced Corporal Krebs and said, "Your job is to get Mr. Vogel to the police chief's home and back here once your mission is completed. If this police chief is not home, the Major wants you to make a reasonable effort to find him and eliminate him, but only if you can complete your mission without getting yourselves killed in the process. We can't afford to lose good men at this stage of the war, so I will leave it up to you to decide, whether you should try and locate this police chief, or rendezvous with me and the other men, so we can try again tomorrow morning."

Then, after pausing, SS Captain Schneider added, "No matter what happens, you must be back here by 0700 hours, or you will have to make your way to Gruben on your own. Just remember, if you have to return without escort, you must make sure that you are not followed."

After acknowledging the order, Corporal Krebs put on a long gray civilian coat, before he turned to the young Werwolf commando and said, "Lead the way, Walter."

As soon as Corporal Krebs and Walter Vogel got on their bicycles, the young Werwolf commando turned assassin led the way toward Oberstdorf, on a cold Tuesday morning. The date was May 1, 1945.

After waking her father up, Anna Sigmann enjoyed a sinfully delicious cup of hot American coffee while she started to prepare breakfast. At this point in the war, the food that the Americans shared with her family were considered luxuries. So many had lost so much during the war, that Anna felt both blessed and a bit guilty, for having access to the kind of food that was issued to the American Army.

When her father entered the kitchen and he placed his holstered

Walther PP pistol on the counter, Anna remarked, "I was hoping that now that you are retired from police work, so you can serve as the Burgermeister, that you would not need to carry a pistol any longer."

While Gunther sat at the table and his daughter filled his cup with American coffee, he looked up and said, "I don't mean to worry you, Anna, but until we deal with these Nazi fanatics who are determined to prolong this war, I will continue to carry my gun. In fact, I left a loaded pistol for you in my desk drawer. Hans and I want you to be able to protect yourself while we're away, especially until the French arrive."

"But Papa, I agreed to help care for the children who were relocated from Munich to Oberstdorf," responded Anna.

After taking a sip of coffee, Gunther never sounded more serious when he said, "Hans and I cannot worry about you, while we do what needs to be done to secure this town."

Gunther Jager should have known better than to argue with his daughter. While Anna removed the skillet from the stove, she let her feelings be known while she served her father a hot breakfast of grilled slices of U.S. Army SPAM and diced potatoes with a slice of crusty black bread. "I'm sorry, Papa, but I am going to the Hotel Mohron to help care for the children and nothing that you and Hans say will stop me from doing so."

After hearing what his only daughter had to say, Gunther looked across the table and said, "You remind me of your mother. I could never say no to her and I can never say no to you. Just do me one favor and let me send someone to pick you up and take you to the hotel. The French Army Captain will be staying with me, while Hans and the Americans go on a patrol of the area. He has a Jeep and plenty of fuel, so it will be no problem for us to come by and pick you up, while we prepare to receive the French Army. In the meantime, I need you to hang white sheets from the upstairs windows, to let the French soldiers know that we pose no threat to the occupation of our town."

Just as Anna remarked, "OK, Papa, I will do as you wish," there was a knock on the front door.

"That must be my ride into town," said Gunther as he stood up at the head of the kitchen table.

"I thought Hans was picking you up?" responded Anna, as she remained seated next to were her father was sitting.

"He's probably busy and had to send someone else," said her father as he went to answer the door.

After putting on his pistol belt, Jim slipped his shoulder bag over his trench coat, before he picked up his steel helmet and his M1 Carbine and left his room. Their plan was to go on a quick inspection tour of Oberstdorf, before they had breakfast with their men and left to conduct a patrol of the outlying area, to include some of the nearby alpine trails.

As soon as Jim left the hotel, he was surprised to see Hans and Al closing the engine hood of a captured German Kublewagen. After seeing that the captured vehicle had its SS markings painted over and the initials U.S. painted in large black letters on the front doors, Jim cracked a smile then said, "I see Al worked his magic and got this Kublewagen running."

"Thanks to Al, this Kublewagen runs just as good now as it did when it left the factory," responded Hans, as he walked around to the right side of the vehicle and opened the passenger side door.

"It's time to check posts, Jim," remarked Al, as he opened the driver's side door, while Hans sat in the front passenger seat.

While Jim opened the left rear passenger side door and took his seat, Al continued and said, "Lord help anyone we catch sleeping on duty, because Hans is gonna do more than write his ass sorry up."

As Jim closed the back door, he wasted no time in responding to Al's last remark. "Sleeping on duty would be a big mistake, as long as we have bad guys running around the countryside."

While Al started the Kubelwagen and drove away from the hotel, Hans checked his watch and said, "I promised Gunther that we would pick him up when we inspected the town's defenses."

"Once a cop, always a cop," responded Al.

"That's correct," said Hans, who quickly added, "Gunther has only been the mayor for a few hours and he already misses being the chief of police."

"He's a good man, Hans. I can tell he cares about the people in this town," remarked Jim from his position in the back seat.

"He certainly does," responded Hans.

As soon as Jim noticed the two backpacks and the German K98 sniper rifle that was stored next to him in the rear of the vehicle, he leaned forward in his seat and said, "I see we're fully equipped back here for our early morning foot patrol."

"You know what Napoleon said, "An Army marches on it's stomach," responded Al.

After cracking a grin Jim added, "I hope you tossed a few Hershey Bars in these backpacks, 'cause you won't make it through the day without your ration of chocolate."

"I sure did," responded Al who quickly added, "I even packed away a few K rations, some extra ammo and plenty of coffee, so we can wash down our chow in style when we stop for lunch."

While Jim leaned forward and patted Al on the top of right shoulder, he looked at Hans and said, "We're in good company, Hans. Not only will you never go hungry as long as Al is around, but he's also one hell of a tough SOB to have on your side, if you ever get into a fight."

As Hans smiled at the antics of the two Americans, he knew that his meeting and helping Al Parker and Jim Beauregard was something that was meant to be. Even his wife Anna agreed, that something special happened, when her husband made it possible for the American Army CID Agents, to take a ruthless cop killing fugitive into custody during the Ardennes Offensive.

While Al continued to drive the Kubelwagen through town, Hans glanced back at Jim and remarked, "I can't tell you how grateful I am, to have you and Al and your men helping to protect this town, from SS Major Kessler and his band of Nazi fanatics. If they get their way, this war will go on long after what's left of Germany surrenders."

"Don't worry, Hans. Major Kessler's days are numbered. He just doesn't know it yet," responded Al Parker, as he down shifted the manual transmission when he negotiated a tight turn."

"The same is true for SS Captain Schneider and anyone else who sides with 'em," added Jim.

The moment Gunther opened the front door, the two men who were sent to kill him brandished 9mm P38 pistols, as they pushed their way into his home without saying a word. While the younger of the two men pointed a pistol at Gunther and called him a traitor, the older of the two who kept watch at the door remarked, "Let's go, kid. Do what we came here to do. The Captain is waiting."

Just as the young teenager cocked the hammer on the 9mm P38 that was issued to him for this mission, Gunther acted as calm as ever when he looked at the boy and said, "I know you. Your Kurt Vogel's son. You came to my home with your father to drop off one of my police vehicles." Then, after pausing for a split second, Gunther quickly added, "No, I'm wrong. You came on two occasions with your father......How is your father?"

"He died a heroes death while serving The Furher in the Luftwaffe," screamed the young man who quickly added, "While men like my father are fighting for our country, you and the other traitors in this town have sided with the enemy!"

From her position in the kitchen Anna knew that if she failed to act, her father would be killed by the armed gunmen who stormed into their home. Because she was the daughter of a policeman and the wife of a policeman, Anna was trained from an early age, how to safely handle the handguns that were carried by German law enforcement officers. With no other options at her disposal, Anna slowly removed the .32 ACP caliber Walther PP Pistol from her father's well worn leather holster and disengaged the safety, by moving the lever up into the firing position. Seeing Germany all but destroyed and losing her oldest son on The Russian Front, also hardened Anna and made her an even tougher woman for the two intruders to deal with.

The second Anna heard the older of the two young men call out, "If you can't shoot this traitor then I will," she stepped into the living room with her father's Walther PP Pistol in hand and opened fire.

The second a volley of .32 caliber bullets struck the young Werwolf assassin in the chest and the other armed intruder in his left leg, the shock of coming under fire, caused Walter Vogel to flinch and discharge a single shot, that hit Gunther in his left arm. As the dead Werwolf fighter fell to the floor, Gunther took cover behind a nearby chair, while SS Corporal Krebs fired two shots at Anna that missed the mark, as he opened the door and limped out of the house.

Gunther Jager proved that he was still a cop at heart, when he asked his daughter if she was OK, while he retrieved the 9mm pistol that was on the floor next to Walter Vogel's body and went after the escaping gunman. After hearing his daughter call out, "Be careful Papa!," Gunther glanced back for a second and yelled, "Stay down, Anna." Once outside, Gunther emptied the pistol at the escaping gunman, as he peddled his bicycle in the opposite direction.

The second Al Parker called out, "Shots fired!" Hans rolled the passenger side window down on the Kublewagen.

After turning his head sideways, Hans remarked, "It's coming from the same direction where we're going."

Hans then turned to face Al Parker, before he looked at Jim Beauregard and added, "I've got a bad feeling about this."

"Me too," responded Jim, as he cycled a round into the chamber of his M1 Carbine, before he leaned closer to the front seat and said, "You better step on it, Al."

"I got the peddle on the floor, Jim. She's giving me all she's got!" responded Al.

A split second later Hans made a hand motion and said, "Next right, Al!"

As soon as the fast moving Kublewagen reached the corner, Al called out, "Hang on!" Given the road conditions, Al did an amazing job of controlling the German Army version of an American Jeep, when the vehicle slid sideways around the turn, then straightened out and drove down the street where Gunther Jager's home was located.

While Hans pointed straight ahead, he called out, "There's Gunther."

Despite his age and the fact that he was wounded, Gunther Jager was trying his best to pursue the escaping gunman on foot. After hearing Hans calling his name, Gunther stopped running and held his wounded arm, while he stood on the side of the road. As soon as the Kublewagon came to a screeching halt, Hans jumped out of the vehicle with a Thompson submachine gun in hand, just as Anna opened the door to her father's house and called out, "Papa! Hans!"

While Jim and Al held their weapons at the ready and provided security, Gunther did his best to speak after pursuing the escaping gunman on foot. "Two gunmen forced their way into the house. The one they sent to kill me was Walter Vogel from Langenwang. Anna shot and killed Vogel with my pistol. She must have hit the other gunman in the leg as well, because he was limping when he left the house and escaped on a bicycle. He just turned left on the corner when you arrived."

As Hans looked toward the corner, he remarked, "I'll bet he's heading to one of the alpine passes, where you and some of your men have observed SS troops and other soldiers carrying supplies."

"I agree," remarked Gunther.

As soon as Anna ran up to her husband and her father, Hans hung the Thompson Submachine Gun over his shoulder, as he turned to his wife and asked if she was all right. Even though she was a very strong woman, it was obvious that Anna was upset about having to shoot and kill one of the intruders when she said, "I'm OK, Hans, but I had to kill the boy who was about to shoot my father."

While Hans hugged his wife, he did his best to reassure her that she was justified in her actions when he remarked, "The Nazis killed that boy when they put a gun in his hand, not you." Hans then turned to his father-in-law and said, "Let me reload that pistol for you, Papa."

When Gunther handed his son in law the empty pistol, Hans removed the empty magazine and slipped it into his coat pocket, before replacing it with the spare loaded magazine that he removed from the P38 holster that he carried on his belt. While Hans completed the reloading procedure and he handed the loaded 9mm pistol back to his father-in-law, he relayed instructions to Anna, "After you call Doctor Bremer for my father, call the Hotel Mohron and let the Americans and Captain Garnier know what happened. Tell them that we are going after the one who got away."

"Promise me you'll be careful," said Anna, before she gave her husband a quick kiss on the side of his face, then stepped back and put her right arm around her father.

"Please, Anna. Do as I say," responded Hans, as he returned to the Kublewagen with the two American CID Agents.

Just as Al Parker put the vehicle in gear and was about to drive away Anna called out, "Promise me, Hans."

"I promise," responded Hans who quickly added, "Now go inside," just as Al drove away.

After hearing the sound of gunshots being fired in town, Captain Garnier, Lieutenant Miller, Lieutenant Kelly and the other American troops at the hotel, scrambled to find out why all hell was breaking loose in Oberstdorf. Once Captain Garnier received a phone call from Anna Sigmann, he instructed the men to take their breakfast rations with them and settle for a quick cup of coffee, so they could get out into the field as soon as possible. The men were also instructed to take extra ammunition along as well.

While the men grabbed extra ammunition and checked their weapons, Captain Garnier showed his map to Lieutenants Miller and Kelly and said, "According to Anna Sigmann, her husband drove off in this direction with the Colonel and Captain Parker in the captured Kublewagen. She described the second gunman as being tall and thin, about 20 years of age with blonde hair. He was wearing a long gray coat and a gray cap. The second gunman is also believed to have been wounded in the leg and was limping when he ran out of the house. He fled the area on a bicycle."

As soon as Sergeant Sam Carubba walked over to the three officers and said, "We're ready, to go, Sir," a dozen shots were heard being fired off in the distance.

"That sounds like pistol fire and rifle fire," remarked Lieutenant Miller.

"It's coming from the south," added Koenraad Berger, the local alpine guide who was assigned by Gunther Jager and Hans to serve as a scout for the Allied troops.

"Lead the way, Mr. Berger," said Captain Garnier, as he picked up his M1

Carbine and took command of the Allied composite unit.

★ ★ ★

As soon as Al Parker brought the Kublewagen to a stop at the check-point, Peter Sigmann and two armed German civilians, who were guard duty on the outskirts of town, approached the vehicle. While Hans remained seated, he spoke quickly through the open passenger side window and explained to his son Peter what just happened at his grandfather's house.

Once Hans was finished giving his son and the other two men a quick rundown of what just occurred in town, Peter leaned over and explained what just occurred at the checkpoint. "As soon as I heard the gunfire in town, I left the other checkpoint that I was inspecting and raced over to this location on my bicycle. I came here to assist the two men on guard duty, because this position is the closest checkpoint to the location in town where the shots were were fired. Shortly after I arrived, a young man on a bicycle shot at us with a pistol, as he approached this checkpoint. As soon as we took cover, we returned fire as he raced by and headed south. I'm sure I hit him, father. Otto and Johan also fired two shots each and may have hit the gunman as well. I believe that's the case, because he slumped over again immediately after they opened fire."

The last thing that Hans wanted, was to see his youngest son Peter go in harms way again, after he managed to survive the war as a German Air Force Officer. Up until now, Oberstdorf was a quiet town, that had escaped the acts of violence that were prevalent elsewhere in Germany. Thanks to the fanatics who were determined to prolong the war, the good people of Oberstdorf were forced to take up arms and engage Nazi troublemak-ers, during what was hoped would be the last days of the crumbling Third Reich.

As proud as Hans was to see his son wearing a German police coat and cap, while he served under his command, he was equally concerned for his safety. Fortunately, his military training served him well and prepared Peter for the challenges of police work. After all, anyone who could survive a number of air combat actions as a fighter pilot, should be equally prepared to survive a ground combat action, while serving as a policeman.

Because they were involved in a time critical situation, Hans instruct-ed his son to assemble two dozen town militiamen and assist Colonel Beauregard's men in following their trail, while they went in pursuit of the escaping gunman and his associates. As soon as Hans finished relaying his instructions, he added, "If we're lucky, we'll find his body up ahead. If not, we'll try and get a message to you and the others to let you know where you can find us."

"Be careful, father," said Peter.

As Hans looked up at Peter, he smiled a bit, then said, "You too, son."

Hans then turned to his left and said, "After you, Captain."

"Here we go," remarked Al, as he put the Kublewagen in gear and drove off into the darkness.

After hearing a number of shots being fired at different times in the Town of Oberstdorf, Captain Schneider checked his watch, before he turned to SS Sergeant Mueller and said, "Tell the men to keep an eye out for Krebs and Vogel. The last four shots that we heard were fired from rifles. Since Krebs and Vogel were only armed with pistols, we have to assume that one, or both of them might still be alive and heading this way. Either way, we'll give them another three minutes, before we return to our camp near Gruben and report to the Major. Pass the word to the men."

As soon SS Sergeant Mueller acknowledged the order, SS Captain Schneider added, "I've got a bad feeling about this mission, Sergeant."

The second they spotted an abandoned bicycle on the side of the trail, the captured Kublewagen came to a stop. As Jim, Al and Hans got out of the vehicle with their weapons at the ready, Jim spoke in a low tone of voice when he addressed Al and Hans. "While you two look around for the one who got away, I'll watch your back."

As soon as Al and Hans grabbed the backpacks and the sniper rifle from the rear seat of the Kublewagen, they began to search the area for a trail that was worth following. When Al and Hans spotted drops of blood on the bicycle and on the ground leading away from the area, Al glanced back and whispered, "We found a blood trail, Jim."

While Jim continued to follow Al and Hans, he spoke just above a whisper and said, "Remember, this guy likes to shoot at people with a pistol, so let's be careful."

When Corporal Krebs stumbled into the security perimeter, that was established by SS Captain Schneider and the men in SS Sergeant Mueller's squad, SS Privates Grueber and Schultz held their fire and grabbed the badly wounded Corporal as he collapsed on the ground. While SS Private Schultz began to apply basic first aid to the Corporal's more serious gunshot wounds, SS Private Grueber ran back to where the main body of the squad was positioned and signaled Captain Schneider and Sergeant Mueller to come forward.

By the time SS Captain Schneider and SS Sergeant Mueller arrived by the side of the mortally wounded Corporal, SS Private Schultz was closing the young man's eye lids, as Krebs passed away. After making eye contact with his squad leader and his Captain, SS Private Schultz reported that Walter Vogel was shot and killed by a woman in the police chief's house and that Gunther Jager was wounded but is still alive.

Without wasting any time, SS Captain Schneider turned to SS Sergeant Mueller and said, "Tell the men we're moving out." The Captain then turned to the two Privates and said, "As long as we're not being pursued, we'll take the Corporal with us and find a place to lay him to rest, when we get to our base near Gruben."

"Yes Sir," responded SS Private Grueber as the largest man in SS Sergeant Mueller's squad picked up the Corporal's body and carried him over his shoulder. Before moving out, SS Captain Schneider turned to SS Private Schultz and instructed him to bring up the rear.

As soon as Al Parker held out his right arm, he spoke just above a whisper when he grabbed Hans by the left arm and said, "I thought I just saw some movement up ahead."

"Let's fan out and take it slow," responded Jim.

After spreading out a bit in a single file formation, the light from the early morning sky, enabled Jim, Al and Hans to see a squad of German troops heading south across open terrain.

"That must be the wounded shooter's friends," whispered Al.

As Jim walked closer to Al and Hans, he also spoke in a low tone of voice when he said, "Since it doesn't pay to engage them at this distance, let's follow them for as long as we can to see where they go."

"Good idea," whispered Al.

The next to speak was Hans. "We should be able to follow them as long as we keep them in sight from a distance."

Once again, Jim took command and faced Hans, as he whispered, "Since you know this terrain like the back of your hand, you should be the one to take point, but don't get too far ahead of us, OK?" "Yes, Jim," responded Hans.

As soon as Al Parker whispered, "They're almost out'a sight."

"OK, Hans. Lead the way," said Jim.

After leaving the French tank crew behind to help a contingent of armed civilians protect the town, Captain Garnier and the rest of the men headed in the direction of the escaping gunman. On the way out of town they met Peter Sigmann. After explaining what happened and telling the Allied troops, that he was on his way to get some additional help, Captain Garnier thanked the German policeman for the report, before he signaled CID Agent Sam Carubba to proceed.

As soon as the abandoned Kublewagen, that was parked near an abandoned bicycle was located, Captain Garnier turned to Sergeant Carubba

as they got out of their Jeep and said, "Take Mr. Berger and see if you can pick up their trail. Sergeant's Coppola and Angelone will accompany you, to provide additional security while you look around. The rest of us will wait here."

Once Sam Carubba acknowledged the order, he turned to Mr. Berger and said, "Let's see what we can find out, Mr. Berger."

The next to speak was Sergeant Coppola, who turned to his partner and said, "Come on, Ange."

It took less than thirty seconds of searching the area around the abandoned bike, for Sergeant Carubba to report that they found a blood trail. As Mr. Berger knelt down by the abandoned bicycle, he looked up at his American Allies, who were standing nearby and said, "The one who escaped is definitely wounded. It also appears that men wearing U.S. Army boots, are on the same trail that is being used by the wounded gunman."

"That must be Colonel Beauregard, Captain Parker and Hans," remarked the French Captain.

After standing up, Mr. Berger pointed toward Gruben and added, "This is just a suggestion, Captain, but if Hans and the two American Officers are following the wounded man on foot, we should probably do the same."

As Captain Garnier addressed the American soldiers from the composite unit, he spoke in a low tone of voice when he said, "I agree with Mr. Berger. Advancing any further with our vehicles could alert the German troops who are known to operate in the area. As bad as that could be for us, it could be twice as bad for the Colonel, Captain Parker and Chief Sigmann."

When he continued, Captain Garnier wasted no time in instructing Sergeant's Carubba, Coppola and Angelone to take point and provide security for Mr. Berger as he led the way.

As soon as the three sergeants acknowledged the order, Sergeant Carubba turned to their guide and said, "We're ready when you are, Mr. Berger."

While Mr. Berger and his security team continued following the trail, Captain Garnier turned to MP Lieutenant Miller and said, "While Lieutenant Kelly and I follow the men on point, I would like you and Sergeant Mulligan to fall in behind us and cover the rear of our column."

"My pleasure, Sir," responded the MP Officer, before he turned to the

XXL size CID Agent and former paratrooper and said, "Let's go, Mike."

As Lieutenant Kelly began walking by Captain Garnier's side, while they followed the men who were taking the lead, the American CIC Agent expressed his frustrations. when he spoke just above a whisper and said, "What is it with these Nazis, Captain? Don't they get it? The war's over."

"You should have seen them in action when they were winning," responded the French Army Intelligence Officer, who had been fighting the Germans, including SS men, the Gestapo and the ruthless pro Vichy French Milice, ever since Paris was occupied by the enemy.

Koenraad Berger and the three U.S. Army CID Agents didn't travel all that far, from the location where the bicycle and the Kublewagen were abandoned, before the alpine guide stopped and knelt down to get a closer look at the terrain.

While the rest of their men fanned out to provide security, Captain Garnier, Lieutenant Kelly and MP Lieutenant Miller waited nearby, as Mr. Berger stood up and filed another scouting report. "The wounded gunman we are pursuing stopped here. It is also obvious that he has lost a great deal of blood. I can also report that he is not alone. There are signs of several men wearing Germany Army boots who were also in this area." Then, as the famous alpine guide pointed to the south, he added, "The men wearing Germany Army boots are still heading south and are being followed by our men."

Sam Carubba was next to speak and said, "Unless they change course, Sir, it looks like they're heading toward the Alpine mountain passes, where Mr. Berger and Mr. Jager spotted German troops carrying supplies."

Even Doc Keller contributed to the exchange, when he looked at Captain Garnier and said, "Excuse me, Sir, but if this gunman is hit that bad, he's gonna slow down whoever is helping him make his escape."

"Doc Keller is right, Sir," interjected Lieutenant Dan Kelly, who quickly added, "This could also make it easier for the Colonel, Captain Parker and Hans to stay on their trail.

"And us as well," remarked MP Lieutenant Miller.

After agreeing with his American Allies, Captain Garnier thanked Mr. Berger for his report before he remarked, "They can't be that far ahead of us. Let's move out and above all, we must be as quiet as possible."

After hearing Lieutenant's Kelly and Miller volunteer to bring up the rear with Sergeant Mulligan, Captain Garnier turned and faced Koenraad Berger as he continued and said, "Sergeants Carubba, Coppola and Angelone will continue to accompany you to provide for your security. The rest of us will follow close behind."

"Thank you, Captain," responded the alpine guide, before he turned to the three sergeants and said, "This way, gentlemen."

After hearing Sergeant Carubba remark, "We're right behind you, Mr. Berger," the alpine scout removed the Mauser K98 rifle from his shoulder, as he turned and headed toward Gruben with the three sergeants from the Paris CID Office by his side.

The moment Jim and Al spotted Hans stop and take cover on the left side of the trail, the two CID Agents advanced in a slight crouch to his position. As soon as they knelt down by his side, Hans turned and whispered, "A lone sentry is positioned up ahead, along the edge of the tree line. I lost sight of the others."

"Even if we eliminated that sentry, it's still three of us against an entire squad," whispered Al.

When Jim responded, he whispered as well. "Now that the sun's coming up, it'll be a lot harder to follow them and virtually impossible to advance on their position, without getting into one hell of a gun battle."

Hans agreed and quickly added, "There's something else that we have to consider." While Hans continued to whisper, he pointed off to the left and said, "There's a small village called Gruben off to the left. According to several members of the Oberstdorf Heimatschutz, including my father-in- law, Koenraad Berger and Mr. Johan Feedler, who serves as an Oberforstmeister with the Forest Service, this is the direction of travel that different groups of troops have taken, while transporting supplies into nearby alpine passes."

While Jim faced Al and Hans, he whispered, "That means that there's a lot more of these holdouts, than the one squad that we followed, operating in this general area."

After nodding his head in agreement, Hans spoke just above a whisper when he said, "Correct."

"I guess that means we better wait until help arrives," responded Jim.

"How 'bout something to eat in the meantime?" whispered Al, as he slowly slipped the pack off his back.

"Good idea," whispered Jim, as Al slowly removed three Hershey Bars from his pack and handed one each to Jim and Hans.

While Hans slowly peeled back the wrapper, Jim leaned closer to Al and joked, "This isn't the breakfast that I had in mind when you said we should eat something."

After taking a bite off the end of his Hershey Bar, Al responded in an equally low tone of voice when he said, "I promise I'll buy you breakfast as soon as we deal with these Nazi troublemakers."

Even though Jim was joking around, he continued to play the straight man when he whispered, "I'm gonna hold you to that, partner."

After following a squad of German troops, who were likely involved in the assassination attack on his father-in-law, Hans was to hungry to care what type of food they ate. Besides, as far as Hans was concerned, even an American Hershey Bar was better than anything that his army provided their troops.

While Hans and the two American Army CID Agents quietly devoured their early morning ration of chocolate, Jim paused to check his watch, before he leaned closer to his two colleagues and whispered, "I'm gonna pull back a bit, so I can let whoever comes out to give us a hand know what the game plan is?"

"Me and Hans will cover you from here," responded Al, as he and Hans put the remains of their Hershey Bars in their coat pockets and picked up their weapons. While Jim slipped his Hershey Bar into his trench coat pocket, he addressed his two colleagues in a very low tone of voice. "Like I said before. This is your town, Hans, so you call the shots. If you want'a wait and see what develops, that's what we'll do. If you want'a engage this squad, or anyone else who shows up, do your best to let me know what the plan is, so we can back your play. In the meantime, you and Al are on point."

As soon as Hans responded and said, "Yes, Jim," Jim got up in a low crouch and pulled back to a position, that was in the direction where they expected help to arrive. After taking a few steps in the opposite direction, Jim stopped and turned to face Al and Hans. Jim never sounded more concerned when he whispered, "Home alive in '45."

While Al tossed Jim a casual salute to signal that he got the message, Jim turned and continued to reposition himself, so he could intercept the men who he hoped would be along shortly.

As soon as Jim spotted Koenraad Berger, followed by three of his men heading his way, he knew he made the right decision about falling back, to meet the personnel who came to their rescue. Doing so, put Jim in a position to brief the responding troops, without alerting the enemy about their presence.

After meeting with Captain Garnier and the other men in their unit, Jim decided to have Lieutenant Carl Miller fall back even further, to keep Peter Sigmann and the men that he was expected to arrive with, from venturing too far forward, until the time was right to do so. Unfortunately, the decision to engage the enemy soldiers was made for them, when all three squads of SS troops came out into the open.

The second Al and Hans spotted three squads of SS troops approaching their position, on the trail that led back to Oberstdorf, Al flipped open the safety cover on his M3 Grease Gun and whispered, "Here we go, Hans."

While Hans slowly retracted the bolt on the American Thompson that he carried, he glanced back and made eye contact with Jim, just as the SS trooper on point spotted the presence of Allied troops off in the nearby distance and opened fire. As soon as Al Parker and Hans jumped up from behind their positions of cover, they opened fire as well and brought down three of SS Major Kessler's men, including the SS Private who was leading the enemy column. Since Kessler's men were all combat veterans, they handled themselves appropriately under fire and were able to initially hold the Allied troops at bay. Unfortunately, the terrain features on the trail that led back to Oberstdorf gave the advantage to the Allied troops that initiated the ambush.

At the rear of the German formation, Captain Schneider made his way under fire to where Major Kessler was reloading his MP40 with another 32 round magazine. As soon as his second-in- command arrived by his side, Kessler was getting ready to continue returning fire, when Captain Schneider crawled up next to him and said, "Sir, Lieutenant Emich is a good officer, but he isn't ready to command the operation that you have planned for this area."

"What are you suggesting, Gerhardt?" asked Kessler.

Without mincing words Captain Schneider remarked, "Take the 3rd Squad with you and head for our camp at Spielmannssau. It will be a lot easier for you to defend that position if you decide to stand and fight. If not, you can direct Lieutenant Emich to disperse his men until he hears from you."

"And I take the 3rd Squad to Kemptner Hutte until we are ready to strike," remarked Kessler.

"That's exactly what I had in mind, Sir," said Captain Schneider.

While the exchange of gunfire continued, it was easy for Kessler to see, that he and his men were facing an Allied force of very competent soldiers, who were doing an excellent job of holding their ground. The situation was further complicated by the fact, that Kessler's SS unit was taking fire from two different directions and had already sustained several casualties. As a result, Kessler had every reason to believe, that if he ordered the withdrawal of all three squads, the remains of his entire unit would be aggressively pursued. Worse yet, was the potential of having the bulk of his men killed, before they made it to trail head, that led to their camps at Gruben, Gottenreid and Spielmannssau. It was the combination of these concerns, that compelled Kessler to reluctantly agree, to have Captain Schneider and the remaining survivors of the 1st and 2nd Squad cover his withdrawal.

As Kessler faced his second-in-command, he did his best to seem more like a friend than a superior officer when he said, "We've been through a lot together, Gerhardt. Without a doubt, this is the most difficult decision that either of us has ever had to make. But you're right. It's what needs to be done."

"I had a good teacher," responded the SS Captain, who became more serious when he added, "Go, Sir, while we can still cover your withdrawal."

"Auf Widersehen, Gerhardt," (Goodbye), said Kessler who instantly transformed into an aggressive combat commander, as he relayed order to Sergeant Mueller and the men in his squad. "Third Squad on me!"

Without looking back, SS Major Kessler got up in a slight crouch and headed toward the trail head. Following very close behind their commanding officer, was SS Sergeant Bruno Mueller and the other members of 3rd Squad.

The situation changed, when Hans noticed SS Major Kessler and eight of his men making a mad dash for the trail head that led to Gruben, while his two remaining squads provided covering fire. Their effort to cover their commander became even more aggressive, when the remaining SS troops threw several hand- grenades in the direction of the American troops, while Kessler and eight of his men withdrew from the engagement.

"Kessler is on the run with some of his men!" called out Hans, as he turned toward Al, while he reloaded his M3 Grease Gun.

"We'll see about that," said Al, as he put his Grease Gun down and he picked up the bolt action German K98 sniper rifle.

By the time Jim arrived by their side, with Sergeant's Angelone and Coppola, Al had a round in the chamber and was aimed in on his first moving target. When the first round fired just missed hitting Major Kessler, Al cycled another round into the chamber, took a breath and exhaled, while he aimed the K98 at the escaping SS Major. The second Al pulled the trigger, SS Private Schmidt fell mortally wounded, when he ran in front of the bullet that was meant for Major Kessler.

"One down!" called out Al, as he loaded a fresh round into the chamber. Once again Al placed the cross hairs of the scope over a target, as Kessler and seven of his men zig zaged away from the area. This time SS Private Grueber was killed with a well placed shot to the center of his back. "Two down" remarked Al, who continued as he put the sniper rifle on the ground. "Kessler and six of his men are in the wind."

"They're heading toward Gruben and Gottenreid," said Hans as he put the empty Thompson down and drew his 9mm P38 pistol.

"Here, take this," said Al, as he presented the K98 sniper rifle to Hans.

After tucking his P38 pistol in his belt, Hans accepted the rifle and a handful of ammunition from Al. As Hans began to engage the SS troops who were aiding in the escape of their commander, he knew he had no choice but to do so, because men like Major Kessler were helping to destroy what little was left of Germany. The fact that Major Kessler commanded the assassination team, that tried to kill his father-in-law and could have harmed his wife, made it ever easier for him, to engage the SS troops behind the attack on his home.

While Jim, Al, Hans and Sergeant's Angelone and Coppola continued banging away at the remaining SS troops, Captain Garnier tossed two smoke grenades toward the enemy. Once the smoke from the two grenades filled the air, the French Captain led the American soldiers he commanded, in a very aggressively executed flanking maneuver. Even though they faced nine battle hardened SS troops, Captain Garnier and the men he commanded were able to execute a successful flanking maneuver, that was expertly supported by Colonel Beauregard, Captain Parker, Hans Sigmann and Sergeant's Angelone and Coppola.

The second the coast was clear, an anxious Hans put the sniper rifle down and picked up his U.S. Army pack as he stood up and said, "I'm going after Kessler. I can't let him get away!"

"Easy Hans," said Jim, as he grabbed the local police chief by the arm and he suggested that they get better organized, before they charge off into the unknown.

While Al put his pack on and he retrieved the German sniper rifle, he agreed with Jim and quickly added, "Remember what you said before, Hans. Your father-in-law, Mr. Berger and their buddy from the Forest Service, have seen a lot more troops than the ones we just encountered, moving up into these mountain passes. That means Kessler and his six men aren't the only Nazi holdouts who intend to keep on fighting."

As frustrated as he was, Hans nodded his head ever so slightly and agreed that they should get better organized, before going in hot pursuit of SS Major Kessler and the other holdouts.

"Now that we got that settled, let's go," said Jim and he led Al, Hans, Anthony Angelone and Sal Coppola over to where Captain Garnier and the other men were searching the enemy killed, wounded and the two prisoners who came out of the skirmish unscathed. While this search was being conducted, Jim asked Al to take control of the prisoners, until Lieutenant Miller arrived with some help from town.

"My pleasure," responded Al as he jogged over to where two captured SS troops who were already completely disarmed and searched were standing with their hands locked behind their necks.

Jim then gently grabbed Captain Garnier's left arm and said, "Charles, have the men place any serviceable captured weapons and any available ammunition in a pile off to the side."

"Oui mon, Colonel," responded the French Intelligence Officer before he relayed the order to make a pile of all serviceable weapons and ammunition.

As soon as the men began to do so, Jim addressed Lieutenant Kelly as he pointed to the area where they initially observed the SS troops emerge from a position of cover. "When we first spotted these SS troops they advanced from a position along that treeline. Take Ange and Sal with you and check it out, but be careful doing so, Dan."

"Yes, Sir," responded the Lieutenant from CIC before he called out to the others and said, "Ange, Sal..let's go!"

While Lieutenant Kelly jogged off with Sergeant's Angelone and Coppola, Jim addressed Captain Garnier as he and the other men continued to conduct a methodical search of the enemy prisoners and those killed in action, "Let me know as soon as you find any worthwhile intel, Charles."

Once again, Captain Garnier responded in a respectful fashion in French, as he conducted a very thorough search of a slightly wounded captured SS soldier, who was standing with his hands locked behind his head. "Oui mon, Colonel." As soon as Captain Garnier finished searching one of the SS soldiers who wasn't wounded, he turned the prisoner over to Captain Parker before moving on to conduct other searches.

While Hans Sigmann rummaged through the pile of captured weapons, he picked up a 9mm MP40 submachine gun and hung the sling around his chest. After checking the weapon and seeing that it was unloaded, Hans removed the empty magazine and tossed it on the ground, before he bent over and retrieved a loaded thirty two round MP40 magazine from a captured ammunition pouch. "It's not much but it will have to do," remarked Hans as he inserted the loaded magazine into the captured submachine gun.

While Hans re-positioned the MP40 on his shoulder, Jim knelt down and removed a Mauser made P38 pistol and the loaded spare magazine from the black leather clam shell holster that was taken from a dead SS trooper. As Jim soon as stood up, he handed the loaded spare eight round magazine to the Oberstdorf Police Chief and said, "Here's an extra magazine for your pistol. I got a feeling it might come in handy where we're gong."

"Thanks, Jim," responded Hans, as he replaced the spare magazine that he used earlier, to reload the 9mm P38 that his father-in-law took from the assassin who raided his home.

After Jim checked to see if the Mauser P38 was loaded, he turned to their alpine guide and spoke as he handed him the pistol. "Here you go, Mr. Berger. It's loaded."

"Thank you, herr Oberst," responded Mr. Berger as he tucked the captured pistol into the leather belt that was secured around his coat.

Jim then turned to Mike Mulligan and asked the XXL size CID Agent to carry the captured MG42 machine gun with a 72 round drum magazine and the can of belted ammunition that was in the pile of captured weapons. As soon as Sergeant Mulligan acknowledged the order and he retrieved the German machine gun and the can of ammunition, Jim knelt down and picked up a German Army issue Walther LP42 Flair Pistol in a holster containing five flairs from the pile.

After standing up, Jim addressed Sergeant Mulligan, as he secured the leather flair pistol holster onto the XXL size CID Agent's M1945 Combat (back) pack. "I hate to load you down with more gear, Mike, but a flair pistol might come in handy before this day is over."

"We're ready for anything now, Sir," remarked Mike Mulligan as he carried his M1 Carbine over his left shoulder, while he held the MG42 in his right hand and the extra can of ammunition in his left.

By the time Hans was minimally rearmed and ready to go, MP Lieutenant Miller arrived with Peter Sigmann and two dozen armed militiamen from Oberstdorf. As soon as Hans and Jim greeted Peter and Lieutenant Miller, Hans asked his son to assign three good men from the town militia to relieve Captain Parker and assume the responsibility of guarding the captured SS troops. At the same time, Jim addressed Lieutenant Miller and said, "Distribute anything in the pile of captured weapons that goes bang to the men from town, except for the four grenades." Then, after a split second pause, Jim added, "Keep two of those grenades for yourself, Carl and give the other two to Peter."

"Consider it done, Colonel," responded Lieutenant Miller, as he motioned to some of the men from town defense force to give him a hand, while he handed out captured weapons and ammunition from the pile that was on the ground. While that was being done, Peter Sigmann selected three men to take over the guarding of the captured SS troops.

When Peter Sigmann returned to where his father was standing with Jim Beauregard, he brought two members of the town militia to meet the American Army Colonel. While the man wearing the partial Luftwaffe uniform, that displayed the rank of sergeant, was obviously disabled, the other individual was a physically fit older gentleman armed with a shotgun, who was wearing a sleeveless brown leather vest, over the gray uniform of an Oberforstmeister of the Reichsforstamt (German Forestry Service).

While speaking in a very respectful tone of voice, Peter addressed the American Army Colonel as he stood in between the two volunteers. "With your permission, herr Oberst, I would like to assign Mr. Johan Feedler and Mr. Otto Krueger to assist Sergeant Mulligan, carry extra ammunition and the other equipment that is needed to support the MG42. Both Mr.

Kreuger and Mr. Feedler speak excellent English, Sir."

"I'm sure Sergeant Mulligan will appreciate the help," responded Jim.

When Peter continued he introduced Oberforstmeister Johan Feedler to the American Colonel. In doing so, Peter explained Mr. Feedler's familiarity with the area, as a result of his duties as a superior officer of the German Forest Service. Peter also identified Mr. Feedler as one of the first men in town, who reported seeing different numbers of German troops, making their way into the nearby mountain passes, to his grandfather and Koenraad Berger.

As soon as Jim thanked Mr. Feedler for his assistance, the German Forest Service Officer proved that he spoke excellent English, when he addressed the American Colonel in a very sincere tone of voice. "If pursuing these soldiers and the fanatics who direct them, brings this war to an end, then this is something that we must do, herr Oberst."

Jim also sounded very sincere when he responded and said, "My men and I understand that this is not an easy thing to do. We also agree that this is something that must be done, in order to end this miserable war."

After nodding his head ever so slightly, Mr. Feedler quickly added, "Thank you for understanding the complexities of this situation, herr Oberst." As soon as he finished speaking, Mr. Feedler saluted the American Army Colonel.

As Jim returned the military courtesy, he thought to himself, that ever since he met Hans Sigmann and others like him, he began to understand, why many Germans were torn between wanting to serve their country, while they questioned its leadership and privately opposed the gruesome dictates of the regime. Others in Germany changed their opinion of National Socialism, when they saw their country being destroyed and the promise of secret weapons that would turn defeat into victory, never materialized. Regardless of when people "saw the light," by this point in 1945, the last thing that Germany needed, was to have armed fanatics and Nazi inspired holdouts preparing to prolong the war.

Jim also understood, that since Germany was run by a dictator, who was supported by a ruthless army of enforcers, it was impossible to voice any objection to the aims of National Socialism, without paying dearly for your actions. To go beyond verbal opposition was considered an act of treason, that resulted in extreme suffering and execution. The fact that any group of Germans would offer any opposition to the representatives of the Third Reich, impressed Jim and his men to no end. As a result, the German citizens who served in the Oberstdorf Heimatschutz were considered to be descent people, who deserved all the assistance that the Allies could provide.

Once Jim saluted Mr. Feedler, Peter introduced the 55 year old flak gunner, who was recently discharged from the Luftwaffe, after he lost his left hand and left eye in an Allied bombing raid. While Mr. Krueger faced the American Colonel, the disabled veteran spoke as he presented Jim with a salute. "It's an honor to serve with you and your men, herr Oberst."

As Jim returned the military courtesy, he spoke from the heart when he responded. "The honor is ours, Sergeant."

Now that the introductions were out of the way, Jim turned to Sergeant Mulligan and said, "Sergeant Krueger and Oberforstmeister Feedler will be giving you a hand, Mike."

"Yes, Sir," responded Sergeant Mulligan, before he motioned Otto and Johan over to where he was was standing. As soon as they arrived by his side, Mike remarked, "Thanks for helping out."

While standing by the American Sergeant's side, Mr. Krueger spoke first and said, "If you like, Sergeant, I can carry that can of ammunition."

Even though Mr. Krueger was no longer serving in the German Air Force, Mike Mulligan gave the disabled veteran the respect that he deserved, when he allowed the one armed man to take possession of the can of ammunition. "Thank you, Sergeant."

As a World War I combat veteran, who was now serving as a senior officer in the German Forest Service, Mr. Feedler didn't need any direction to know what needed to be done. While speaking in a friendly tone of voice, the Oberforstmeister pointed to the pile of weapons that were on the ground and said, "I will retrieve the other equipment for us, Sergeant."

Sergeant Mulligan also gave Mr. Feedler the respect that he deserved, when he used the English version of the Forest Service Officer's rank, to address the Oberforstmeister, when he sprang into action and he retrieved a belt of ammunition, the spare barrel carrier and the bi pod for the MG42 from the pile on the ground. Just as Mike Mulligan faced the Oberforstmeister and said, "Thank you, Chief," and the Oberforstmeister responded by saying, "You are most welcome, Sergeant," Captain Garnier returned to where Jim was standing with the others. While pointing off to his right, Captain Garnier reported that they found a seriously wounded SS Captain at the rear of the formation.

"That must be Captain Schneider," remarked Hans.

Just as Hans finished speaking, Jim remarked, "Aren't you glad you waited?" just as Al Parker walked over while he reloaded a 30 round Grease Gun magazine.

"He got you that time, Hans," said Al, while Jim turned to the French Captain and said, "Lead the way, Charles."

While Jim, Al and Hans followed Captain Garnier over to where SS Captain Schneider was being treated by Doc Keller, Lieutenant Miller and Peter Sigmann had the other available members of the Oberstdorf Heimatschutz fan out to provide security. As soon as Jim and the others arrived by the mortally wounded SS Officer's side, Doc Keller was closing Gerhardt Schneider's eyes.

"Sorry Sir," said Doc Keller, who quickly added, "He was too badly wounded for me to keep him alive."

As Sam Carubba stood up, he made everyone's day, when he handed his commanding officer a folded map and said, "I found this map on this SS Officer, Sir."

"Here, Hans. You better take charge of this," said Jim as he handed the map to Hans.

As soon as Hans opened the map, he couldn't believe his eyes. "This is too good to be true," remarked Hans, as he pointed to the line marked in pencil, that ran from a position near Spielmannssau to the location marked Kemptner Hutte.

"What's Kemptner Hutte?" asked Jim.

"It's pretty high up that's for sure," remarked Al, as he leaned over Hans's shoulder and added, "That looks like some pretty steep terrain between Spielmannssau and Kemptner Hutte."

"Steep enough to need mules to haul supplies to this resort when it's open for business," responded Hans, before he turned to his right and called Mr. Berger over.

"I haven't been up there in years," said Hans, who quickly added, "But

Mr. Berger knows this terrain better than anyone in town next to Mr. Feedler."

While Mr. Berger walked over to join them, Jim couldn't resist and teased Hans again by saying, "Aren't you glad you waited?"

"He got you again, Hans," said Al while he finished reloading the Grease Gun magazine and they were joined by the famous alpine mountain guide.

Hans had been a cop long enough to know, that cops liked to tease each other and joke around. Since Hans knew that Jim was reacting to his anxiousness, to pursue Major Kessler before they were ready, he took being teased in the right frame of mind and said, "I deserved that. And yes, I am glad I waited."

"OK, Hans. I teased you enough," said Jim. "What's our next move, Chief."

After pointing off to his left, Hans referred to the captured map when he responded and said, "We can move as one unit until we reach Spielmannssau. From there a small group of us can go on to Kemptner Hutte, while the bulk of our men remain behind and secure Spielmannssau until we return."

As soon as Hans showed the map to Mr. Berger and asked for his opinion, the famous alpine mountain guide pointed to the map and said, "We must be careful, Hans, because Gunther and I, as well as our friend Johan Feedler, have observed dozens of troops transporting supplies, into the alpine trails and passes that lead to Gruben, Gottensreid and Spielmannssau. In fact, Kemptner Hutte would be the most remote of all these locations, for SS Major Kessler and his followers to establish a camp."

When Jim turned and faced the Chief Forest Service Officer and he asked if could add anything to their conversation, Mr. Feedler remarked, "My friend, Koenraad, is correct, herr Oberst. I have personally observed different numbers of German troops, including those from the SS, transporting large amounts of supplies into the alpine passes, using bicycles, mules and wooden carts. On each and ever occasion, the boy who escorted these troops is the one who tried to kill Gunther. After I reported these observations to Gunther and Koenraad, the three of us continued to observe more troops making their way around Oberstdorf and taking the trail that leads to Gruben. As far as Kemptner Hutte is concerned, it is an ideal location to avoid detection, while waiting for the time to strike."

As soon as the senior Forest Officer finished and Jim thanked him for his comments, Hans folded the captured map as he addressed Jim and said, "I'll send three men back to town with the four prisoners. That should be enough since two of the prisoners are wounded. Once they head back, we can leave as soon as we hear from Lieutenant Kelly."

"Speaking of Lieutenant Kelly. I wonder what's taking them so long to scout that area?" remarked Jim.

Just as Hans called out to his son and he relayed the order to have three men take the captured SS soldiers back to town, Al pointed off to the right and said, "Here comes, Ange and it looks like he found more souvenirs to bring home."

Even though he was loaded down with his own issued weapons and a pack, Sergeant Angelone also carried a captured German MP40 submachine gun, a Walther P38 pistol and two 32 round magazines for the MP40, as he jogged over to where his commanding officer was standing,

When the winded young CID Agent stopped to catch his breath, Jim remarked. "As soon as you settle down, Ange, you can tell us where you found the heavy hardware?"

While still a bit short of breath, Sergeant Angelone pointed off to the area that he helped to search when he filed his report. "Lieutenant Kelly sent me to tell you, Sir, that we found a well camouflaged camp on the other side of those rocks and trees. It's filled with all kinds of German weapons, ammo, rations, clothing and even some medical supplies."

"That must be one of the camps that Kessler and his men set up, as a base of operations to launch attacks against Oberstdorf," said Hans.

As Jim turned to face the others he wasted no time in saying, "I think we should take advantage of the situation, especially since there wasn't much in the way of captured spare ammunition left, after our encounter with the troops who covered Kessler's withdrawal. It also wouldn't hurt for us to better equipped with other supplies, when we go after Kessler and the other holdouts."

To show that he had the same sense of humor that American policemen had, Hans remarked, "Now I'm really glad I stayed."

While Al Parker grinned and patted Hans on the back again, Jim turned to Sergeant Angelone and said, "As soon as you turn that burp gun over to Peter Sigmann, you can show us the way back to this camp."

"Yes, Sir," responded who immediately complied with the order and passed the 9mm MP 40 submachine gun to Peter Sigmann. Once Sergeant Angelone handed the two spare MP40 32 round magazines to Peter, Jim made a hand gesture toward the area where the enemy camp was located and remarked, "OK, Ange...lead the way."

Jim then turned to Al and said, "Move 'em out, Al."

While Captain Parker waved his left hand in the air, he called out, "We're moving out! Let's go."

By the time Jim and the others arrived at the well concealed clandestine campsite, that was covered in netting and contained two tents, Lieutenant Kelly and Sergeant Coppola had several crates lined up near the larger command tent. Both inside and on top of these crates were bolt action K98 rifles, leather belts loaded with pouches containing five round stripper clips of Kar 98K 7.52x57 8mm Mauser ammunition, six 9mm Walther P38 pistols with spare 8 round magazines in black leather clam shell holsters, three 9mm MP40s with leather pouches containing 18 loaded spare 32 round magazines, two semi automatic K43 magazine fed rifles, that could be loaded using two five round K98 stripper clips of 8mm ammunition, several hundred boxes containing loaded 5 round stripper clips of 8mm ammunition, two loaded 72 round drums and ten cans of belted MG42 ammunition, thirty 16 round boxes of 9mm ammunition, six entrenching tools, a case of grenades, a large supply of German Army food rations, a dozen German Army blankets, a stack of folded camouflaged clothing, including reversible white and green Winter Splinter smocks, two dozen German Army issue Model 1941 Rucksacks, assorted medical supplies, a dozen canteens, extra pairs of gloves, six German Army issue flashlights, a dozen mess tins and two sets of German Kochgerat 15s (Cooking Equipment 15/ designed to prepare food for up to 15 troops).

"This is some stash," remarked Al.

"And we're gonna put it to good use," said Jim as he, along with Al,

Hans, Captain Garnier, Peter Sigmann and Sergeant Angelone approached Lieutenant Kelly and Sergeant Coppola.

"It looks like you and your assistants hit pay dirt with this find," said Jim.

While Sergeant Angelone joined Sergeant Coppola and Lieutenant Kelly on their side of the line of wooden crates, Lieutenant Kelly responded as he picked up a captured Walther P38 and tucked the pistol in his belt. "And the price was right, Sir."

After turning to face Al, Hans, Captain Garnier and Peter Sigmann, Jim spoke with a sense of urgency when he said, "As soon as we pass out these weapons and supplies, we'll take off after Kessler and the others."

As Jim looked across the line of crated supplies and equipment, he picked up one of the empty Germany Army packs and addressed Lieutenant Kelly and Sergeant's Angelone and Coppola. "As soon as I get everyone's attention, you and your two assistants can issue everyone who doesn't have a pack, one of these German Army rucksacks. Fill each pack with some German Army rations and some of these other supplies. We'll also pass out as much of the ammo that the men can carry. Anyone who wants an extra weapon is welcomed to take one."

When Jim continued he pointed to an assortment of other captured German equipment, "Let's also pass out extra clothing, as well as these entrenching tools, bayonets and these flashlights to the men from the town militia. Our men can also help themselves to whatever they might need and that includes Doc Keller, taking some of these captured medical supplies."

Even though he was standing further down the line of crated supplies, Doc Keller heard what his commanding officer said and wasted no time in calling out, "I heard you, Colonel. I'll take as much as I can carry, Sir," as he began making a pile of German medical supplies to take along.

"Thanks, Doc," responded Jim as he picked up one of the captured German canteens and shook to see if it was full. Once Jim determined that the canteen was full, he addressed Lieutenant Kelly again and said, "We should also take all the water we can carry."

"Will do, Sir," responded Lieutenant Kelly as he and his two assistants started filling captured German rucksacks, while Lt. Colonel Jim Beauregard addressed the men from the mixed unit consisting of his troops and members of the Oberstdorf defense force. Once Jim instructed everyone to line up to pickup supplies and extra ammunition, he added that his men should take whatever they might need as well, before they moved out. Jim then addressed Sergeant Mulligan, who was standing nearby and said, "Get some additional help, Mike and take as much ammo as possible for that MG42."

"Yes, Sir," responded the XXL size former MP who was now serving as a CID Agent before he turned to his two assistants and said, "Come on, guys."

"I'll give you a hand, Mike," remarked Sergeant Carubba as he followed Sergeant Mulligan, Otto and Johan, over to the location where Lieutenant Kelly and Sergeant Coppola stockpiled the extra MG42 ammo and additional spare barrels.

While facing his son Peter, Hans remarked, "That MG42 will likely prove to very useful when we come face to face with Kessler and the men he commands. Select two more volunteers from the Oberstdorf Heimatschutz to help carry everything needed to support Sergeant Mulligan's MG42."

While the members of the town militia began drawing extra equipment and supplies, Peter Sigmann directed Kurt Fisher and Herman Becker to assist Sergeant Mulligan. Without hesitating, the two older men, who saw service in the Kreigsmarine during World War I, shouldered their rifles and joined the other men who were loaded down with ammunition and other accessories for the MG42.

While the last of the men from Oberstdorf were being better equipped, and some of his troops were picking up some additional supplies, Jim noticed Sergeant's Angelone and Coppola loading the captured K43 semi automatic rifles. As Jim made his way over to where the two CID Agents were standing, they had the K43s fully loaded and were in the process of filling U.S. Army haversacks with 5 round stripper clips of ammunition.

By the time Jim arrived by their side, Sergeant's Angelone and Coppola were securing the shoulder bags that were slung across their chests. "I see you boys are loaded for bear," remarked Jim who quickly added, "Are you sure you'll be able to carry two heavy rifles and all that extra ammo and equipment?"

As Sergeant Angelone responded, he carried the German K43 over his left shoulder, while he held his M1 Garand in his right hand, "We don't have a choice, Sir."

"You see, Sir, we used up half our .30 cal ammo for our M1s dealing with those SS troops," added Sergeant Coppola

"How much ammo did you boys scrounge up for those cannons," asked Jim, as he pointed at the K43 that Sergeant Coppola had hanging from his left shoulder.

As Sergeant Sal Coppola patted the rather heavy looking haversack that was filled with 8mm ammo he responded and said, "Twenty stripper clips each, Sir."

"An extra hundred rounds won't last long if we get into another gunfight," remarked Jim.

When Sergeant Angelone responded he held up one of the five round stripper clips. "There's a lot more of this stuff available, Sir, but we can only carry so much."

After nodding his head ever so slightly, Jim remarked, "I'll see what I can do about taking more of that German ammo with us."

"Thanks, Colonel," responded Sal Coppola.

"Let's hope you won't need those rifles, but if you do, use 'em in good health, boys." said Jim.

"Will do, Sir," responded Sergeant Angelone.

"Don't worry, Sir. We'll make every shot count, Colonel," added Sal Coppola.

"I know you will. Carry on, men," said Jim.

As two of the most colorful men in his unit walked away, Jim walked over to Al and said, "If we get into a fight on some alpine trail, we're gonna wish we were a lot better armed. I'm also not sure how our volunteers from Oberstdorf are gonna hold up if we run into trouble."

"The men are carrying as much as they can, Jim. Besides, this isn't gonna be a walk in the park," responded Al, who quickly added, "As far as how the men from town are gonna hold up under fire goes, we won't know until the shooting starts."

After Jim looked at the mixed formation consisting of his men and the civilians from the Oberstdorf Heimatschutz and he saw how overloaded they were with weapons, other equipment and packs filled with supplies, he grabbed one of the empty German rucksacks and said, "You're right. We can't ask the men to carry anymore than they already have."

As Jim began filling the German rucksack with five round stripper clips of 8mm ammo, that were designed to be used in the bolt action K98 and the semi automatic K43, Al spoke up and said, "Are you getting that bad feeling again. You know, the one that good officers get before they lead men in battle?"

While Jim stopped filling the rucksack with 8mm ammunition, he faced Al and said, "We won round one because we had Kessler and his men boxed in. We may not be that lucky the next time. Kessler may also have a lot more help, when we tangle with him on ground of his choosing."

"And Kessler's help is made up of trained military personnel, who have probably seen their fair share of combat in recent years, where many of our allies from the Oberstdorf Heimatschutz haven't been in combat since World War 1," responded Al.

"Correct," said Jim.

After hearing what Jim had to say, Al grabbed one of the empty German backpacks and remarked, "Let me give you a hand with that," as he began filling the pack with five round stripper clips of 8mm ammo.

Once Jim and Al finished loaded the two rucksacks with extra German rifle ammo and they approached the mixed formation, Jim directed Sergeant's Angelone and Coppola to standby to take point with Mr. Berger. Jim then turned to Captain Garnier and said, "Charles, you and Lieutenant Kelly can fall in behind the men on point?"

"Qui mon Colonel," responded the French Intelligence Officer, before he turned to Lieutenant Kelly and said, "It looks like we are going for another walk in the countryside."

Jim then turned to Al and said, "You and me are with Hans. We'll keep Doc with us as well.

"Right Jim," said Al as he adjusted the position of the captured K98 sniper rifle that rested on his left shoulder.

Jim then turned and addressed Sergeant Mulligan, Sergeant Carubba and the four men from the town defense force, who were weighed down with the MG42, several cans, drums and belts of ammunition, two canisters containing spare barrels and a bi pod. "Why don't you and your machine gun team fall in behind me, Captain Parker, Hans and Doc."

As soon as Sergeant Mulligan acknowledged the order and he lifted the machine gun onto his right shoulder, Jim turned to Hans and asked where he would like Peter and the men from the town militia to be posted. Without hesitation Hans responded and said, "Why don't we have them fall in behind Sergeant Mulligan and Sergeant Carubba."

"Good choice," remarked Jim.

After turning to face his son, Hans didn't have to say anything when Peter repeated, "I'll have the men fall in behind Sergeant Mulligan."

As soon as Peter finished speaking, Jim turned to MP Lieutenant Miller and said, "Carl I want you to stay close to Peter and his men."

"You got it, Colonel," responded the MP Officer.

Jim then turned to four town militiamen who were assisting Sergeant Mulligan and said, "Are you gentlemen ready?"

Despite their ages, the four members of the town defense force appeared to be ready, willing and able to serve alongside the Allied soldiers who wore uniforms. "Yes, herr Oberst. We're ready," responded Herman Becker, the oldest of the four militiamen, who volunteered to help rid the area of Nazi holdouts.

Jim then faced Hans and said, "With your permission, Chief, I'll move the men out?"

After receiving a friendly nod from Hans, Jim called out, "OK, move out and keep your eyes open. We're heading into Indian country from here on in."

As Mr. Berger led the way with Sergeant's Angelone and Coppola serving as his bodyguards, everyone else fell in line as directed and began heading up the trail toward Gruben.

CHAPTER 8

IN HOT PURSUIT OF ANOTHER FRONTLINE FUGITIVE

As soon as Major Kessler and his depleted squad of six SS troops, including Sergeant Mueller, reached their camp near Gruben, they stopped to rest for a few minutes before moving on. After looking through his binoculars, Major Kessler turned to Sergeant Mueller and said, "Get the men moving, Sergeant. We can rearm once we get to our camp near Gottenreid."

When the senior non commissioned officer asked if there was any sign of Captain Schneider, Major Kessler remarked, "No."

Sergeant Mueller didn't have to be told twice to get the men moving. After telling Private Mittenberger to take point, the men moved out in an orderly fashion, while Major Kessler took one more look through his binoculars.

After removing his MP40 from his right shoulder, SS Major Kessler fell in behind his men, as they made their way at a quick pace to their next stop. While they proceeded on their journey to their clandestine camp near Gottenreid, all Kessler could think about, was how fortunate he and his men were to have stashed supplies at Kemptner Hutte.

Shortly after Panzer Grenadier Lieutenant Albert Emich and the men he was training returned to their camp near Spielmannssau, SS Major Kessler and the remaining members of his SS unit arrived as well. As shocked as everyone was about the loss of such an elite number of SS troops, Major Kessler never showed any signs of defeatism and wasted no time in addressing the rest of the men.

"We sustained losses today, but as you all know, such things happen in war," said the Major before he went in to say, "Now it's our turn to inflict losses on the enemy, but in order to do so we must change our tactics. Rather than stand and fight, we can accomplish more by dispersing our forces into a nearby alpine pass and choosing our time to strike. Standby for your orders."

SS Major Kessler then turned to Lieutenant Emich and said, "Have your men prepare to move out in five minutes. They are to carry as much as they can, into one of the alpine passes where you have been conducting your training." As Major Kessler produced his map of the area, he continued and said, "I want you to show me the locations on this map, where you and your men can set up a chain of smaller camps, that are in relative close proximity to each other. I'll meet you in three to four days, once things quiet down in Oberstdorf."

Lieutenant Emich was a competent officer, who knew that a portion of their supplies were recently moved to another location. As far as he was concerned, if Major Kessler wanted to confide in him about his plans he would do so. Lieutenant Emich also knew better than to question the SS Major, who was commanding this mixed contingent of German soldiers, who were willing to fight on. After receiving his new orders, Lieutenant Emich continued as he pointed to a nearby alpine pass, that was ideally suited as their new base of operations. "This is were you can find us, Sir."

While Major Kessler folded his map, he looked at Lieutenant Emich and remarked, "The rest of us will do our best to deal with the enemy troops who attacked our camp near Gruben."

After hearing what the SS Officer just said, Lieutenant Emich couldn't help but remark, "Excuse me, Major, but you only have six men, Sir."

Rather than explain himself, SS Major Kessler repeated his previous response and said, "I'll see you and the others in three to four days."

"Yes, Sir," responded Lieutenant Emich, who quickly added, "Good hunting, Sir."

After saluting the SS Officer and having his salute returned, Lieutenant Emich turned and directed his men, to pick up all the supplies that they could carry and prepare to move out.

As soon Jim, Hans and their men arrived at the clandestine camp near Spielmannssau, it was easy to see that this location was recently abandoned. When Mr. Berger reported that there were signs of a small number of men heading toward Kemptner Hutte and a much larger number of men heading into one of the nearby alpine passes, Jim turned to Hans and said, "You know what they say about splitting your force to pursue two different objectives?"

While Peter Sigmann and Lieutenant Miller had the men fan out to provide security, Hans checked the captured map, before he addressed Jim, Al, Captain Garnier and Mr. Berger. "If the bulk of Kessler's men headed into one of the nearby alpine passes, it makes sense that this SS Major and the six men that he escaped with, are on their way to Kemptner Hutte."

After looking at the two American Army Officers and their French ally, Hans continued and said, "While I am confident that a relatively small number of us can deal with Major Kessler, I would hate to see the rest of the men go after what could easily prove to be a numerically superior force."

"You're right. We would be crazy to send the men from Oberstdorf, after what could turn out to be a well equipped numerically superior force," responded Jim.

Rather than make this decision on his own, Jim wanted to hear from the man he was close personal friends with. After facing his Army buddy, Jim said, "What'a you think, Al?"

As usual, Al Parker proved to be a level headed thinker when he responded and said, "With the exception of our men and Peter Sigmann, the bulk of the men that we'd be sending in harms way, have no recent military training or experience." Then, after pausing for a split second, Al added, "I agree. We're better off dealing with Major Kessler with a group of our best men and mop up the rest when we're in a better position to do so."

As soon as Jim asked their French ally what he thought, Captain Garnier agreed with Jim and Al and added, "This SS Major is like the head of the snake. Once we deal with him, it will likely be a lot easier to deal with the others."

Under the circumstances, Hans didn't argue with the logic that was put to him by men that he respected. "Why don't we take a dozen or so men with us and leave the rest to secure this campsite until we return. By doing so, we'll have a large enough armed force positioned at this location, to cover us when we move on Kessler and his men at Kemptner Hutte. If for some reason Kessler is not at Kemptner Hutte, we can send for reinforcements from the French troops, who are expected to arrive in Oberstdorf sometime today."

"That sounds like a plan," remarked Jim.

Because of his intimate knowledge of the area, Jim turned to their alpine guide and said, "Tell us, Mr. Berger, is there anything we need to know about this place called Kemptner Hutte, before we move against SS Major Kessler and his men?"

"Yes there is, herr Oberst," responded the experienced alpine guide, who continued as he knelt down and used the blade of his belt knife, to sketch a rough layout of the resort on the ground. "Kemptner Hutte consists of two main buildings, that are positioned on a flat plateau, in a clearing that offers unobstructed views of the entire area." [30]

While Jim, Al, Hans and Captain Garnier knelt down in a semi circle facing Mr. Berger, the experienced alpine guide went on to say, "Due to the terrain features, this SS Major and his men would have to lose the use of their eyes not to see us coming, if we launched an attack in broad daylight. In fact, it would not take much, for a handful of well trained soldiers, like this SS Major and his men, to prevent us from getting within striking distance of Kemptner Hutte, if we attacked during the day."

As soon as Al Parker spoke up and said, "It sounds like our only option is to make a night assault," Jim immediately asked Hans how he felt about executing an attack at night?

"Both Al and Mr. Berger are right, Jim," responded Hans, who went on to say, "I'm afraid we would sustain heavy casualties, if we attempted to attack Kemptner Hutte after sunrise, or before sunset."

After making eye contact with their alpine mountain guide, Jim asked Mr. Berger about the feasibility of executing a night assault over such difficult terrain. "You're the expert, Mr. Berger. Without you, we can't pull this off, so we need to know, if you can you get us into position, so we make the final advance to Kemptner Hutte under the cover of darkness?"

"It can be done, herr Oberst," responded Mr. Berger, who quickly added, "I suggest the men get something to eat and get as much rest as possible before we leave. The men must also dress warmly, because it will get a lot colder, once we make the climb to an altitude of 1839 meters, especially after sunset."

"OK, that's it," said Jim before he turned to Al and said, "Can you take care of getting the men something to eat and some hot coffee before they get some rest?"

"I'll get right on it," responded Al.

"I will give Captain Parker a hand," said Captain Garnier.

"So will I," remarked Hans as everyone stood up and got to work.

Once they finally arrived at Kemptner Hutte, SS Major Kessler instructed Sergeant Mueller to put one man on guard duty, while the rest of the men had something to eat before they were allowed to rest. While a pot of water was boiled for ersatz coffee, SS Sergeant Mueller opened a crate containing German Army rations and handed out cheese spread and dried sausage.

After relieving the man on sentry duty, SS Major Kessler accepted a cup of hot ersatz coffee and some food from SS Sergeant Mueller, who joined him by the front door of the main building. When Sergeant Mueller remarked, "One thing is certain, Major. We have enough supplies to remain here for some time," Major Kessler nodded his head in agreement, while he ate his rations in silence.

After sipping some ersatz coffee, the Major seemed a bit perturbed when he finally spoke up. "I still can't believe that Captain Schneider allowed an Allied patrol to follow you and your men back to our camp near Gruben?"

In an effort to defend the recently deceased Captain, Sergeant Mueller responded in a respectful tone of voice and said, "Just like Captain Schneider reported, Sir, the woman who was in the Police Chief's home surprised our men, killed the boy and wounded Corporal Krebs. By the time the Corporal shot his way through a checkpoint on the outskirts of town, our mission was completely compromised." Then, after waiting to see the Major's reaction, Sergeant Mueller added, "The simple truth, Sir, is that whoever followed us from Oberstdorf was very experienced in such matters, because at no time would we have returned to our camp near Gruben, if we knew that we were being pursued."

Rather than belabor the point, Major Kessler decided to end the conversation. One reason he did so, was because he could not change the past. Major Kessler also needed time to think about how he was going to proceed, after losing the bulk of his best troops. As tired as he was, Major Kessler had too much on his mind to sleep. Instead, he turned to face the non commissioned officer and said, "Get some sleep, Sergeant."

"Yes, Sir," responded Sergeant Mueller, as he stood up and left to join the men who were resting in a nearby room, in the resort known as Kemptner Hutte.

Because they planned to execute a night assault, Al Parker handed the captured K98 sniper rifle to Lieutenant Miller. "Hold onto this for me will you, Carl?" said Captain Parker.

"Sure thing, Captain," respect the Military Police Lieutenant.

When their commanding officer walked over to where they were standing, Jim addressed Lieutenant Miller in a very down to earth tone of voice when he said, "You know what to do if any unfriendly company shows up before we get back."

"Yes, Sir," responded the MP Lieutenant.

"You and Peter Sigmann make a good team, Carl. It's clear that both you and Peter command the respect of men from Oberstdorf. Having that respect, can mean the difference between victory and defeat, if you end up in a fight with the enemy."

"Thanks, Colonel. And don't worry, Sir. We'll be OK," responded the MP Officer.

Even though Jim was always concerned about his men, he did his best to make his subordinates feel, that he had complete confidence in their abilities to perform as soldiers. While doing his best to present the right disposition, Jim presented the MP Lieutenant with a casual salute as he said, "You're in charge, Lieutenant. Carry on."

"Will do, Sir," responded Lieutenant Miller as he returned the salute.

After turning to face Al Parker, Jim continued and said, "OK, Al. It's time. Move 'em out."

As soon as Captain Parker relayed the order to move out, the men who would be advancing on Kemptner Hutte took their positions and began to walk toward the trail head.

While Koenraad Berger led the way, Sergeant's Angelone and Coppola provided security for the man on point. Following close behind was Jim, Al, Hans, Captain Garnier, Lieutenant Kelly, Doc Keller, Sam Carubba, Mike Mulligan and his four assistants from the Oberstdorf militia. This left MP Lieutenant Carl Miller and Peter Sigmann to command the remaining number of civilian militiamen, who were assigned to secure the abandoned campsite near Spielmannssau. In order to let Colonel Reynald know what they were up to, Jim instructed two of the militiamen to deliver a handwritten message to the French Colonel, who should have arrived in Oberstdorf earlier in the day.

When the terrain became more difficult, Jim suggested that they stop and take a break before advancing any further. While doing so, Jim asked Mr. Berger to produce a more detailed layout of Kemptner Hutte, so they could plan their assault with precision before it got dark. After kneeling down, Mr. Berger used rocks and other items to represent the layout of Kemptner Hutte. Once Mr. Berger finished providing a detailed description of the resort, Al Parker turned to Jim and said, "Any idea how you want'a handle this, once we get into position?"

As Jim knelt facing the others, he sounded as if he had been mulling this idea over in his head, ever since they decided to execute a night assault on Kemptner Hutte. While speaking with complete confidence, Jim pointed to the mock layout of the resort, as he explained what he had in mind. "I think we should kick things off by making lots of noise and doing as much damage as possible, before we enter the building."

When he continued, Jim turned to Mike Mulligan and his four assistants and said, "Once we get into position, Mike and his machine gun crew are gonna kick things off, by firing a flair over the top of the resort, before they rake Kemptner Hutte from one end to the other with machine gun fire. While Mike shoots the resort up with that captured MG42, Ange and Sal will put their M1 Garands to work. Once their M1s run dry, they'll use the two captured K43s that they brought along. Sixty seconds after they open up, Mike and his team, along with Ange and Sal, will concentrate their fire on the larger half of the resort, that's situated on the left side of Kemptner Hutte. This will enable the rest of us to safely advance toward the main entrance of the smaller building, that's located on the right side of the resort.

Before we enter the building, we'll toss grenades through the shot up windows, while saving some in case they're needed when we get inside."

Jim then turned again to face Mike Mulligan and his four assistants. "Once you hear those grenades go off, I want you to take your team around to cover the back of the resort. Ange and Sal will go with you and will cover the left side of the building, while also being in a position to assist you and your men if you run into trouble. That will put the seven of you in a position to intercept Kessler and any of his men, if they try to escape out the back door, or from one of the side windows."

As Jim continued his pre-raid briefing, he looked at the members of the entry team and said, "The rest of us, with the exception of Mr. Berger, will enter the main building and clear room after room, until we have either captured or killed SS Major Kessler and his men."

When Mr. Berger spoke up and said, "Herr Oberst. I would like to go with you and your men when you conduct your search. After all, herr Oberst, I am the only one here except for Johan Feedler, who has been inside this resort, since certain changes were made in 1931. And since Johan is assisting Sergeant Mulligan, I could be of service, especially since you and your men will be entering Kemplner Hutte at night."

After considering his request, Jim responded and said, "OK, Mr. Berger, but only if you agree to bring up the rear with our medic Doc Keller."

As soon as Mr. Berger responded and said, "I will do as you say, herr Oberst," Jim turned to Hans and said, "Did I leave anything out?"

Without hesitating, Hans remarked, "It's a good plan."

"OK then," said Jim, who looked at their alpine guide and added, "Lead the way, Mr. Berger."

While SS Sergeant Mueller stood by the window near the front door, he used his field glasses to examine the alpine pasture, that presented an unobstructed view of the surrounding area. In a few minutes the sun would set. Once that happened, the light from the stars would be the only natural illumination, that would allow a sentry to see anything around the perimeter of Kemptner Hutte.

"That's quite a view. Isn't it, Sergeant?" asked SS Major Kessler, as he joined the NCO by the window.

"Yes, Sir, it is," responded Sergeant Mueller, as he lowered his binoculars and turned to face his commanding officer.

While Mueller waited for his commanding officer to continue, Major Kessler remarked, "Even though I doubt anyone will be stopping by to pay us a visit, I want to keep one man on sentry duty at all times, even at night."

"Yes, Sir," responded Sergeant Mueller.

After checking his watch, Major Kessler seemed to be in better spirits, when he addressed Sergeant Mueller in a more down to earth tone of voice and said, "It's been a long day. Let's get some food prepared. The men could use a good meal."

Once again the veteran non commissioned officer responded like a good soldier. "You're right, Sir. It has been a long day. I'll get the men working on some supper for us."

Once the sun set over Kemptner Hutte, Mr. Berger led the way as Jim Beauregard, Al Parker, and Sergeant's Mulligan, Angelone and Coppola followed close behind. The purpose of this reconnaissance mission, was for the key players to get a chance to see the target location, before they went operational.

As soon as Mr. Berger came to a stop, the American troops who were following his lead, belly crawled up to the position of cover, where the alpine guide was positioned. "That my friends is Kemptner Hutte," whispered Mr. Berger.

"That's some spread," whispered Captain Parker.

While speaking in an equally low tone of voice, Jim faced their alpine guide and said, "You did one hell of a job of describing this place, Mr. Berger. It's just like you said it was."

"Thank you, herr Oberst," responded Mr Berger.

Of all the people present, Jim Beauregard was glad that he got the idea, to get a look at Kemptner Hutte, before they launched the actual assault. After turning to his left, Jim addressed the three sergeants, who would be responsible to kick things off, by using an MG42 and their rifles to shoot up the resort.

While continuing to speak in a low tone of voice, Jim pointed at the resort as he addressed the three sergeants, "I wanted you men to see this place before we went operational, so you can get a better idea of what you need to do when you open fire."

As the three sergeants examined the resort, Jim looked at Sergeant Mulligan and said, "The extra ammo we brought along for the MG42 is gonna come in real handy, when you go to town on Kemptner Hutte, Mike."

"We'll do as much damage as possible, Sir," responded Mike Mulligan.

As soon as Sergeant Mulligan finished speaking, Jim addressed Sergeant's Angelone and Coppola. "Every window in that place that Mike doesn't break is all yours. As soon as Mike fires the first flair, I want you to concentrate on the windows by the main entrance. We'll make our move toward the main entrance, right after you shift your fire, to the left side of the resort."

"You got it, Sir," whispered Sergeant Angelone.

"OK, let's stay low when we head back to get the others," said Jim.

"After you, Mr. Berger," whispered Al.

After nodding his head to signal that he heard the American Captain, Mr. Berger remained in the prone position, as he slowly backed up, before he turned and led the way back to where the other members of the raiding party were located.

★　★　★

The sudden presence of a flair burning over the resort turned night into day, while the machine gun bullets and rifle fire that struck the wooden building and smashed windows, forced Major Kessler and his six remaining SS troops to dive for cover. Immediately after Kessler cursed his attackers, he called out to the SS Private who was on sentry duty to get down. As the SS Private fired his MP40 through one of the windows by the front door, a stream of rifle fire killed him instantly and took him out of the fight.

The second the enemy machine gun and rifle fire shifted to the left side of the building, SS Major Kessler knew what would happen next. Shortly after telling Sergeant Mueller to fall back from the main entrance, two hand grenades came flying through a ground floor window near the front door and exploded.

Just as the SS Major and SS Sergeant Mueller made their way into the hallway, that led to the other side of the resort, Kessler knew that an assault force would be raiding the building in a matter of seconds. The sound of another grenade going off by the main entrance signaled that they were about to have company.

In order to respond to this threat, Kessler instructed SS Sergeant Mueller to count to five and toss a grenade into the main room, as they withdrew to collect their packs and equipment. In addition to acknowledging the order, SS Sergeant Muller went a step further and volunteered to remain behind and provide covering fire for the withdrawal. As soon as Mueller did so, Major Kessler patted the NCO on the side of his right arm and said, "OK, but only for a minute or so, then meet us out back."

As Major Kessler and his men headed into the section of the resort where they kept their equipment, Sergeant Mueller removed the Stielhandgranate (wooden handle stick grenade) that was tucked into the side of his pistol belt. After arming the grenade, SS Sergeant Mueller tossed it into the main room where the entrance was located, just as another flair illuminated the area around the resort.

The second Al Parker kicked the front door open, he stepped back when he heard the distinctive sound of something hitting the ground and sliding across the floor of the main room.

"Grenade!" yelled Al, as he held his left arm out to prevent anyone else from entering the resort until it was safe to do so.

The second the grenade exploded, Al stepped into the main room and sprayed the area with a stream of .45 caliber bullets from his M3 Grease Gun. While Al reloaded, Jim fired five shots in rapid fire succession from his Paratrooper Model M1 Carbine into the darkness, before he turned to Sergeant Carubba and said, "Send one their way to clear this room."

As everyone stepped aside, Sam pulled the pin on a grenade and tossed it toward the entrance to the hallway, that led to the other side of the resort. Once the grenade detonated, Jim, Hans and Al took turns stepping into the corridor and firing into the dimly lit passage way. A split second later the sky above the resort was illuminated again, when Sergeant Mulligan fired another flair into the night's sky. This gave the raiding party enough light to advance further into the building. While they did so, Jim turned toward Mr. Berger and said, "Any suggestions?"

While speaking fast and in a low tone of voice, Mr. Berger responded and said, "That corridor leads to a larger room, herr Oberst. From there Kessler and his men can easily escape out the back door."

"We need to clear that hallway but let's be careful doing so," said Jim.

As Jim and the other members of their raiding party advanced along the outer walls toward the corridor that connected one side of the resort to the other, Hans spotted something that caused him to open fire with his MP40. The second Hans did so, SS Sergeant Mueller was hit twice in his right hip and leg as he stepped back out of the line of fire. Even though his wounds forced him to move slowly, Sergeant Mueller lifted his right leg high enough to remove the stick grenade, that was tucked into his right boot.

After removing the cap that secured the bottom of the grenade, Sergeant Mueller pulled the cord that set the charge, before he tossed his last Stielhandgranate at the raiding party. This time it was Jim Beauregard who called out, "Grenade!" as he and the other members of the raiding party took cover to avoid the blast, that occurred in just under five seconds.

Now that he was wounded, SS Sergeant Mueller decided that he would do a better job of serving the Major and their men, if he stood his ground and prevented the raiding party from advancing any further inside the resort. While SS Sergeant Mueller did his best to ignore the pain from his wounds, he began firing burst after burst from his MP40 at the raiding party.

In an effort to move things along, Al Parker removed his last grenade from the musette bag that he carried. When Sam Carubba produced one of his grenades, Jim whispered, "Wait for him to reload, then Hans and I will cover you."

The moment the attacker who was blocking their advance stopped firing, Jim and Hans opened fire, while Al and Sam pulled the pins and tossed their grenades into the darkness. Now that his men were ready to make a run for it, SS Major Kessler looked back and made eye contact with Sergeant Mueller, just as the two grenades hit the floor and rolled closer to where the NCO was leaning up against a wall. After presenting the Major with the Nazi salute, SS Sergeant Mueller stepped out into the hallway and opened fire just as the two grenades exploded.

As soon as the SS Sergeant was blown off his feet and killed, Hans led the way as the raiding party advanced deeper into the resort. By the time they passed by SS Sergeant Mueller's dead body, the sound of gunfire was heard emanating from behind the building.

Once again, the night sky above the resort was illuminated by a flair, that was fired by Mike Mulligan. "It sounds like Kessler and his men are pinned down behind the building," said Hans, as he ran faster through the building with his MP40 at the ready.

As soon as SS Major Kessler made their through the back door of the resort, he and his men came under immediate fire from a combination of Allied troops and four armed German civilians. After taking cover behind two wooden carts and stacks of wooden crates, Kessler was returning fire, when SS Private Mittenberger got hit with a burst of submachine gun fire and fell over dead. The moment Kessler spotted a German Policeman reloading his MP40, while he stood by the open back door of the resort, the SS Officer fired a short burst from his MP40, that came within inches of hitting Hans Sigmann.

"That was a close one, Hans," said Al, as he and Jim took turns firing at the SS troops who were pinned down in the yard behind the resort. As soon as Hans reloaded his MP40, he leaned out of the open doorway enough to spot some movement in the darkness.

When Sergeant Angelone called out, "Hey, Mike, fire another flair," Sergeant Mulligan responded and said, "Last one. Here goes!"

As soon as Major Kessler heard that the Allied soldiers had one flair left, he turned to his remaining four men and said, "Get ready to move on my command. If we get separated, I want you to make your way to where Lieutenant Emich and his men are located."

After exchanging another volley of gunfire with the Allied troops and armed German civilians, Kessler and his men took off running like men who had nothing to lose, by attempting to escape. As soon as Major Kessler and his men began shooting their way to freedom, Mike Mulligan stopped to reload the MG42, just as Sergeant's Angelone and Coppola used the light from the flair before it burned out, to kill two SS Privates as they ran behind their commanding officer.

From his position by the open back door of the resort, Hans was reloading his last 32 round magazine into his MP40 when he turned to Jim and Al and said, "They're on the move!" A split second later, Hans was off and running in pursuit of the SS Major and the last two men in his unit. Once Hans emptied his MP40 at the escaping SS men, he tossed the empty submachine gun to the ground and drew his 9mm P38 pistol, as he led the way, with the other members of the raiding party following close behind.

Even though it was dark out, there was enough light from the stars to see shapes and shadows off in the distance, as SS Major Kessler and an SS Private ran around the resort and headed toward the trail head. While the men in the Allied raiding party took pot shots at the two escaping SS men, Hans continued to run with his pistol in hand, as if he was a rookie cop pursuing his first criminal.

When Major Kessler and the only surviving member of his three squads of SS troops reached the steeper terrain, Kessler turned around and emptied his last full magazine at the men who were pursuing him. Whether it was a lucky shot or not, four of the 9mm bullets that Kessler fired, struck Hans Sigmann in his left thigh, stomach and left shoulder and caused him to drop to his knees and collapse on the ground.

Even though he was winded from running after the escaping SS men, Al Parker could not believe his eyes when he saw Hans get hit and go down. "Hans is hit!....Doc, come quick!" screamed Al, as he knelt down to steady his aim, when he fired his M3 Grease Gun until it was empty. A split second later Jim and the rest of the men stopped running and emptied their weapons into the darkness, in the last known direction of the fleeing SS troops.

When Sergeant Carubba called out, "I think one of 'em is hit!" Al Parker dropped his empty Grease Gun, drew his 1911 pistol and racked the slide to load the chamber, before he removed his flashlight from his belt and took off into the darkness. As soon as Al took off, Jim made eye contact with Sergeant's Angelone and Coppola and said, "Keep the Captain company. We'll be along shortly."

By the time the two Sergeants took off to assist Captain Parker, Doc Keller arrived by his patient's side and examined his wounds. When Jim asked how Hans was doing, Doc Keller used his flashlight to give his patient a quick examination, before he responded and said, "I need to get him inside, Sir."

The second that several shots were fired off in the distance, Jim instructed Mike Mulligan and his four assistants to help Doc Keller carry Hans back to Kemptner Hutte. Jim then turned to Mr. Berger, Captain Garnier, Lieutenant Kelly and Sam Carubba and said, "Let's go."

While Sergeant's Angelone and Coppola moved in to take the wounded and last remaining member of Kessler's SS unit into custody, Al Parker was involved in a running gun battle with the wounded SS Major, who was doing his best to limp down the trail to safety. Even though Al's eyes had adjusted to the darkness, it wasn't easy to score a hit, when his target was limping at a fast pace and shooting back at him. Kessler's situation was considerably worse, because the gunshot wounds to his right leg and buttocks were incredibly painful and were making it harder for him to make his escape.

The SS Officer was also running low on pistol ammunition. This forced him to conserve his ammunition and fire fewer shots at the American, who seemed determined to capture or kill him. It was also a bit unnerving from a psychological perspective, when the SS Major heard his pissed off American pursuer call out, "You shot my friend. You're a fucking dead man, Kessler!"

By the time Jim Beauregard and the other members of the raiding party arrived by their side, Sergeant Angelone was just finished searching their prisoner, while Sergeant Coppola covered the POW with the captured K43 rifle that he was armed with. After hearing Sergeant Angelone report that Captain Parker took off after Major Kessler, after they took the wounded SS Private out of the fight, several shots were heard being fired further down the trail.

"That sounds like a forty five, Sir," remarked Sam Carubba.

As Jim looked down the trail, he seemed to be genuinely concerned for Al Parker's safety, when he checked the chamber of his M1 Carbine and said, "Let's go."

While Lt. Colonel Beauregard left with the others, Mr. Berger stepped forward with his pistol in hand, as he addressed Sergeant's Angelone and Coppola. "I will be happy to guard the prisoner, so you can assist herr Oberst and Captain Parker."

"Thanks, Mr. Berger," said Sergeant Coppola before he turned to his buddy and said, "Let's go, Ange.

After leaving the wounded prisoner with Mr. Berger, Sergeant's Angelone and Coppola took off down the trail to join the others.

Being involved in a shootout at night on a cold alpine trail, that was illuminated only by the light from the stars in the sky, was proving to be a challenging experience for all parties involved. When the pain from his wounds became unbearable, Major Kessler decided to try and ambush the American, who seemed relentless in his efforts to pursue him.

As soon as Major Kessler limped over to the side of the trail, he did his best to make himself the smallest target as possible. Kessler accomplish this by easing himself down into a kneeling position. Doing so, enabled the SS Officer to stretch out his wounded right leg, while he aimed his 9mm P38 pistol in the direction that his pursuer would be taking.

After two plus decades in law enforcement and his experience as a combat soldier, Al Parker had developed excellent instincts. The second he stopped hearing noise up ahead, Al sensed that something was wrong.

As Al held his Army issue flashlight in his left hand and his 1911 pistol in his right, he moved more carefully along the alpine trail. When Al heard Jim calling his name, he decided to use his flashlight to illuminate the trail for a split second, to see if it was safe to proceed. The second Al did so, two shots rang out, with one of the bullets striking him in his left side.

As soon as Al emptied his forty five in the direction of the muzzle flashes, he tucked the 1911 in his pistol belt and drew the revolver that he carried in a shoulder holster. The moment Al charged his attacker, a third shot rang out, just as Al had his flashlight back on and was drawing a bead on Major Kessler's chest. When a forth shot was fired and Al was hit again, he fired two shots from the short barreled Smith & Wesson Military and Police (M&P) revolver, that he had been carrying since the early 1940s.

Even though he was wounded, Kessler had no intention of surrendering, especially to a Negro American Army Officer. After dropping his empty pistol, Kessler drew the knife that he carried in his right boot, while he was in the process of getting up on his good leg. A split second later, Al Parker tackled Kessler like a linebacker on a professional football team. When Kessler tried to stab his American attacker, Al blocked his effort to do so, just as the SS Major grabbed Al Parker's gun hand to prevent from being shot.

While Major Kessler used his last ounce of strength to break free and try one more time to thrust his knife into his attacker's side, Jim Beauregard stepped out of the darkness and fired two shots from his M1 Carbine at point blank range into the SS Officer's right foot. The second Kessler cried out in pain, Al Parker used his steel helmet to head butt his opponent in his face. Doing so, enabled Al to pull his gun hand free and shove the two inch barrel on his S&W .38 caliber revolver under Kessler's chin and pull the trigger.

As Major Kessler's dead body went limp, Jim Beauregard knelt by Al's side and asked if he was hit. While Al Parker remained on all fours over Kessler's dead body, he nodded his head ever so slightly, before he responded and said, "Yes, Jim. In my left side. My left leg feels kind'a funny too."

As Jim gently placed his right arm around Al's back, he called out to their men and said, "Give me a hand with the Captain, fellers."

Once they helped Al up on his feet, Jim checked his friend's wounds and said, "Once we get some sulfur power and a bandage on those wounds, we'll get you back to Kemptner Hutte."

"We'll take care of the Captain, Sir," remarked Sergeant Angelone as he produced a packet of sulfur power, while Sergeant Coppola removed a bandage from his Carlisle medical pouch.

While the two CID Agents tended his wounds, Al turned to Jim and asked about Hans.

Jim never seemed more serious then when he responded and said, "I don't know, Al. Doc Keller had him moved back to the resort to work on him. We'll know more once we get back."

While Al kept pressure on the gunshot wound that grazed his left side, Jim helped him make his way back to Kemptner Hutte. In order to keep Al from going into shock, Jim handed his M1 Carbine, shoulder bag and his pistol belt to Sam Carubba, before he took off his Army Officer's Trench Coat and placed it over his wounded friend's shoulders. When a shivering Al Parker tried to give Jim back his coat, Jim remarked, "I'm gonna tell Mary on you if you don't behave."

While Al limped along and grimaced in pain, he responded and said, "OK, Jim. You win. I'd rather be court martialed than have Mary pissed off at me."

★ ★ ★

When Al Parker woke up in the morning he found Jim Beauregard sitting next to him, while he sipped a canteen cup of hot coffee and puffed on his pipe. As soon as Al spoke up and said, "That coffee smells good," Jim turned around and faced his buddy and asked how he felt.

"I'm OK. How's Hans?" asked Al.

While Jim put his canteen cup on top of a nearby ammo crate, he responded in a somber tone and said, "I'm sorry I have to tell you this, Al, but Hans died last night. Doc did everything he could for him. He was just hit too bad to stop the bleeding."

While Al's eyes swelled with tears, Jim continued and said, "Before he passed away, he thanked us again for getting him and his son out'a that POW Camp and for taking them home." Then, while Jim put his pipe down next to his cup, he went on to say, "It also meant a lot to him, that he had the chance to see his wife again."

As Al used his right hand to wipe the tears from his eyes, Jim remarked, "I feel the same way. I can't believe he's gone. His passing hit the men pretty hard as well. Everyone liked Hans, including our French Allies."

While Al used his right hand to wipe his eyes again, Jim retrieved the metal flask that was positioned with his buddy's personal affects on the table next to the cot. After unscrewing the top, Jim spoke in a soft tone of voice and said, "Here ya go, Al," as he handed the flask to his friend.

After taking possession of the flask, Al remarked, "To Hans," before he took a healthy drink of whiskey. As soon as Al handed the flask back to Jim, Jim raised the flask into the air and continued the toast. "It was an honor to know you, Hans. You were a cop to us, not the enemy."

As soon as Al was in better shape to travel, Jim and the rest of their patrol used a wooden cart to help him travel down the trail head. Now that the French Army was occupying Oberstdorf, the local militia was authorized to hunt down the remaining number of holdouts, who were operating under the command of Lieutenant Emich. The day they returned from Gruben in a convoy of Jeeps, a long line of German prisoners were being herded out of the mountains by members of the Oberstdorf Heimatschutz and a contingent of French troops. Leading the Oberstdorf militia was their new police chief, Peter Sigmann.

Thanks to Colonel Reynald, a message was sent to SHAFE that requested a C47 to land to deliver supplies to his American Liaison Unit and pickup a wounded U.S. Army Officer. As the C47 made it's way to an open pasture near Oberstdorf, Jim and Al paid their respects to Anna Sigmann and her father, at the grave site where Hans was laid to rest.

Despite her loss, Anna Sigmann expressed her gratitude to the two American Army Officers, for all that they did to help the German people, who had no use for the Nazis, or their plans to continue the war. When Anna continued, she looked at Jim Beauregard and Al Parker and said, "I also want to thank you for bringing Hans and Peter home to me. After being apart from Hans for so long, my time with him these last few days were a precious gift, one that I will always cherish."

When Jim asked Anna to say goodbye to Peter for them, she promised to do so and added, "Hans would be very happy to know, that Peter is staying on here in Oberstdorf as our police chief."

The sound of the C47 flying overhead meant that it was time for the two Americans to leave Oberstdorf and continue on their mission. After saying goodbye to Anna Sigmann and her father, Jim helped Al over to their Jeep. Once Al was settled in the front passenger seat, Jim drove their Jeep over to the open pasture that was selected for the C47 to land.

While their men lined the LZ with their vehicles, Jim broke the news to Al, that he was being flown back to Paris, so he could fully recover from his wounds. When Al objected and said that he was staying with the unit and was going on to Berlin, Jim looked at his buddy and said, "Captain Murphy was right. You never followed an order in your life. That changes today, because this is one order that you're gonna follow. You're going back to Paris."

As soon as Al started to tell Jim that he was feeling good enough to make the trip, Jim became very serious as he looked at his good friend and said, "Seeing Hans get badly wounded and being with him when he died took a lot out of me. I also lost a few years off the tail end of my life, when I watched you pull that crazy stunt, that enabled us to capture Ivan Larson. Seeing you go running off into the darkness after Major Kessler and not knowing how bad you were hit just about finished me off. To be quite honest, I don't know how much more of this crap I can take. I certainly can't lose you, so please don't argue with me and get on the damn plane."

As soon as the C47 came to a stop and the crew chief opened the door, Jim, Al and the rest of the men were surprised to see General Tremble and Major Tommy Savino get off the aircraft. Once everyone came to attention and saluted the superior officer, General Tremble returned the salute and wasted no time in saying. "I'm here for two reasons. One is to congratulate the two of you and your men for the outstanding job that you've done. The detailed report that our French Allies sent to SHAFE, is being used as the justification to decorate each and everyone of you for your service in the Invasion of Southern Germany. I'm also here to relieve the two of you and see to it that you are both reassigned to the states. The Joint Chiefs want a detailed briefing on black market activities in the ETO, as well as on this Werwolf business and you two have been selected by SHAFE to make this report in person."

As soon as Jim started to object and said, "But, Sir, I thought you wanted me to command the first CID detachment in Berlin?" General Tremble held up his right to signal his subordinate that this order was not debatable. "I'm sorry, Jim, but your war is over," remarked the General, who quickly added, "You and Al will be returning to the states on priority transportation orders. Major Savino is being promoted in the field to Lieutenant Colonel and will assume command of your detail."

After changing his demeanor and becoming considerably more soft spoken, General Tremble continued as he handed Jim a letter and a copy of cable traffic. "I also have some mail for you, Jim. You might want to read this in private."

After examining the letter that was addressed to him, Jim looked at Al and said, "It's a letter from my son Peter from his new ship." Jim then opened the cable and began reading. As soon as he did so, Jim had a hard time swallowing the lump in his throat, as his heart sank to a level that he never thought possible for a human being to endure. While Jim walked away in shock, Al knew something was terribly wrong and remarked, "I'm afraid to ask what's in that message?"

"It's his oldest son, Peter," responded Tommy Savino, who continued speaking in a low tone of voice and said, "He was initially listed as being wounded in action, after a Jap plane crashed into his destroyer escort. Jim's son passed away several days later, after being transferred to a hospital ship. When Jim's wife received the second Western Union Telegram, she contacted Colonel Richmond in New York and asked him to send a message to Jim at our office in Paris. Once I got the news, I contacted the General."

As a father who knew what it was like to see a son wounded in battle, Al could not imagine what it must be like to lose a child under any set of circumstances, especially in what was believed to be the closing days of a world war. After excusing himself, Al limped over to where Jim was clutching the cable, as the tears streamed down his face.

As Al placed his right hand on Jim's shoulder, he did his best to comfort his friend when he said, "I'm sorry, Jim. I can't imagine what you're going through. Bea will need you now more than ever. So will your son Michael. I guess it's a good thing that we're going home."

After using his Army issue handkerchief to wipe the tears from his face, Jim did his best to regain his composure as he said, "We better say goodbye to the men."

After being briefed by the recently promoted Lt. Colonel Savino, the men in the detail lined up at attention, as Lt. Colonel James Beauregard and Captain Al Parker shook hands with every man and wished them well. As difficult as it was for him to speak, Jim did his best to control his emotions as he faced his men and said, "It was an honor to serve with each and everyone of you. Both Captain Parker and I look forward to the day, when we hear that you're all back home and living the rest of your lives in peace. Take care of each other and always remember that what we did during this war made a difference."

The second Jim and Al snapped to attention and saluted their men, the men returned the salute.

As the engines on the C47 started up, Jim shook hands with Tommy Savino and congratulated him on his promotion. Once Al Parker and Tommy Savino said goodbye to each other, General Tremble addressed the men in the detail and their new commander. "You boys be careful. I'll see you in Berlin."

After returning the salute to the men in American Liaison Unit, General Tremble reached out and grabbed Al Parker on his good side and said, "Let me give you a hand, Al."

As Jim and the General helped Al, as he limped over to the cargo door of the plane, all three of them realized that a lot had changed since the first time they met. Jim's father was right. Time heals all wounds.

After arriving in Paris and checking back into his hotel room, Jim wondered who was knocking on his door at such a late hour. When Jim opened the door, he was surprised to find General Tremble holding a bottle of scotch in his hand.

"I know it's late, Jim," said the General, "But I thought you might join me for a drink before we hit the sack."

As Jim stepped aside and he invited the two star general into his room, he accepted the bottle and poured two healthy shots into the clean glasses that were next to a pitcher of water. After handing the glass to General Tremble, Jim raised his glass and said, "Your bottle, your toast, Sir."

Of all people, Jim was surprised to hear the General make the following toast. "To our sons, Jim, the ones who made the ultimate sacrifice, so we would be victorious in this God awful war."

As soon as Jim offered the superior officer a chair, General Tremble sat down and explained why he stopped by. "My oldest son Nathan was a B17 pilot in the Eight Air Force. He was killed in action on the second raid to knock out the ball bearing factory at Schweinfurt. That was back in October of '43. The day Nathan died, over 640 other men were killed in action on the same mission. Everyone of those men had a family and friends who would grieve their loss for many years to come."

After pausing to take a quick sip of scotch, General Tremble continued and said, "Whenever I start to feel sorry for myself, I read the names from the Eight Air Force casualty list for the Schweinfirt- Regensberg Mission. Doing so doesn't bring my son back, but it helps put things in perspective.

Even my wife seems to find some relief in knowing that we're not alone and that our oldest son died in very good company."

As the two star general continued, he removed several pages of folded paper from his jacket pocket and handed them to Jim. "I asked an Admiral I know in Naval Intelligence to get me a copy of the casualty list from the Battle of Okinowa. I hope that you and your wife will find some comfort, when you see your son Peter's name on such a distinguished list of American heroes, who were killed in action during this horrific battle."

After downing the contents of his glass, General Tremble stood up and placed his empty glass on the dresser in Jim's room. When Jim asked if the General had other children who were serving in the war, General Tremble removed his wallet and showed Jim two photographs. As the General spoke, he sounded like a proud father. "Our son Frank is a tank commander in the Third Army. I try not to think about the fact that Frank's had a total of three tanks shot out from under him, since he landed in France."

After pointing to the second photograph, General Tremble went on to say, "Our youngest son is a rifleman in The Eighth Army. After Danny landed on Palawan Island, he participated in the Invasion of Mindanao." Then, after pausing for a second, the General seemed to lighten up a bit when he added, "I actually had to write Doug Mc Arthur and ask him to tell our youngest son to write his mother, or I was coming to the damn Philippines to kick him in his pants. Three weeks later my wife received two letters from Danny and I got a Jap flag in the mail. It cost me a case of French Champagne and a German Luger, but Doug Mc Arthur came through for me and for that I will always be grateful. Our youngest son now writes on a regular basis."

Seeing Jim crack a smile was all that General Tremble was hoping to achieve. After hearing the General remark, "Keep the bottle. I'm sure we'll finish it before you and that crazy sidekick of yours leave for the states. I'll see you and Al for breakfast. I'm buying."

As Jim stood up, he extended his hand and said, "Thank you, Sir. And you're right about this list. It doesn't bring them back, but it does put things in perspective."

After nodding his head in agreement, General Nathan Tremble said, "Goodnight, Jim," as he left his hotel room. As soon as Jim closed the door, he examined the casualty list and began to read the names of the U.S. Navy personnel who were killed in action, as well as the names of the ships that were damaged and sunk to date during the Battle of Okinowa. The sad part was, that this list didn't include the names of the other Allied military personnel, who would be added to the list of casualties, when the Battle of Okinowa would eventually end on June 22, 1945.

As Jim reviewed the casualty list, it was equally overwhelming to think about the military personnel who were seriously wounded and would be disabled in some way for the rest of their lives. After pouring himself another drink, Jim thought about the people who were tortured, imprisoned and executed by the enemy in cold blood. Millions more would be displaced for some time to come and had to rebuild their lives from scratch. The good news was, that the Allies were winning the war, for had the outcome been different, the forces of evil would have ruled the earth for some time to come. Al was right. They needed to go home. Their war was over.

On May 7th, 1945 the German Armed Forces unconditionally surrendered to the Allied Forces in Reims, France. A second surrender ceremony also took place in Berlin on May 8th, 1945 which is officially recognized as VE Day (Victory in Europe). The war in the Pacific ended on August 14, 1945 with the unconditional surrender of Japan to the Allied Forces. It took the dropping of not one, but two atomic bombs, to convince the Japanese militarists to agree to the surrender terms. A more formal surrender ceremony took place on the U.S.S. Missouri in Tokyo Harbor on September 2, 1945.[31] (*31) 30. Tourismus Oberstdorf Prinzregenten-Platz 187561 Oberstdorf. 31. V-J Day. History.com

CHAPTER 9

THE POST WAR YEARS

Eleven months after Cal Parker and Michelle Dumont Parker were married, Michelle died while giving birth to a healthy baby boy. Rather than make any immediate decisions about the future, Cal decided to have Michelle's parents care for the infant, who was named Benjamin Greene Parker after the man who saved his father's life.

While Jim Beauregard and Al Parker rotated home after serving in The Invasion of Southern Germany, Cal Parker served as as CID Agent in Berlin. Doing so, enabled Cal to visit his son and Michelle's family, while he served with the occupation forces in the American sector.

After being discharged from the U.S. Army, Al Parker returned to his duties as a Detective with the New York City Police Department. In 1947, Al was promoted to Detective 2nd Grade and was assigned to the Chief of Detective's Office, where he spent the remainder of his career working with Frank Angelone, Johnny Mc Donald and Pat Murphy Sr. When Al retired in 1950 he devoted his time to his family and his motor vehicle repair business. His business really expanded, when Al began restoring old cars and trucks and renting them out to the film industry.

Shortly after Cal Parker returned to the United States and was discharged, he joined the New York City Police Department. While guarding a prisoner in Harlem Hospital, Cal met a young medical school student, who he would later marry. In addition to raising Cal's son Benjamin, the couple would have two of their own sons. All three Parker boys would follow in their father and grandfather's footsteps and join the police department. The Parker's and the Dumont family also remained in contact after the war. Doing so enabled Retired Chief Inspector Francois Dumont and his wife to maintain a relationship with their grandson Benjamin.

In 1947, Jack Parker transferred into the newly formed United States

Air Force and would go on to serve in the Korean War and the Vietnam War. Jack Parker would also marry and have two sons and a daughter. During his career in the Air Force, Jack Parker proved to be an outstanding leader of fighter pilots and moved up in rank. After becoming one of the first African Americans in the USAF to achieve the rank of full colonel, Jack Parker continued to make history when he was promoted to the rank of Brigadier General while serving in Vietnam.

When a Presidential Order directed that the U.S. Armed Forces would no longer be segregated, Jim Beauregard's four part book series The Frontline Fugitives became a best seller. In the 1960s Hollywood took notice of the fact that The Frontline Fugitives was the perfect fit for a television series, in a day and age when TV shows and movies about police work and World War II were very popular. The fact that The Frontline Fugitives also touched on social issues surrounding the civil rights movement, added to the human interest aspects of this story.

As the author, who was also a Retired Deputy Chief of the Atlanta Police Department, Jim was the perfect person to hire as the script consultant and technical adviser to the show. Jim also made sure that Al Parker was hired by the production company, to provide the vehicles that were used when the crew filmed on location in New York. When the crew filmed scenes relating to the time that Jim and Al spent in Paris, Francois Dumont served as the French Police consultant to the show.

While filming on location in Paris, the Beauregards, Parkers and Dumonts spent most of their free time in The Paris Cafe, with Gabby Allaire as their gracious host. They even had the chance to spend some time with Peter Sigmann, his wife and his mother Anna. Clearly, these were five of the best years of their lives.

After the war, Michael Beauregard joined the Atlanta Police Department and married a girl that he met at a USO dance when he was stationed at Ft. Bragg. The couple would have three sons, with their first being named Peter after Michael's brother, who was killed during the war. Michael's oldest son Peter followed in his uncle's footsteps and served on a U.S. Navy PBR Boat during the Vietnam War. His other sons served in the U.S. Army, with one becoming a helicopter pilot and the other a CID Agent.

During his police career, Michael advanced in rank and served as a patrol sergeant, a detective sergeant and as a lieutenant of detectives. In keeping with their family tradition, Michael and his wife continued to run the family farm and made a good living by selling farm fresh eggs, fresh produce, beef and pork to local markets.

Becoming a grandmother enabled Beatrice Beauregard to better cope with the loss of her son Peter. Even Jim Beauregard benefited greatly by being a loving grandfather. On many occasions, Jim would take his grandsons for a ride, on the same horse drawn wagon that he rode on as a kid. Whenever Jim did so, he told his grandsons stories about a long list of heroes, that included men like, Al Parker, Patrick Murphy Jr., Pat Murphy Sr., Frank Angelone, Johnny Mc Donald, Andy Dubrowsky, Fred Richmond, Joe Coppola, Jack Donovan, Don Lorenz, Jimmy Scott, Kevin Klein, Sal Jacobi, Kevin Kalb, Tony Giordino, Billy Davis, Mike Kirby, Chester Wright, Tommy Savino, Hank Blair, Doc Keller, Chris Jacko, Mike Mulligan, Phil Martin, John Gramacki, Steve Dickenson, Danny Cabrerra, Raymond Polanski, John Reader, Nathan Tremble, Cal Parker, Benny Greene, Anthony Angelone, Sal Coppola, Sam Carubba, Bill Hayes, Charlie Golovan, Carl Miller, Billy Barnes, John Lew, Dan Kelly, Fred Janowski, Rusty Morgan, Steve Dalton, Tommy Baines, Captain Marcel Badeau, Colonel Andre Reynald, Captain Charles Garnier, Hans Sigmann, Peter Sigmann, Gunther Jager, Koenraad Berger and a number of French policemen, including Francois Dumont.

Taking these long rides on an old farm wagon enabled Jim's grandsons to receive an education about subjects that were not always covered in school. Clearly, Michael Beauregard's sons learned a lot about life and American history whenever they spent time with their grandfather.

Unfortunately, tragedy struck when Beatrice Beauregard became sick and ended up bedridden for the last year of her life. Even though a private nurse was brought in to care for Bea, Jim never left his wife's side and did all of the household chores that his wife had performed during their marriage. The day Beatrice Beauregard passed away, Jim was grateful that the most beautiful woman he ever knew and loved was going to a better place.

After the war, all of the men who served in CID returned to civilian life and enjoyed long careers in a variety of law enforcement positions. Of all the men who served together during the war, Anthony Angelone and Sal Coppola remained partners for the bulk of their careers on the New York City Police Department. Both of these men rose though the ranks of the Detective Division and retired after thirty years of service. Sam Carubba also had a long career in civilian law enforcement and retired after 28 years of service as a Captain of Detectives with the Baltimore Police. After returning to the Dallas Police Department, Bill Hayes became a Texas Ranger. By 1947 Hank Blair was discharged from the Army and joined the Los Angeles Police Department. During his 25 year career he served as a Detective and as a Patrol Sergeant. Mike Mulligan, Charlie Golovan, Mike Butler, Joshua Fermi and Chris Jacko also returned to civilian life and had long careers in police work.

Billy Davis remained in the Air Force and retired with the rank of Brigadier General after serving three tours in the Vietnam War. Carl Miller also remained in the U.S. Army and served as an MP Officer in the Korean War, in Germany during the Cold War and in Vietnam.

After the war, Doc Mel Keller went to medical school and became an emergency room physician and a trauma surgeon. In 1947, Tommy Savino returned to his position with the Providence, Rhode Island Police Department, where he rose through the ranks and retired as captain of detectives. Don Lorenz also went home after serving in post war Germany and returned to his position in the New Haven, Connecticut Police Department.

After serving as the Police Chief in Oberstdorf, Peter Sigmann joined the West German Federal Police. In 1946, Charles Garnier also returned to his previous position with the French National Police, where he spent the remainder of his career working with Chief Inspector Francois Dumont. As a result of his service during the war, Colonel Andre Reynald remained in intelligence work until his retirement. While Private George Zangolas was killed in action during the Invasion of Germany, Charlie Monacco survived the war and married Paulette. Charlie and Paulette lived happily ever after in Paris, where they ran a profitable business. Jardan Moreau also survived WWII and went on to serve with the French Foreign Legion in Algiers and Vietnam. After his retirement, Jardan ran a very exclusive security company that was based in France. When Francois Dumont retired from the French National Police, he and his wife spent most of their time living and working on their family farm.

After receiving a phone call from Mary Parker, Jim Beauregard packed a bag and made reservations to fly to New York on the next available flight. Rather than have his aging father travel alone, Michael Beauregard took a few days off from the Atlanta Police Department and escorted his dad on what would be a very demanding trip. The year was 1972.

Despite his own health problems, Jim was determined to be by his old friend's bedside before he passed away. Based on what Mary said, Al's cancer had spread rather rapidly. The fact that he had heart problems only made a bad situation worse.

When Jim and his son Michael arrived at New York University Medical Center, he met Mary Parker and Cal's wife, who was a senior physician on staff at the hospital. A few minutes later, Cal Parker, his oldest son Benjamin and Cal's brother Jack arrived in the visitor's waiting area. All three members of the Parker family were wearing their uniforms. Cal was dressed in his blue police lieutenant's uniform, his son Benjamin in his police officer's uniform and Jack in a blue U.S. Air Force uniform, that displayed the insignia of a brigadier general.

It had been almost three years since their last reunion. At the time, Cal was a detective sergeant and his son Ben was walking a beat, in the same police precinct where his grandfather spent the bulk of his career. In January of 1972, Jim was laid up for some time, after he lost his balance and broke his ankle. During the same period of time, Al had his first heart attack. A few months later Al was diagnosed with cancer. As a result of their declining health, Jim and Al stayed in contact via telephone and through handwritten letters.

As Jim warmly greeted Cal, his son Ben and his brother Jack, it was easy to see that they were old friends. Michael Beauregard had also met the various members of the Parker family over the years and was no stranger in their homes.

When Mary looked at Jim and said, "You should've seen Al smile when I told him you were coming to visit," Jim knew that he would not be able to through this without breaking down. After all that he and Al had been through, the thought of seeing his old friend, for what might be the last time, was proving to be more than he could bear.

As Jim's eyes swelled with tears and he remarked, "Al doesn't deserve this. Not after all that he's done," his son Michael gripped his father's left arm and said, "Hang on, Pop."

After nodding his head ever so slightly up and down, Jim patted his son's hand, as he responded and said, "I'll be alright, Mike," before he used his cane to steady himself, as he walked slowly into Al's hospital room.

Seeing Al lying in a hospital bed, made Jim do his best to act as if nothing was out of the ordinary, as he made his way toward his old friend. As soon as he arrived by Al's side, Jim reached out and gently placed is right hand over his best friend's right arm. Rather than say anything, Jim stood next to the bed and waited for Al to notice that he had a visitor.

The moment Al opened his eyes, he smiled when he saw his old Army buddy standing by his side. While Jim did his best to hold it together, Al turned his head a bit to the right, as he spoke in a low raspy voice and said, "Mary made my day when she told me you were coming to visit."

"I got here as soon as I could, Al," said Jim, before he went on to say, "My son Michael came with me. He's visiting with your family while we shoot the shit."

"There's something I have to tell you," whispered Al, who paused to catch his breath, before he continued in a low tone of voice. "Before we left for Paris in early 1945, Sister O'Rourke called and asked me if I would meet her. When I did, she handed me a letter from Ivan Larson. He asked me to forgive him for killing Pat Murphy Jr. and for everything else that he did wrong. He sent a similar letter to Captain Murphy."

Once again, Al paused when he found it difficult to breath. After catching his breath, Al continued and said, "I couldn't do it, Jim. I was filled with too much hate. I kept that letter and every year on the anniversary of young Patrick's death, I read it and tried my best to forgive Ivan Larson and Shorty Mc Ghee for what they did, but I couldn't do it."

While continuing to speak just above a whisper, Al went on to say, "Last night I had dream about what we did together. It was one of those vivid dreams in living color. I remembered that ride that we took in that glider. It was strange because I knew it was winter but I wasn't cold. At one point I saw myself running away from that SS unit, so I could circle around and ambush them from behind. You were there, so was Hans, Ivan Larson and General Tremble. Just before I woke up, I was dreaming about the trip back to the states, when we had Larson in custody. I remembered seeing the look on Captain Murphy's face, when we stepped off the plane and he got a chance to see the young kid who killed his son Patrick. When I woke up, I thought about my talk with Sister O'Rourke and the letter that Ivan Larson asked her to give me before he was executed."

Once again, Al paused to catch his breath, before he picked up where he left off. "I forgave him, Jim. I can't explain it, but there's no doubt in my mind, that if Ivan Larson and Shorty Mc Ghee could do it all over again, things would'a been different for a lot of us, including them."

As a man who had an equally long career in law enforcement, as well as in the Army in time of war, Jim did his best to sound as reassuring as possible, when he looked at Al and said, "As my father used to say, "Time heals all wounds, Al."

After seeing the tears streaming down Jim's face, Al's eyes also began to swell with tears, as the two men who became best friends under unusual circumstances faced each other for the last time. As Jim swallowed hard, Al whispered, "I'll never forgot what you did at that train station down south, when we saw those German POWs being treated better than those Negro soldiers. You made a difference that day, Jim. It may not have seemed like much at the time, but you moved the ball forward and for that I will always be grateful."

"Thanks, Al, but I don't feel very proud of myself," responded Jim, who quickly added, "I didn't do enough."

After hearing what Jim just said, Al raised his raspy voice an octave and said, "My sons and my grandchildren have a better life than I did, because of men like you, the Murphys and the other good cops and soldiers that we served with. We even became close friends with enemy soldiers like Hans and his son Peter. Forgiving Ivan Larson and Shorty Mc Ghee put the finishing touches to my journey as a mortal man."

After thinking about what Al just said, Jim remarked, "I thought for sure that when my book series got published and people read how well we worked together and how brave you, Cal and Benny Greene were, that folks would wake up and realize that African American cops and soldiers were no different than the rest of us. Even when the TV series came out, not much seemed to change for the better. There were still too many riots and people objecting to the Civil Rights movement."

"Don't be so hard on yourself," whispered Al, who paused for a split second before he added, "You did a lot more than you know."

Under the circumstances, all Jim could bring himself to say was, "Thanks, Al."

When Al continued, he sounded like he was having an even harder time talking. "Do me a favor and call Mary from time to time to make sure that she's all right. Now that the kids and the grand kids are older, she's not as busy as she used to be. Besides, she always worries about how you're doing after Bea went to be the Lord."

When a lightening bolt of searing pain shot through Al's cancer ridden body, Jim reached out and held his best friend's hand and said, "Hold on, Al. I'll get Mary and the doctor."

While doing his best to speak, Al whispered, "Stay, Jim. Tell Mary that I love her and I'll wait for her on the other side."

A split second later, Retired Second Grade Detective Al Parker, who served as a commissioned officer in the United States Army during World War II, passed away. Not since Jim heard that his son Peter was killed in action and his wife Bea died, had he felt this much of a loss.

When Al's family and Michael Beauregard entered the room, they found Jim bent over and embracing his best friend's lifeless body as he sobbed uncontrollably. As emotional as everyone else in the room was, Michael Beauregard did his best to comfort his father by saying, "Captain Parker's in a better place, Dad. He'll never be in pain again."

After hugging his son, Jim turned to Mary and said, "I'm sorry, Mary, but when I went to get you and the doctor, Al stopped me and asked me to tell you how much he loves you."

Mary Parker proved that she was a truly amazing woman, when despite her own grief, she had the strength to comfort the man who became one of her husband's closest friends. "It's OK, Jim," said Mary, as she embraced the man her husband served with. When Mary stepped back, she continued as she faced Jim. "You and Al did more than just serve together. You made history and in the process of doing so, you became brother's-in-arms and the very best of friends." Unable to respond, Jim nodded his head up and down every so slightly, while his son Michael patted his father gently on his back.

After attending the funeral for Al Parker and delivering the eulogy, Jim Beauregard and his son Michael returned home to Atlanta. In December of 1972, James Beauregard died in his sleep on the anniversary of the capture of Ivan Larson. THE END

FINAL COMMENTS FROM THE AUTHOR

T he "surprise" that I mentioned earlier in the Author's Comments was to include Hans Sigmann and his son Peter in the story line for The Frontline Fugitives Book IV. I decided to do so, because rescuing Hans and his son from a POW Camp was something that I would do, if I was in the position that Jim Beauregard and Al Parker were in during World War II. Other veteran law enforcement officers that I briefed on this aspect of this story, agreed with my decision to include Hans and Peter in Book IV.

The proof that Jim and Al acted correctly, can be explained by the simple fact, that Hans Sigmann acted like a fellow law enforcement officer and not like a German soldier, when he allowed the Americans to take custody of a captured American glider pilot, who was wanted for killing a New York City Policeman and other serious crimes. As I point out in some of the dialogue in Book IV, Hans Sigmann could have paid a very high price, if his superiors and or the Gestapo, learned that he intentionally allowed a group of American soldiers and a captured U.S. Army glider pilot to go free. A bad situation would have been made worse, if Hans Sigmann's superiors learned, that these same Americans successfully engaged and wiped out an SS unit. As a retired federal agent, who also served as a police officer, I understand the bond that exists between law enforcement officers and acted accordingly, when I included Hans Sigmann's character in the expanded story-line for Book IV. There are also historical references that verify, that "professional courtesies" and acts of kindness were performed by Allied and German combatants during World War II.

Including Hans Sigmann, his wife Anna, their youngest son Peter and Anna's father and other anti Nazi German characters in Book IV, also served as a guide of sorts, to help frame the end of the story, when the Allied composite unit led by Jim Beauregard, pursued a band of Nazi holdouts into the Alpine mountains near Oberstdorf, Germany. Even though aspects of this part of Book IV are a dramatization of actual events, the intent was to represent a part of history, that tends to get very little attention in books and war movies.

Even if their numbers were relatively small, in comparison to the overall population, the German people who resisted the Nazis and aided the Allies in any way deserved to be recognized. As a result, it seemed prudent to create a cast of fictional characters, who could help tell a story, that is based in part on historically accurate events. Even the fictional "bad guy" characters who are included in Book IV, represent the type of die hard Nazis and supporters of National Socialism, who were determined to continue fighting at all cost. Fortunately, after a great deal of death and destruction, the Allies were victorious over the Axis forces.

In summation, let me say, that it is never an easy decision for a writer to have primary or main supporting characters die or get killed in action. Unfortunately, when you write a historically accurate fiction book series, about crime fighting and combat actions that take place in time of war, bad things happen to good people. As a result, it would be unrealistic and historically inaccurate, to have all of the "good characters" survive the war. In fact, it's through the tragic death of men like Tony Giordano (Book 1), Patrolman Patrick Murphy Jr. (Book I), Lieutenant Chester Wright (Book II), MP Private Garcia (Book II), Marcel Badeau and Jacques Bayard AKA L' Artist (Book III) and Benny Greene, Hans Sigmann, Nathan Tremble Jr., Peter Beauregard and Michelle Dumont Parker (Book IV), that we can better appreciate the impact that their loss had on this world.

NOTES

CHAPTER 1

1,2,3,4,5,6 *Other Losses* by James Bacque was used as a main research
source to develop the scenes and the dialogue between certain
fictional characters involving the Rhine River Open Air POW
encampments. This reference source was also used to help develop
certain scenes and dialogue between fictional characters involving
the treatment of massive numbers of POWs and Disarmed Enemy
Personnel in the European Theater of Operations toward the end
of WWII, as well as after the war.

CHAPTER 2

7 *The United States Army in World War II-The Quarter Master Corps:
Operations In The War Against Germany* by William F. Ross and
Charles F. Romanus.

CHAPTER 3

8,9,10,11 *The French Invasion of Germany 1945*, Cinema Department of the
French Military translated by Nettemperur.

CHAPTER 4

12 *Hitler's Weherwolves by Charles Whiting* as well as the book
Werwolf–The History of the National Socialist Guerrilla Movement by
Perry Biddscombe.

13 *Hitler's Wehrwolves* by Charles Whiting as well as the book
Werwolf–The History of the National Socialist Guerrilla Movement by
Perry Biddscombe.

CHAPTER 5

14 *WW2 French Invasion of Germany 1945* (Video) Cinema
Department of the French Military. Translated by Nettemperur, as
well as *The Last Days of The Reich–The Collapse Of Nazi Germany,*
May 1945 by James Lucas .

15 *Werwolf–The History of the National Socialist Guerrilla Movement* by
Perry Biddscombe.

16   *WW2 French Invasion of Germany 1945* (Video) Cinema Department of the French Military. Translated by Nettemperur, as well as *The Last Days of The Reich–The Collapse Of Nazi Germany, May 1945* by James Lucas .

17,18,19   *Werwolf–The History of the National Socialist Guerrilla Movement* by Perry Biddscombe.

20   *WW2 French Invasion of Germany 1945* (Video) Cinema Department of the French Military. Translated by Nettemperur.

21   *The Last Days Of The Reich–The Collapse Of Nazi Germany*, May 1945 by James Lucas.

CHAPTER 6

22,23   *The History of the National Socialist Guerrilla Movement* by Perry Biddscombe and *Neimandsland–A History Of Unoccupied Germany 1944-1945* by Gareth Pritchard.

CHAPTER 7

24   *American POWs In Oberstdorf, Germany* by Alfred Gene Flowers EX POW Biography National Headquarters, 3201 East Pioneer Parkway #40 Arlington, Texas 76010-5396. Hq@axpow.org and *Werwolf–The History Of The National Socialist Guerrilla Movement 1944-1946* by Perry Biddiscombe.

25   *Werwolf–The History Of The National Socialist Guerrilla Movement 1944-1946* by Perry Biddiscombe.

26,27   *Werwolf–The History Of The National Socialist Guerrilla Movement 1944-1946* by Perry Biddiscombe and *The Last Days Of The Reich-The Collapse Of Nazi Germany, May 1945* by James Lucas

28   *Werwolf–The History Of The National Socialist Guerrilla Movement 1944-1946* by Perry Biddiscombe.

CHAPTER 8

29   Hotel Mohron Martplatz 6, Oberstdorf, Germany Website

30   Tourismus Oberstdorf Prinzregenten-Platz 187561 Oberstdorf

31   V-J Day. History.com Additional reference source: "The Joy of Field Rations" (Blog) Wednesday, December 19, 2012 Makeshift Cooking, German Army, WW2